After Dinner Conversation
"Best of 2024"

Philosophy | Ethics Short Story Fiction

After Dinner Conversation – "Best Of" 2024

After Dinner Conversation publishes fictional stories that explore ethical and philosophical questions in an informal manner. The purpose of these stories is to generate thoughtful discussion in an open and easily accessible manner.

ISBN# 979-8-9924170-2-9 (Print)
ISBN# 979-8-2306360-4-5 (Digital)

Library of Congress Control Number: 2025931851

https://www.afterdinnerconversation.com

After Dinner Conversation is an independent nonprofit publisher. We believe in fostering meaningful discussions among friends, family, and students to enhance humanity through truth-seeking, reflection, and respectful debate. To achieve this, we publish philosophical and ethical short story fiction accompanied by discussion questions.

Table Of Contents

Apple Pi

Adam Strassberg

* * *

Martin and Mari married the year after graduation. Martin was a tall, thin White man with black glasses. Mari was a short, fat Black woman with white glasses. It was a mixed marriage—sort of—they both majored in mathematics, however, Martin minored in statistics, whereas Mari minored in accounting.

They had a remarkable romance—they had never had a fight, not even a small one, never a disagreement, nor even raised their voices to one another. They were committed to absolute fairness and equality in all aspects of their relationship. It was a match made in Heaven, or at least the Euclidean domain equivalent of such.

Martin trained as an actuary, Mari as a CPA. They loved the small suburban starter home they purchased together soon after their wedding. It had a slate black roof with a white picket fence, enclosing a lush green yard with a lovely old apple tree in the center. Martin was a bit relieved to not be beholden to lifting Mari over the threshold. Rather, after they got the keys, they unlocked and opened the front door together, then held hands and jumped across the threshold simultaneously.

They soon discovered that they agreed on most things most of the time, but not on everything all of the time.

Martin and Mari were excited to set up their new bed, but both of them wanted to sleep on the left side. "Let's toss an even coin for it," Martin suggested, taking a nickel from his pocket. "It's fifty-fifty, so it's fair." He flipped the coin into the air, called heads, and won. Martin set his night table to the left side of the bed, Mari set hers to the right.

Later that night, when Martin kissed Mari, then tickled her in their usual prelude to coitus, Mari denied him. "I'm sorry, Martin. I don't know why, but I'm just not in the mood."

"Let's flip for it. It's fifty-fifty, so it's fair."

"How about we pass tonight, and instead I'll give you fifty-five to forty-five odds for this in the future?"

Two months later, their first car broke down, and the repairs cost more than the vehicle. Martin wanted a new sporty convertible; Mari wanted a new practical minivan. She removed a coin from her purse, but before she flipped it, Martin interrupted. "How about we swap some odds? Let's go with forty-sixty odds for the new car type—convertible versus minivan—but let's up it to sixty-forty odds for intercourse each night?" Mari assented and Martin removed from his coat pocket his favorite icosahedron, a black metal twenty-sided Dungeons and Dragons game die. Mari rolled a success—"Nat 20, Critical hit"—and so they purchased a new minivan.

Martin hated the minivan, particularly the challenge of parking it in the supermarket lot. He remembered back to simpler times. He and Mari were so happy back in college. They lived on the same floor in identical dorm suites right next door to one another. They met on the first day of orientation, bonding over their vision, their eyes. They were both nearly blind without their glasses, yet amazingly, they had the same prescription and could even wear each other's frames. They were otherwise physically distinct but so alike in every other way. They had the same major and so took most of the same classes. They had the same friends and enjoyed the same nerdy games. Their dorm took to nicknaming them the twins. By the end of the year, they alternately slept in each other's bedrooms, and their friends kept gifting them matching pajamas!

Martin returned with the groceries, and Mari had finished picking this week's apples from their big tree. It was seven years now—eleven from the year they first met—and they still had never had a fight. They had no conflict just calculations, no arguments just adjustments. Martin wanted to make applesauce, but Mari wanted to bake an apple pie. There were not enough fresh apples to do both. This was today's conundrum.

Martin frowned. He really loved applesauce.

Mari kissed him on his forehead. "How about we up it to twenty-five to seventy-five for sauce versus pie in exchange for seventy-five to twenty-five for bedtime sex?"

Martin nodded his head and rolled the usual twenty-sided die from his pocket. It was decided. Mari later served him a slice of homemade hot apple pie with vanilla ice cream on top. He disliked this, but he ate it, and it was utterly delicious.

The years passed faster and faster. By the time they had both entered their fifties, when most married couples had sex weekly, if at all, Martin and Mari coupled nightly—he had managed to negotiate the odds ratio up to ninety-five to five for each bedtime!

One night, after rolling the die, Martin kissed Mari but his erection did not follow. He had won the roll, but his libido seemed lost. And Mari was as sexy to him as the first day they had met, even more so!

Martin met with his doctor the next day and learned about erectile dysfunction and midlife andropause. There was so much that could be done, and Martin left hopeful with a Viagra prescription gripped tightly in his hands.

When Martin explained this solution to Mari, she disagreed with the plan. She loved him but there were risks to the medication—priapism, heart attacks, stroke, and even blindness. She was very concerned about Martin's vision because, while hers improved over the years, his had only worsened. Martin sighed, then reluctantly took out the twenty-sided die from his pocket. He held it in his palm. The decades of so many daily rollings had abraded the many triangular faces of the icosahedron into a nearly smooth ball, but it still rolled true and fair. The digits from one to twenty embedded on each triangular face had faded, but they were still inked and legible. After thirty years of marriage, Martin had managed to trade up the odds for everything in Mari's favor, all in exchange for that one particular thing most important to him and most men. Mari let Martin roll for the medication—but the odds of every other decision now were five to ninety-five in Mari's favor—and so it was 5 percent for filling the prescription versus 95 percent against. Martin rolled—"Nat 1, Critical fail." Mari took the prescription and fed it through their paper shredder.

Martin and Mari enjoyed a happy marriage to the end of their days. For Martin, it was indeed happy but never again joyful. He drove Mari's car, relaxed on Mari's couch, ate Mari's meals, watched Mari's movies. Martin seemed just to live Mari's life now, at least 95 percent of the time. He often puzzled over the same mystery, but try as he might, he just could not see it. How had their marriage, which had always been fair, somehow become so unequal? But then he would just roll his die and hope for the best.

* * *

Discussion Questions

1. Are Martin and Mari in love? What is it about their relationship that leads you to your conclusion?

2. What role should "fairness and equality" play in a relationship? What's wrong (*if anything*) with wanting fairness and equality in a relationship? Are joy, happiness, and success in a relationship contingent on fairness and equality?

3. What (*if anything*) is a better way to deal with relationship conflict than the flip of a coin when the parties want different things and there is no middle ground? If accommodations are voluntary, how do you know the other party will also give and take and not simply take advantage of the other?

4. Martin and Mari never fight. Should couples fight? If so, how do you know if you are having the right, or wrong, kind of fight for a healthy relationship?

5. What would you say to a potential partner who suggested a disagreement be resolved with the flip of a coin? How often would this have to be the solution for it to be a relationship warning sign?

* * *

Bubblegum Prayer

Dawn Muenchrath

* * *

He said later that he knew almost immediately—knew before he'd finished reading it through before he'd even reached the third stanza. That happened sometimes, every once in a long while: a piece of art—a movie, a novel, or a poem, as it were, in this case—that didn't reveal its treasures slowly but instead all at once, bowling you over with the staggering force of its insight, the words leaping off the page to take your hunched shoulders and shake them, to remind you not just why you loved art, but why you loved life, or why you *had* loved life and could again.

For the first time in thirty-five years, Elroy packed his papers (yes, he still insisted on *hard copies* of everything) into his briefcase and left the office early. It was June, raining, and he didn't have an umbrella or a proper jacket, but he marched into the street with his head held high. He gazed upward and laughed in wonderment as fat drops smacked his forehead and flowed in rivulets down the lines of his face.

He walked from the office towers to the park with the pond and followed the paved path along its perimeter. He admired the new leaves trembling on the elms, the brown ducks preening in the water, and even smiled at the smattering of fellow walkers and joggers sharing the path—these health-conscious people who normally irritated him. For over an hour, he walked until the storm had cried itself dry, the sun had cut through the clouds, and petrichor wafted from the concrete. Then he headed east, out of the park, and up the hill to the old brownstone, the one that had made sense when there were five of them: his wife, the two girls, and the dog, but now seemed excessive. Inside, he peeled off his wet clothes, dried with a towel, and tied on a robe. Then he took the poem from his briefcase and sat to read it again.

The next morning, he showed it to Alina. Of all the young girls who worked at the office, Alina was the one he liked best. She had long, dark hair, green eyes, and a small, thin mouth. She reminded him of his eldest daughter but also a little of his wife when she was young and beautiful. Standing by the coffee machine, he waited patiently as she read from the page, her eyes flitting back and forth rapidly, lips wordlessly mouthing the verses. She looked up, wiped a tear from her eye.

"My god, Elroy." She sniffled.

"What did I tell you?" he said with a smile.

"*My god*," she repeated.

By ten o'clock, everyone in the office had read it. Theirs was a respectable, mid-sized magazine, but the Arts & Literature section was small, getting smaller by the year, and so, most people in the office reading the poem now were people who had not read a poem in quite some time. One woman proposed that she hadn't read a poem since "Flanders Fields" in the fifth grade, and there was a murmur of agreement. No matter. It didn't take an expert to see that this poem was something special—a winner and then some.

"It's like," one woman began, and everyone turned to her eagerly, poised to agree, "it's just like so much *yes*."

Everyone laughed.

Someone else tried: "It's *this* moment. It's *now*. But, also, it's... so much more."

"It's what we've all been thinking."

"It's what we've all been *feeling*."

"It's what no one has been able to put into words before."

"It's going to go viral."

"So viral."

They were curious, naturally, about the poet. The name on the online submission form read, cryptically, L. P. Page, and the gender, age, and ethnicity options had all been left blank. Since Elroy was the managing editor of the section, it fell to him to contact the winner of the Poem of the Year prize. Typically, alongside the winning poem, they printed a photograph of the poet and a blurb about how they'd arrived at this particular piece.

Elroy settled himself in his chair and sipped some water preparatorily. He was imagining the poet as a young woman, twenty-something, with dark hair and a nice smile. He supposed he was imagining someone like Alina, who was an aspiring writer herself. He picked up the phone, dialed the provided number, and listened to the ring. This was the best part of the job. Delivering good news. Making someone's day. Perhaps changing, however slightly, the course of her life.

After five rings, the call went to voicemail. The canned voice that told him to leave a message belonged not to a young woman but a man—no, a boy, a teenage boy. He sounded entitled. Bratty. Elroy hung up.

Determining he would try again after lunch, he pulled out the copyedits he was working on for the interview with a very famous author, but he found he couldn't bring himself to care about the author's current favorite writing destination. Who had thought that was an interesting question?

All he could think about was the poem.

He had to know.

He called again. He called five times, and then, finally, someone picked up.

"Hello?"

"Good after—er, good morning," Elroy said. "I'm calling with regards to the poem, 'Bubblegum Prayer,' which was submitted to our Poem of the Year Contest. Are you the writer?"

There was a pause, rustling. A chuckle. "Shit, did it win? Is that what this is about?"

Elroy looked around his desk, at his copy, at the framed photograph of his daughters barefoot on the dock by the lake, and considered hanging up. He closed his eyes and counted to five.

"Yes, that's right," he said.

"Holy shit. Holy shit." A pause. "And there's some cash with that, right?"

"There is a monetary prize associated with the winning

poem, yes—"

"Awesome. Do you need my banking deets? Or will you guys just send a check?"

"Someone will be following up about all that," Elroy said. "For now, however, I'd just like to say *congratulations*—"

"Thanks."

"—and I was hoping you could provide, on the record, a short statement to be included alongside the poem."

"Come again?"

"In the past, writers have commented on their inspiration, their influence, their writing process..."

"Ah. Okay, okay." The line went silent. Then, there was the sound of a door. Traffic.

"Hello?"

"Yeah, sorry, still here. I'm just thinking. 'Bubblegum Prayer,' that's the poem you want? You're not just messing with me?"

"Do I sound like the type?"

The boy laughed. "Okay. Okay. Cool. Well... I didn't write it, the poem. I'm the *creator*, but I'm not the *poet*. I programmed the code that wrote it. How's that for a statement?"

Having ended the call, Elroy remained in his chair, motionless, for some time. It occurred to him that if he happened to forget this unpleasant revelation, everything might go on as normal. He, Elroy, could make up something else, a harmless quote, to put in the blurb. The boy on the phone might not even care. He seemed mostly concerned with the money and, further, not particularly precious with his words. Then again, he could have easily kept that bit of information to himself. He'd told Elroy for a reason.

Elroy called Alina into his office. At first, she didn't believe it. It wasn't possible. That poem had spoken to her *soul*. Elroy loved her even more for her romanticism.

He was not, as a general rule, one to solicit advice, but he asked her then what she thought should be done.

She raised her hands in supplication. "This is over our heads," she said.

By two o'clock, the editor in chief, another senior editor, Gerrie, and three junior editors, including Alina (it was sensed that the young people might have some special insights on the matter of *technology*), had been called into Elroy's office for an emergency meeting. Like Alina, the others were initially disbelieving. It was an insult to their own sophisticated literary sensibilities to think they might have been fooled by a computer. Once the matter of pride had been put aside, the contest rules were dug out from one of Elroy's dusty cabinets and read aloud. Twice. The issues of authorship and originality were not even mentioned.

It was assumed.

The six faces grimly exchanged glances around Elroy's desk. Alina looked down at her hands. The editor in chief cleared her throat and suggested, with unusual hesitancy, that, perhaps, it was their duty to share this poem—regardless of its origins—with the world.

There were a few nods.

Gerrie straightened in her chair, shaking her head. "What about our duty to protect the value of true art?" she said.

"But what *is* true art?" Alina said, her face flushing pink from the attention.

No one had an answer.

The editor in chief got up and walked to the window. Today, the sky was blue and cloudless. She turned back to them.

"Well," she said, "the way I see it, our hands are tied. With the writer notified, we have no choice but to go ahead and break the story, warts and all. Otherwise, he's liable to blab to someone else. Another publication."

No one said anything, and instinctively, the group turned to Elroy, who had said little since the meeting began.

"If anything could use a good scandal to shake things up, it's poetry, isn't it?" he said with a shrug. On this, everyone agreed.

They went public with the story—in print and online—that Friday. They published the poem, alongside the so-called poet's admission that he'd coded a program to write it (he refused to provide a photograph), and a lengthy essay meditating on the meaning of art and authorship, but, judging by the comments proliferating on social media, most hadn't bothered with the essay. They had their own opinions.

By midnight, the story had been picked up by all the major news stations in the country, as well as many internationally. The poem itself had been translated into fifteen languages (in some cases, with the help of a computer program). In the coming weeks, the paper received some praise and considerably more condemnation. Several talk shows reached out for an interview with Elroy or the editor in chief, but they both declined. The boy, L. P. Page, was similarly evasive. By some reports, he had received as many as fifty death threats and fifteen marriage proposals.

At the end of the month, Elroy, on his therapist's recommendation, took leave for a month to go to Los Cabos and "decompress."

He invited Alina along and paid for her ticket.

He was sitting beachside sipping black coffee and reading an old, dog-eared copy of Dickens one morning when she came running down from the hotel, flip-flops smacking against the rock path, phone clutched in hand.

"Elroy! Did you see the news? Did you hear?" She was wide-eyed, breathless.

He set down his cup and said, not unkindly: "If it's about that poem, I don't want to hear it."

"You'll want to hear this."

She passed him her phone and sat in his lap as he adjusted his glasses to read the article, which was distracting given that she was in a bikini and a thin floral wrap.

The boy, the programmer, the bogus poet, had been found dead in his home. Police said the place had been ransacked, the computers stolen.

Oddly, Elroy felt neither shock nor sadness. He felt as if he'd known all along this was coming. He said something appropriate about the senselessness of a young life lost, and then they headed back up to the main restaurant on the resort to have breakfast. Over their toast and egg-white omelets, they talked less than usual. It seemed everything about the issue had already been said. When the waiter came to clear their plates, Alina said she wanted to go for a swim in the ocean, and Elroy said he'd meet her there. He just wanted to stop at the room for a moment first. There, he set his suitcase on the bed and unearthed a small square of folded paper from beneath his clothes. The mattress squeaked as he sat down, uncreasing the folds in the paper. For perhaps the hundredth time, he reread the poem "Bubblegum Prayer," and when he was through, he felt better.

He refolded the sheet, returned it to its spot at the bottom of his suitcase, and changed into his swim trunks. Then he headed out into the sunshine to meet Alina.

* * *

Discussion Questions

1. Is something art because of what it means to the creator or what it means to the consumer? Can something be art without the creator intending it to be?
2. What (if anything) is the distinction between using a computer program to write a poem, Photoshop to make a photo, or a camera obscura to create a painting?
3. Do you think the literary organization should have retracted the poetry award? Why or why not?
4. Would it matter at all if the computer program had produced dozens of poems and the programmer selected his favorite to submit, discarding the others? What if he had made minor word changes to the initial draft prior to submitting it? Is there some minimal level of choice that makes a computer-generated poem a human creation?
5. Would it matter to your analysis if the boy, L. P. Page, was a computer programming genius and others would not have been able to create a computer program that would have produced such an impressive poem?

* * *

Disconnect

Julia Meinwald

* * *

It's 7:12 p.m., and Simone has this guy in the palm of her proverbial hand. Technically speaking, it's not her hand. The guy is on a date with Alexis, one of Simone's most loyal clients at Connect2. Simone is clicked into her terminal three miles away. Alexis has flipped the switch, giving Simone full control over her actions and words and full access to her thoughts and sensations. Each client feels different to pilot. If the client has joint pain or a headache, the pilot feels it. Many pilots find their first week on the job an almost spiritual experience, feeling the similarities and differences in how various human bodies move through the world. Simone, one of the most respected, in-demand pilots at Connect2, has inhabited over two hundred people.

Piloting Alexis is fun for Simone. Alexis has the sharpest sense of smell Simone has ever encountered, and her near-constant pulse of nervous energy feels energizing to Simone. Alexis is a well-oiled Porsche, and Simone is a racecar driver. Or something. Simone doesn't really care about cars, but Alexis has some strong memories associated with her father's prized Maserati. It's not Simone's job to unpack this. It's her job to make this guy fall for Alexis.

It doesn't hurt that Alexis is beautiful. She's gorgeous in a predictable, blonde and leggy way. She has a nice laugh, too, which Simone deploys now to show this guy that she gets his Vonnegut reference. Simone hasn't actually read Vonnegut, but she knows enough to recognize popular characters and ideas. Guys never want to talk about the books anyway. They just want to throw down the reference to see if their date picks it up. "You're funny," she says to the guy. This is a bit on the nose for Simone, but she's calculated right; the guy preens and, as if repaying a social debt, asks her about herself. Or rather, he asks her about Alexis. Or, rather, he asks "Alexis" about Alexis.

If Alexis were in control right now, she would demur. She can't stand talking about herself and honestly finds a question as broad as "Tell me about yourself" borderline aggressive. Simone, however, has no problem with this. In her own life, she can happily monologue about the flurry of worries and amusements filling any given day. It's only slightly more difficult to do this for someone else. She tells the guy about the book Alexis is reading, about Alexis's sister's impending wedding, and transitions seamlessly into a story about a business lunch that draws attention to the impressive company where Alexis works in HR. She's careful to speak in Alexis's syntax. The less successful pilots at Connect2 go too far, making their clients perfect embodiments of charm. When the client flips the switch back and tries to take over, the discrepancies are glaring, and the subsequent dates are disastrous. Connect2 estimates that close to 15 percent of first dates in Los Angeles involve a pilot, but getting caught as a passenger on a date is still considered a red flag in the dating world. The trick is to present Alexis as faithfully as possible—just amping up a few parameters to make a better first impression.

Simone has just revealed where Alexis went to college, and the guy makes a face that both women read as patronizing. Simone feels Alexis's impulse to flinch, but she stifles it. She pauses for a moment to see if Alexis is going to signal that she'd like to take control of the date, but she doesn't. Generally, clients flip the switch to take control mid-date in two situations: when they want to end the date prematurely or when they want to get physical. Every now and then, Simone gets someone who wants her to pilot the first kiss, but anything beyond that is forbidden by the Connect2 code of conduct. In Alexis and Simone's first few months together, Alexis would constantly flip the emergency override switch—forcibly seizing control against Simone's advice. A guy teasingly mocks her order? Emergency override. A guy doesn't get Simone-as-Alexis's funny joke? Uber is en route. After enough dates like this, though, Simone has earned Alexis's trust.

This guy seems judgmental, but Simone has gotten some positive bio-signals from Alexis. Part of Simone's job is to debrief with Alexis after the dates. To help her clarify her own feelings about a guy and choose a course of action. The consulting part is fun, but what Simone loves most are the dates themselves. Some of her friends think that piloting is like a superpower, but in truth, it's easier to see (and be) what someone else wants when you don't have to tend to your own personal desires. A surprising number of pilots at Connect2, including Simone, are single.

"I'm honestly shocked how many girls I go on dates with who just *don't read*," the guy is saying.

"Okay," says Simone, "I could be wrong, but is that tattoo on your wrist a literary reference?"

* * *

The day after the date is Alexis's twenty-ninth birthday. She knows it's not a big deal birthday. Next year, she might force herself to throw some sort of party for the big three-O. To pick the best, quietest, quirkiest bar in Silverlake, spend twelve hours crafting the perfect three-sentence email invite, then despair when only ten people show up and no one stays past midnight. Probably, though, she won't. Alexis doesn't act, she reacts. She receives, she waits, she happily makes the second move. It's a safer, easier way to move through the world.

Alexis doesn't list her birthday on social media, but it still feels like a personal affront that she's only gotten a handful of birthday greetings so far. None of them feel at all personal to her. She's got messages from her parents and her sister on the family text chain, but those feel rote, too. Alexis can't help but read this as a referendum on the quality of her personality. If she were smarter, funnier, kinder, she would probably be surrounded by gifts, confetti, and people who love her.

Her twenty-eighth birthday wasn't bad. Her boyfriend at the time took her to dinner, but just at their local Italian place, which had paper napkins and fewer cheese and pepper flake shakers than tables; the wait staff would ferry them back and forth between diners as needed. They talked, as they usually did, about his fantasy hockey league and how unethical and stupid various politicians were. The quotidian quality of the date made Alexis wonder if he was planning on dumping her. A few months later, he did indeed end things; Alexis was never sure if the lackluster birthday dinner was an early warning sign or not.

In an effort to celebrate herself (something culture seems to want her to do), Alexis takes a cupcake from her fridge and a birthday card from work out of her bag. All her coworkers have signed it, but the closest thing to a personalized message is the drawing of a rat wearing a party hat that her colleague Meredith drew in the card's lower right-hand corner. Meredith draws *Birthday Rat* on everyone's cards, but at least it has more personality than the usual "Happy birthday" and "Hope you have a fantabulous day!"

Her doorbell rings as she's stoically waiting for her cupcake to warm up and lose that cold fridge feeling. She springs to the door with an embarrassing dose of optimism. She's greeted by an old Asian woman bearing two dozen roses, which Alexis signs for and brings to the kitchen with cumbersome happiness. The card informs her that the roses are from Connect2. She's disappointed that they are from a company and not a person, but she has to admire their customer service.

Alexis suspects she's probably one of Connect2's most active users. She had hated dating before, but dates piloted by

Simone are fun, and the debriefs are even better. Sometimes Alexis even accepts a date with a guy she knows she's not interested in, just so she can make fun of him with Simone after the fact.

Alexis's phone dings. It's an email from Simone listing twenty-four things to love about Alexis—one for each rose in the bouquet. Alexis lifts the cupcake to her lips, reading the list again and again with each chocolaty bite.

* * *

Alexis shows up twelve minutes early for her debrief with Simone, sits in her car until she is only four minutes early, then enters the Connect2 building. The door to Simone's office is open, and Simone has implanted herself into a beanbag chair with two coffee mugs in front of her. Alexis lowers herself into the other beanbag as Simone exclaims, "Girl! You're wearing the sweater!" Simone and Alexis spent a good ten minutes going over the pros and cons of purchasing a turtleneck, debating whether Alexis could pull it off, and delving into what the larger ramifications of such a sartorial choice might be. Alexis shrugs with some pleasure.

"It looks so good!" says Simone. "You look like a stylish bunny rabbit. Can I touch it?"

Alexis nods, and Simone runs her hand down the length of Alexis's arm. To Alexis, it feels like the kinesthetic equivalent of ASMR. "Mmmmm," says Simone. "Softness."

"This is my first time wearing it," says Alexis.

"I'm honored I get to see it on its maiden voyage!" says Simone. "So, obviously, we have an agenda, but can I tell you a story first?"

"Always," says Alexis, settling into her beanbag.

"Okay, so I had an intro session with a new client yesterday. A really rich guy who just decided to open his marriage and wants to find a new sidepiece, these are his words, 'as efficiently as possible.' So, we finish up the regular intake stuff, and then he asks me... if I'll cut his hair."

"What?" Alexis laughs.

"Yeah, I was like, my dude, that is not part of this service, but best of luck to you."

"I might have done it," says Alexis, picking up the mug Simone has set out for her and inhaling deeply.

"Do you know how to cut hair?" asks Simone.

"A little. I cut some friends' hair in college. I've always thought there's something kind of romantic about it. In the right context, I mean. Something about how they trust you. It's like you're doing a loving act of service."

"Plus, you're kind of molding the person into a new version of themselves. New do, new you."

"Right. Like in those spy shows where the woman gets a new haircut and suddenly no one recognizes her."

Simone laughs. "So, shall we discuss our first order of business? Thumbs up or thumbs down on our Great Literary Mind?"

Alexis does a sideways thumb, and Simone lets out a theatrical groan. "Alexis!" she says. "They can't all be sideways thumbs! Seriously, is there *any* chance *this guy* is your soulmate?"

"There's a chance this coffee is my soulmate," says Alexis, making the kind of joke Simone makes and liking how it tastes in her mouth.

* * *

Simone clicks into her terminal for Alexis's next first date, and when she sees who the date is with, she almost chokes. Alexis is on a date with Jason. Neurotic, goofy, charming Jason. It's not unheard of for pilots to encounter someone they know in real life while on the job. The Connect2 code of conduct doesn't forbid it; you just need to fill out an extra form disclosing your situation. Simone knows immediately she will not be truthful when she fills out the form about Jason. She has harbored what could only be referred to as a tragic crush on him for close to two years. Members of the same running club, they often fall into pace with each other, and have even grabbed breakfast together after their runs on occasion. Simone has hinted pretty aggressively that she is interested, but Jason, a paragon of tact, has never acknowledged her overtures. He's perfected his Friend Face—a look that says *I adore you, but nothing interests me less than seeing you naked.*

Simone as Alexis goes through the basic opening pleasantries with Jason, asking about his day and how he chose this place. She is always invested in getting a good outcome for her clients, but for the first time, she feels nervous. It's strange seeing Jason in date mode. His hair is still wet from a shower, and she's never seen this plaid shirt before. She feels a strange mixture of jealousy and titillation.

"There's this painting," Jason says. "I don't know the name of it or who painted it, but it's of this woman in a field, sort of looking over her shoulder at the painter or at someone. It's weird, but I keep thinking you look just like that woman in the painting."

"Where did you see the painting?" she asks.

"I had a postcard of it in my room growing up," Jason answers.

"I had postcards in my room, too!" She gets a quizzical burst from Alexis, who never collected postcards. Simone doesn't think including this one personal detail from her own life will blow the facade. She has never felt this tight, focused kind of energy from Jason before. There's no harm in enjoying it for a moment.

"I'm so afraid of rambling on and sucking all the oxygen out of the room," says Jason. "Tell me about yourself." Simone goes through her basic intro to Alexis spiel. Jason asks if she wants to stay for another cup of coffee. Simone does.

* * *

The next day, after a 5K, the whole running group goes out drinking. Simone and Jason are sharing a massive plate of nachos, the bar is playing one of Simone's favorite albums in its entirety, and life is good. Even though she knows she did not actually go on a date with Jason the day before, she feels closer to him. She shifts her weight under the table, rubbing her toe up the leg of Jason's jeans. He stands abruptly, saying the next round is on him. Their friend Diane approaches and starts talking about whether or not she should quit her job. Simone looks to the bar, catches Jason's eye, and he makes a face at her like *we know the same thing*. She knows it's not a great sign that when she flirts with him, he pulls away, but her gin and tonic is delicious, and she is invincible. Jason sits back down with Simone and Diane, and the three of them go over the few pros and numerous cons of her job.

"Simone, you like *your* job, right?" slurs Diane.

"Being a professional Cyrano?" teases Jason. "Who wouldn't like that? Simone gets paid to date."

"And I get glowing reviews," Simone preens. "Promoted three times in as many years, *and* my picture is on our recruiting pamphlet."

"The face of the faceless," Jason says.

"Let's play a game," says Simone. "Everyone think of a secret about the person to your left and whisper it to the person to your right." She leans close to Jason and whispers, "There's someone at this table I want to kiss more than Diane."

Jason smirks and bonks Simone on the top of her head. "Good secret, drunko." He leans over to Diane and whispers, loud enough for Simone to hear, "Simone has two levels, totally sober and totally wasted. Nothing in between."

Diane leans into Simone and whispers, "I fucking *hate* my job." She has not fully understood the assignment.

They stay out until closing, and Simone and Jason are the last two standing on the curb, waiting for their Ubers. Simone keeps reaching for Jason's hand, and he keeps holding it for a few seconds, then letting it go.

"I think you're just the cat's meow," says Simone. Then, taking his hand again, "I'm not tired yet."

"Simone. Not tonight," says Jason.

A minute or so later, his Uber shows up, and he gets in. Simone knows rejection when she hears it. But she can't help coming back to the possibilities that all non-tonight nights might still hold.

* * *

Simone is still feeling cocktails four through six from

the night before when she meets Alexis for their next check-in. Alexis is paying three dollars a minute to meet with her, wrapped into her monthly bill, but Simone often gives her an extra ten minutes or so for free because Alexis is one of the sane ones. Simone genuinely would like to see a happy ending for her.

"For me, Jason is a pass," Alexis says, once they've briefly compared notes on the previous night's episode of *The Bachelor.* "He was so in his head. I felt like we were both so nervous; it was hard for me to get comfortable."

Simone is genuinely surprised. It's hard to picture someone not liking Jason. "To be fair," says Simone, "you don't usually feel comfortable when first meeting someone."

"I didn't take an official tally," Alexis says, "but I think he apologized to me, like, ten times over one coffee." Simone guffaws.

"Yeah, he did seem pretty eager to impress," says Simone. "If you want, next time I can keep an official 'I'm sorry' count from my terminal. We can make an over/under bet, and if you win, I'll let you give me a haircut."

"I think if I win, you should give *me* a haircut," says Alexis.

"You may find the results alarming, but yes, I'm in," says Simone, shaking Alexis's hand.

"So, you really think I should see him again?" asks Alexis.

"Has he reached out to you?" Simone asks, trying not to sound overly invested.

"He asked if I'm up for dinner on Friday," Alexis confirms.

"Tell him yes," says Simone.

* * *

Getting dressed for her second date with Jason, Alexis is thinking about soulmates. As part of the intake process at Connect2, clients have to describe how they picture their soulmate. Most people jot down a few sentences about being someone's priority or feeling sparks that mature into smoldering embers. Alexis wrote close to a thousand words. Alexis thinks a soulmate is someone who knows all of your thoughts and still accepts you. She thinks a soulmate gives you small doses of optimism when you can't get out of your own head. She thinks things that are hard for you will be easy for your soulmate. Where Alexis is shy, her soulmate will have chutzpah. Things that Alexis fears will be welcome challenges for her soulmate. Simone, trying to lighten the mood, proclaims all sorts of people and things to be her soulmate: the deli cat next door to Connect2's offices, the writer of that one SNL sketch that was actually really good, comfortable shoes, a nice breeze. The message, Alexis thinks, is that her soulmate might be right under her unusually sensitive nose. Alexis thinks Simone may be right about this.

* * *

When Simone clicks in for Alexis and Jason's dinner date, she sees that Alexis has not even worn one of her top ten date outfits, but Jason is looking sweaty and serious in a way that Simone finds lovely.

"I've got you," Simone says to Alexis, as she always does right before she flips the switch to take control. "This is going to be a good night."

* * *

Over dinner, Jason asks Alexis question after question. He asks if she can hear him chewing (she can), if she has ever gotten so mad she's wanted to hit someone (she hasn't), if she thinks David Lynch is going to make any more films (she doesn't care). As Simone's words come out of her mouth, though, Alexis realizes that Simone cares. She cares about David Lynch films; she teases Jason with a warmth Alexis doesn't feel. Alexis learns more about Simone on this date than in all of their debriefs together.

Alexis lets her mind wander, thinking about how strange being piloted is. She smells the flowers Jason has brought her, thinking *I am letting Simone smell flowers.* She raises her hand to her cheek. *Simone is touching my face. Simone tastes the sweet whipped cream I'm swallowing.* Simone has access to these thoughts, but is focused on the guy sitting across from Alexis.

The check comes, and Jason looks down. "So, I don't know if you'd want to, I dunno, go for a walk or maybe come to my place for a drink?" he says.

* * *

Simone has seen Alexis's engagement drifting as dinner has worn on, but she feels like she's on one of the best dates of her life. Especially when the conversation turns philosophical, and she can push aside Alexis's biographical specifics and share more of her own views. When she makes Jason laugh, she feels like a queen.

Simone doesn't see what harm a quick postprandial walk could do. She gets that Alexis isn't attracted to Jason, but she hasn't flipped the switch to take control and end the date.

"You live near here?" Simone asks as Alexis, knowing

that he does.

"Just a couple blocks away." Jason smiles.

It has rained, leaving the air cool and the streets glistening. They cut across a park and, in a few minutes, arrive at Jason's building. Simone tries to soak in each second, knowing that Alexis will take control and end the date at any moment.

"God. I can't get over how beautiful you are," says Jason. Then he kisses her. It's a kiss Simone has been thinking about for over a year, and just the fact of it finally happening is mind-blowing. She kisses him back.

* * *

Alexis does not like kissing this loud-chewing, ever-apologizing guy. His lips feel gummy against hers. She's fascinated, though, by the idea that both she and Simone are in the same kiss. How strange, she thinks, to be a conduit for someone else's pleasure. Jason's hands are all over her now. His touches are all too gentle like he's trying to tickle her. Meanwhile, Simone is using Alexis's hands in ways she never would. She's pulling handfuls of Jason's hair, biting his lips. Alexis concentrates on being there but not there. She imagines herself as the spoke of a wheel, perfectly still, warmly wrapped in the embrace of perpetual motion.

* * *

Here are the things Simone most likes remembering from her night with Jason. The way that he put his hand between her head and the backboard of his bed so she wouldn't bang it against the wood. The fact that after taking off her blouse, Jason folded it and put it on his nightstand. Sure, it's not her blouse, not her head, but the experience was immersive. Her favorite memory is the few seconds of silence after they'd slept together, broken by Jason saying, with a goofy smile, "So, that was fun." Alexis hadn't flipped the switch until they'd finished coffee and a crossword the next morning.

She knows that if her supervisor digs into the logs for this date, it won't be good. Alexis's biodata didn't align with the choices Simone was making for her, and Simone has violated a clear rule against piloting a sexual encounter. Technically, it's a fireable offense, possibly even one with legal consequences. She's confident, though, that if Alexis really wanted to take back control, she would have. Maybe, Simone thinks, Alexis was even giving her some sort of gift—intuited Simone's investment in the moment and decided not to take it away from her. Simone knows she's done something wrong, but until an outside party tells her how wrong, she's going to assume the transgression was minor.

* * *

That Sunday, Simone sits across from Jason, digging into diner eggs after a run. Simone keeps trying to steal potatoes off Jason's plate, and Jason keeps pushing her fork away.

"What's up with you this morning?" Simone finally asks.

"It's nothing," says Jason. Then, after an uncharacteristic silence between them, "I kinda get the feeling that you don't love it when I talk about my romantic life."

"That's crazy. You can talk to me about anything."

"Okay. Well, I guess I'm in a funk because I went on

what I thought was a really great date with this girl, but she ghosted me."

Simone fills her lungs with courage. "I mean, I know I'm not this amazing girl who ghosted you, but *I'd* be pretty into taking you on a date sometime." Jason looks at his eggs. Too many seconds pass. "Maybe a romantic trapeze lesson?" she appends lamely.

Finally, Jason arranges his features into Friend Face. "You're such a loon," he says, taking a forkful of potatoes and plopping them onto Simone's plate. "Eat your eggs and stop prying into my sad love life." Simone has been drunk on the great flood of serotonin coursing through her ever since the date. Here, in this overbright diner, rejected once again, she crashes hard. They finish breakfast in relative quiet, both thinking back to their own separate versions of the same night.

* * *

Alexis brings macaroons to her Monday session with Simone. For some reason, she wonders if Simone will bring some kind of confection herself—if they will be faced with an embarrassment of desserts—but when she arrives, Simone is empty-handed, slumped in her beanbag.

"So," Alexis begins, "crazy date, huh?"

Simone smiles weakly, then seems to resolve to engage and sits up a bit straighter. "I counted twelve on the apology tally, so I think I owe you a haircut," says Simone, but her eyes aren't fully smiling. The excitement Alexis had felt on the drive over starts to evaporate. It's not that she'd imagined passionately kissing Simone. She hadn't even imagined Simone thanking her. She'd just pictured the two of them sipping coffee and dissecting their shared experience.

"I don't think there's going to be a third date with Jason," she says carefully.

"Well, you can't force yourself to be into someone you're just not into," says Simone. Alexis wonders if Simone is referring to her own disdain for Alexis. She wonders if Simone thinks she is pathetic. To be rejected by someone who is literally paid to spend time with her would be a new low.

Meeting with Alexis usually energizes Simone, but today even Alexis's open face, her receptivity to all Simone has to offer, isn't enough. Simone knows what Alexis wants from her, abstractly at least. If she was piloting someone else in her shoes, she would give Alexis a hug, tell her the date had been wild and she'd never done anything like that before. Tell Alexis that she'd love to get dinner sometime, just the two of them. As both pilot and passenger, Simone can't get any of this out.

"What're all these boxes for?" Alexis asks.

"Well, my friend, it's the end of an era," says Simone. "Today is my last day at Connect2."

"Oh, did you...."

"My manager reviewed the logs from your date with Jason."

"Weren't you pilot of the month last month?"

Simone is briefly impressed with Alexis's memory. "Yeah, for the third time. But, they take the code of conduct seriously."

"I wasn't... I would have taken back control if... I mean, I think it was an interesting night for everyone." Alexis can't quite articulate why she let things go so far. It has something to do with the overfull sensation of being touched by one person while your thoughts stream to someone else. It has something to do with grasping for the only kind of connection you can reach.

"Being a star employee was sort of *my thing,*" says Simone. "But, at the end of the day, I'm just a girl who gets fired for cause. Anyway, I guess they'll assign you a different pilot."

"I don't really want another pilot."

"Yeah," Simone sighs, with a roll of her eyes. "I'm basically irreplaceable." She takes a half-hearted bite of the macaroon Alexis brought. "These are good. You didn't have to do this."

"Oh, I know," says Alexis. "I wanted to." Then, reaching shyly into her bag, "I brought something else." Alexis pulls out a hairbrush and a simple pair of cutting scissors. She guides Simone from the beanbag to a proper chair, spreading an old sheet she brought from home on the floor around them. She smooths Simone's hair. She runs her fingers across Simone's scalp. She brushes out Simone's wild mane until it is a cloud around her head. She begins to cut.

"New do, new you, right?"

Simone feels herself relax, if only a little. She tries to breathe out Jason, breathe out her manager's disappointment, and breathe in the feeling of Alexis's hands at work. To embrace the idea that a macaroon and the friend who brings it to you is a thing of great value.

"This haircut is my soulmate," Simone says. She's not entirely wrong.

* * *

Discussion Questions

1. If you could have someone "pilot" you on a date, would you allow them to? At what point in the date would you want to take over control? After how many dates would you no longer want them to pilot you? Would you ever tell your partner you were piloted at the start of the relationship?

2. Is there a difference between being "piloted" by another person on a date and being the date version of yourself on a date? (*energetic, interested, funny...*) If so, what is the difference in presenting these two false versions of yourself?

3. Connect2 asks clients to describe how they picture their soulmate. How would you describe your soulmate? To be truly happy in a relationship, must a person date their imagined soulmate? Is a person settling for less if they date someone who doesn't exactly meet those ideals?

4. Given that Alexis could take back control at any time, did Simone do anything wrong by continuing the date through sexual intercourse?

5. If you could, like Simone and Alexis, share the experience and sensations of a sexual encounter with someone else, would you? Who would you share that experience with? Would you be obligated to tell your partner two minds inhabited the one body in front of them?

* * *

Echo

C.M. Selbrede

* * *

Thirteen Stars

Once, during a depressive episode, Stanley cut out thirteen small paper stars and taped them to the ceiling of his cluttered bedroom. They were made from the construction paper left over from his youth, stored away in a basket on a shelf in the basement, forgotten until that very moment. He was seventeen.

Stanley had seen glow-in-the-dark stars online and had always thought they'd make his room look cooler. But he didn't have any of those, and he was depressed, super depressed, because Gavin and Bartholomew had been shit-talking him behind his back, and that sucked, so hey, why not make paper stars to cheer him up.

Life didn't work that way, Stanley knew. But he wasn't sure exactly how life worked.

A knock at the door. Stanley's sister, an older woman

with kind eyes and frizzy hair, peered at him from the doorway. "Hey, Stan. What's up?"

"What do you mean?" Stanley said flatly from where he was lying on his bed, staring up at the lame paper stars as if they meant something.

"You don't do arts and crafts unless you're upset," Lizzy said, shrugging. She stepped over the mounds of unread comics and books carefully, making her way to the bed and sitting down next to him. "Talk to me."

Stanley hesitated, but he knew there was no chance tonight didn't end with him spilling his guts to Lizzy. They had that kind of bond. "Have you ever heard of something called Echoing?"

"Capital *e* Echoing?" Lizzy wrinkled up her nose. "Gross."

"So you have," Stanley said.

"Of course I have," Lizzy said. "It's all anyone can talk about at work. Personality transplants. They say it can help deal with violent or dangerous criminals."

"Yeah," Stanley said, swallowing. He let the silence linger for a moment before saying, "Apparently, Gavin and Bart think I should get Echoed."

"What?!" Lizzy recoiled. "Excuse me? Why?"

Stanley shrugged. "Word on the street is they're thinking it can be used for people with autism and depression too. People like me."

Lizzy shook her head in disbelief. "You don't need to change, Stan. Not for anyone."

"I know," Stanley said. Another charged silence followed until he cleared his throat. "But do you think I'd be happier?"

"Why would you be happier?" Lizzy said.

"I just... wonder sometimes. If I knew when to dap up my friends instead of just high-fiving them. If I had the confidence to go shirtless at the beach. If I—"

"You can't spend your life thinking about what ifs," Lizzy said. "You'll miss the whole thing."

"But that's all I do," Stanley said. "I imagine a life where fitting in isn't painful. Where happiness isn't fleeting and rare."

It was Lizzy's turn to be silent. "Do we need to make another appointment with Dr. Bramble?"

Stanley shook his head. "I'm fine," he said.

A blue paper star detached from the ceiling and fluttered to the bed, a splash of color on a sea of gray sheets. Stanley watched it, wondering if he should've made a wish as it fell.

Lucky Number Twelve

Stanley lay on his bed, staring up at the blank ceiling of his college dormitory. Part of him missed his paper stars. The rest of him was grateful he hadn't brought them. He wasn't sure they'd be able to stand to see what he'd become.

It was 11:15. Stanley's class had started at 11. He was missing it again. Not for any good reason. His ADHD and depression had just been flaring up, so he'd been missing a lot of classes, spending his days stewing in regret instead of being a productive member of society.

It wasn't just class. Stanley had joined the club rugby team a semester ago, and he was okay at it. Lucky number twelve, in fact... a center. But he hadn't been to practice for weeks. He knew the guys were talking about him, but why wouldn't they? He'd never fit in at the socials. The first few times Stanley was drunk, he'd walk around the mucky, frat-like basement backward because, for some reason, that seemed like the kind of thing a drunk person would do. That was weird. Stanley was weird. The memory of his stupidity hurt, almost physically. It stabbed him from the inside out until he was sure his throat was filled with knives.

Stanley's phone buzzed. It was Oscar. He groaned.

Oscar was probably Stanley's best friend. They'd met during orientation on the mandatory hike through the gross Maine wilderness, and Oscar had fallen into a pond by accident. Stanley had helped fish him out, and for some reason, they just felt like friends afterward. So they were.

Oscar was the kind of person Stanley wanted to be: confident, outgoing, athletic, competent. Stanley could go on. Oscar wasn't perfect—Stanley knew that—but Oscar knew what he wanted from life and was determined to get it.

He also didn't walk backward while drunk.

Muttering to himself, Stanley answered the phone. "Hello?"

"Oh, sick, you're up," Oscar said over the line. "I have something crazy to tell you."

"What is it?" Stanley did his best to sound interested, even though on the inside, all he could think about was how he was just a collection of rotting cells, growing and deteriorating and choking the Earth even though he was only going to be alive for a short period of time and—

"My neighbor, Elena," Oscar said, "she's nonspeaking,

right? That kind of autism. Well, she got Echoed."

Stanley sat up in his bed, suddenly distracted from his impending demise. "What?"

"Yeah. She talks now. She's... normal. Completely normal."

"Oh," Stanley said, trying not to sound too wistful. "Is that...?"

"I dunno," Oscar said. "I don't think anyone really knows what to think. Her dad is ecstatic, but her mom, she's shattered. Says there's a piece of her forever missing."

Stanley wondered what it felt like to be somebody else. It was probably easier. It had to be.

Eleventh of November

Stanley stared at the piece of paper sitting on his desk. It was an invitation... frilly and golden and sparkling in the worst way. "You are cordially invited to the wedding of Oscar Jackson Nunez and Kelly Ursula Young on the eleventh of November, blah, blah, blah..."

Oscar was getting married. He'd met a girl, fallen in love, and proposed, all before Stanley had gotten his first kiss. Stanley was happy for Oscar. He really was. But goddamn it.

"Goddamn it." Stanley swore, chucking the invitation behind him. He'd be there. Of course he'd be there. Even though he wasn't one of Oscar's groomsmen like he'd always thought he might be because Oscar and Kelly both had several brothers, and they could only have so many groomsmen, and yeah, that was true, but it was also probably true that Stanley just wasn't good enough.

Which wasn't surprising. He was a screwed-up English

major living at home, working a part-time job and writing a novel nobody would ever care about. It was no wonder nobody from the dating apps stuck around.

If Stanley thought about it, what were the chances, cosmically speaking, that he'd find "The One"? There were only so many gay guys out there, fewer who were willing to date a guy without abs, fewer who were willing to date an autistic one, probably even fewer who were willing to date an autistic guy who self-harmed once every couple of months just to feel alive. Here Stanley was, hurtling around the Earth at a breakneck speed, an ugly sack of cells just like he always thought he'd be.

Stanley's phone buzzed. He reached for it, half expecting it to be Oscar, but no, Oscar was too busy these days. It was just some social media app sending him a pointless push notification. Sighing, Stanley unlocked his phone, hoping to make it go away, but he tapped on it instead.

At the top of Stanley's feed was a picture of a woman he'd never met, Elena, Oscar's neighbor who'd been Echoed. She was visiting Paris or somewhere similar, Stanley guessed, because the backdrop of her photos were those cluttered streets you only saw in Europe. She was holding some woman's hand in a way that indicated more than friends. She looked happy.

Stanley wished he remembered what happy felt like.

Ten of Diamonds

Stanley hated card games. They required focus and foresight and the ability to think quickly, skills he'd been short on for as long as he could remember. But here he was, at Oscar's bachelor party at the casino, trying to figure out if a ten of diamonds was good or bad in this situation.

Stanley wasn't surprised that Oscar had chosen not to do the standard strippers-and-such for the event, but he had been surprised that he'd picked a casino. Stanley had never been to a casino before, but after a few hours surrounded by polished wood, bright neon signs, and the smell of booze, he was starting to get the sense he didn't like them very much.

That wasn't to say things were all bad. Oscar had been sure to spend a lot of time with Stanley even though it was his night. They'd had a few drinks and a couple of laughs. But Oscar's (fraternal) twin brother, Oliver, was driving Stanley crazy in the sense that he was somehow exactly Stanley's type and also a complete and utter douchebag.

"It's not too late to get a stripper in here," he said for the thousandth time that night. Oliver thought he was really funny. If Stanley was a lesser man, he would've laughed, tried to get in Oliver's pants. But Stanley knew that was a pipe dream.

Sighing, Stanley took another sip of his martini. This was going to be a long night.

Nine out of Ten

One martini turned into two, and then three, and the next thing Stanley knew, the world was swimming, and he was sitting next to Oliver at the bar, just chatting. They'd warmed up to each other significantly since they'd become the drunkest men at the affair and had abandoned the pretense of gambling for the reality of slurred words and slimy commentary.

"She seems like a nine out of ten," Oliver muttered, jerking his head toward a girl playing blackjack at a nearby table.

"Really?" Stanley tilted his head. "I don't see it."

"You must be blind, then, bro," Oliver snickered.

"Nah," Stanley smirked. "Just gay."

Oliver's eyes widened. "Oh, you're gay! No shit, bro. I'm bi. Here, here... do me."

Stanley blinked. "What?"

"What am I out of ten?" Oliver smiled a wide, messy grin. "How do you rate me?"

"I don't rate cute guys out of ten," Stanley slurred, realizing too late what he'd said.

"Oh! I'm cute now, aren't I?" Oliver grinned.

"Puh-lease." Stanley looked away. His eyes half-focused on Oscar, who was watching the two of them from afar. Probably nervous they'd pass out. Not that it was outside the realm of possibility.

Oliver laughed... a cute laugh, the kind that made Stanley want to kiss him. Something like courage welled up inside of Stanley. He cleared his throat. "What would you rate me?"

"Not my type," Oliver said a little too quickly. Stanley recoiled.

"Shit, man," Oliver ran a hand through his hair. "I didn't mean that, I just..."

"It's fine..." Stanley got to his feet. "I should go to bed."

Eight Thin Lines

Eight thin scars ran horizontally across Stanley's wrist. They were old—old enough—but for some reason, they stung tonight.

Stanley's torso wasn't much better. Not exactly fat but not exactly skinny, he was average at best, his shoulders and back dotted with an absurd number of acne scars. He used to say he was star-speckled. The fact was, he was just ugly.

Stanley regarded himself in the mirror carefully. He thought about all the different people he always thought he could be growing up and how now he was just this. No do-overs, no chance at escape. Just hurt.

Unless...

A card rested on the hotel room dresser. An advertisement for an Echo Facility. One of the guests at the wedding ran one. Stanley studied the card carefully... it held a lot of promise for such a small, minimalist piece of paper. It could change the direction of his life forever. All he had to do was make the leap.

"You're scared, aren't you?" Stanley said to himself. "You don't want to lose who you are. But remember how miserable you are."

Taking a deep breath, Stanley picked up the card. "This is how you fix things."

Hands shaking, Stanley pulled out his phone and called the number on the card. "Hello? Yes, I'm interested in the procedure..."

Seven Hundred Dollars

"Seven hundred dollars?" Lizzy's voice quivered as she looked him up and down. "That's how much you're paying to lobotomize yourself?"

Stanley had returned home from the wedding fully prepared to tell Lizzy about his choice. Or so he'd thought.

Nothing could've prepared him for how upset she was.

"It's not a lobotomy," Stanley muttered, but Lizzy was having none of it.

"You're replacing yourself with a person you think you have to be," she said. "I mean, come on! How stupid can you be?"

"I'm not stupid," Stanley said angrily. "Just sad. And besides, even if I am stupid, I won't be after this."

"You can't be serious," Lizzy laughed a hollow laugh. "Come on, Stan. This is real life. There is no magic reset button."

"This is close enough," Stanley said.

"What personality did you even pick?" Lizzy spat. "What could you get for seven hundred dollars?"

"Just one of the defaults, nothing fancy," Stanley coughed.

"You're getting a *default* personality?" Lizzy was getting hysterical. "God, Stan. What does that mean?"

"It means I have the chance to be happy," Stanley said. "To be the person I've always wanted to be."

"We're not supposed to get everything we want in life." Lizzy shook her head. "That's for a reason."

"Now you just sound bitter." Stanley rolled his eyes.

"I am bitter," Lizzy said. "My only brother is killing

himself, and not only is he doing that, he has the nerve to warn me about it beforehand. Unbelievable."

"This is what I want," Stanley repeated lamely. He wondered if he was trying to convince Lizzy or himself.

6:33

Stanley's watch said 6:33. His appointment was supposed to be three minutes ago. There was still time to change his mind.

He wasn't going to.

It didn't matter how afraid Stanley was. It didn't matter how much he wanted to turn around and leave, to walk out of there and just resume the plodding countdown to death he'd been participating in all his life. He was going to be Echoed. He was going to know peace.

The waiting room at the Echoing Facility was almost completely empty. The only other human was the nurse at the front desk, a buff man with tattoos and scars. A few minutes ago, he'd asked if Stanley was okay.

"Yeah, just... nervous, I guess," Stanley had said.

"No worries, I was too," the nurse had responded. "But now I live a better life. I used to be dangerous. A bad person. Now, I just go home and watch *Doctor Who* reruns while drinking my favorite chamomile tea. It's crazy stuff, Echoing."

"You don't miss the person you used to be?"

"I don't know if I'm capable of that," the nurse admitted. "That's not how they wire us."

"Stanley Rhimes?" Another nurse appeared in the doorway, distracting Stanley from his thoughts. "So sorry for the delay. They're ready for you."

"Thank you," Stanley said, taking one last look at the outside world before he followed the new nurse into the office.

Five Things to Know

It was like sinking, sinking into a sea of unfamiliar thoughts. It was overwhelming, suffocating. Stanley tried to hang on to who he was, but soon, he couldn't tell which thoughts were his and which were the Echo's.

1. My name is Stanley Rhimes.

1. My name is Lee Rhimes.

2. I'm very unhappy.

2. I haven't found a way to be happy yet.

3. I like to keep to myself.

3. I like to have a good time.

4. I don't understand social cues.

4. Social cues come naturally to me.

5. I am a freak of nature.

5. I am a decent person.

The last of Stanley began to drown, and one final regret took hold. He wished he could've seen this new world as himself. But this was the choice he'd made.

With that, Stanley left the room.

New World

Whenever people asked Lee about the procedure, he wasn't really sure what to say. The whole thing was awkward to him. He remembered being Stanley, but those choices, those thoughts, didn't make sense to him anymore. He wasn't sure why anybody would choose to overwrite themselves like that. He was grateful for the chance to be who he was, really, but he couldn't help but feel a bit weird about the whole thing.

Nobody would let him forget he'd been Echoed, either. Everywhere he went, old acquaintances and distant friends stared at him like he was a three-headed extraterrestrial instead of a lovable goofball who loved baseball and the gym. Like... come on. Lee hadn't chosen this. He couldn't remember if Stanley had either. The personality he'd been presented with back then hadn't seemed quite so obsessive about baseball cards and getting laid.

And his close friends and family didn't want to be around him. They didn't say it to him outright, but Lee could tell. He was perceptive that way. Lizzy was furious whenever he walked into the room. She'd clench her jaw ever so slightly. It made Lee somewhat averse to being around her, in turn, and soon, they weren't nearly as close as they'd used to be.

Oscar, meanwhile, seemed on the verge of tears whenever they spoke. Apparently, he "blamed himself," whatever that meant. If this was anyone's fault, it was Stanley's. Not that Lee was complaining. For all his complex thoughts and feelings, he loved being himself.

Even if who he was wasn't really who he was.

What Changed?

"So... you're a writer?" asked Lee's date, Art, a muscular man who would've never given him the time of day before his Echoing. They were in Lee's apartment, having come home from a terrifying movie and a delicious dinner, and Lee was looking forward to whatever came next.

"Used to be," Lee shrugged, peeling off his shirt.

"What happened?"

"I changed," Lee said. He walked over to Art, who was paging through Stanley's old journal. Stanley would've died if anybody had read it. Lee really didn't care.

"Wow, man," Art shook his head. "This shit is dark. You good?"

"Yeah, bro, I'm fine." Lee walked over and threw an arm around Art's shoulder. "It's like I said. I changed."

"Yeah, but it's kind of beautiful too." Art looked up. "The line about feeling lost in the world hits hard."

Lee didn't remember that line, but he'd take Art's word for it. "Whatever," he said. "Let's get naked."

"You seriously don't remember any of this shit?" Art ignored him.

"Uh..." Lee was starting to feel like this night was going to depend entirely on how he answered this question. "...Maybe?"

"I've been feeling kind of like this, bro," Art pressed. "Lost. Aimless."

"You shouldn't," Lee said. Art frowned.

"No shit, Sherlock."

"Crap, I'm not good with feelings anymore. If you're that sad, just get Echoed like me."

Art blinked. "You were Echoed? Well... that makes more sense than I'd like to admit." With a sigh, Art put down his journal. "I don't think I'll be staying the night."

Crap.

"Why?" Lee tried not to sound too upset.

"It's too weird for me," Art admitted. "My cousin,

Archie, was one of the default personality models for the procedure. And yeah, he was happy, but he was also one of the least interesting, least meaningful people I've known in my life."

"That's kind of a rude thing to say about your cousin," Lee said.

"Is that what you think?" Art asked. "Or is that what the procedure thinks?"

Lee rolled his eyes. "Be for real, man. If you had the chance to cure yourself of your problems... to be happy like everyone else... wouldn't you take it?"

"I don't want to be happy like everyone else." Art shrugged. "I want to be happy like me. Besides... you can't cure mental illness. It's a part of you, the same as your smile or your eyes or the fears that keep you up at night. All you can do is live with it. Or, in your case, kill yourself in some twisted attempt at taking an easy way out."

"You think this is easy?" Lee laughed.

"Yeah, man. I do," Art said. "You don't have to take responsibility for any of the darkness you've felt. You don't have to feel it. You don't have to feel anything."

"Right now, I'm feeling pretty pissed that you're being like this." Lee snorted. "Come on. You don't know me."

"And I never will," Art said. He turned, grabbed his keys, and left Lee's apartment.

Askew

"You know," Lee slurred his words as he sat down at the edge of the water. "I was never happy. Not when I barely graduated college with only a few friends and very few happy memories. Not when I was ghosted by the seventh guy in the span of seven days. It felt like I was pulling something heavy through life. The weight of being me was unbearable. Every memory seemed tinted with shades of regret. Everything hurt. Everything was wrong."

Lee sighed. "But it's still wrong, isn't it? I cut myself while shaving the other day. I used to cut myself on purpose just to feel. Now, the blood means nothing. It belongs to someone else.

"Was the dude whose personality I jacked happy? Or was he just better at pretending? Am I happy? Is this happiness even mine? And more importantly... why can't I get myself to care?"

Lee got to his feet. "I'll never feel the things I used to feel, I guess. I don't even care that everyone hates my guts. It's just their loss. I feel like I should feel differently, but I don't. It's an echo of a feeling."

A distinctive chime from Lee's phone. It was some dude he'd been texting. Maybe seeing this man's body would make him feel better about the fact that his had been hollowed out.

Lee turned and left the water and the night sky behind. If he'd looked up, he would've seen that the stars were resting askew, as though they'd been taped to eternity by God himself.

* * *

Discussion Questions

1. Do you think Stanley did the right thing by getting Echoed? If you do think he did the right thing, what new piece of information in the story was the tipping point that convinced you and why?

2. If Echoing was a real thing, what rules and regulations would you put in place (*if any*) before a person could have the procedure?

3. Under the "Five Things to Know" subheading, Stanley is imbedded with a series of rephrasing. Do you think a person could Echo oneself just by positive self-talk? If yes, then why don't people do this more often?

4. Are happy people inherently less deep and/or less interesting? Can great art/creations be made without depression and pain?

5. If cheap and universal Echoing was a real thing with no legal restrictions, what percentage of the population do you think would get Echoed? What is your reasoning/justification for your choice?

* * *

I'll Not Risk Myself

Noelle Canty

* * *

My phone reception is better outside the laundromat, so I spend most of my time waiting for laundry on the bench near the door. I don't talk with my friends, but I surf the news. I like to know what's going on. I don't like people to know about me, though, even if I have known them for a while. Even my daughter doesn't know much, but maybe it's just because the drugs made me distrust her.

I'm reading about changes in EPA guidelines for wetland preservation, which might affect Indiana, when my daughter's name appears on my screen. She's calling me.

When your daughter is a drug dealer, you don't pick up, especially when you've gotten rid of a ten-year addiction to meth. Just recently, I checked out of rehab. Proud to say, I never bought drugs off her, but she was into coke, and I just stayed out of her business, out of her room. Most seventeen-year-olds have their moms on their backs, telling them to clean their rooms. Even though I know this isn't a good thing, I didn't tell her shit. I was a cool mom. School, homework, boyfriends, the Pill, whatever—I left her alone, and I thought we had a good relationship. Anyway, it gave me more time to work on myself. Which is what I need now.

Two weeks ago, my dentist was going to prescribe me an opioid for getting a tooth removed, but I said no. Apparently, too many young people are going around getting prescription painkillers just by purposely getting perfectly good teeth removed. And now we've got the young-adult population of our southern-Indiana county walking around with gaps in their mouths. That dentist isn't going to be trusting no one. Not for some time, at least. I don't need to get mixed up in nothing like that.

"Mom?" my daughter had asked, kind of pitifully, when her stepfather and I kicked her out of the house.

"I don't need a drug dealer living in my home when I'm trying to stay clean," I said, and Bill, my husband, silently backed me up.

I still feel guilty about it, and my finger strays near the name on the screen.

Pick it up, pick it up.

But she's bad news.

But you're a bad mom.

But you need to stay clean.

But you're strong enough for this.

Deciding that I am strong enough, I pick up the call, but I wait to let her speak.

"Um, hi."

"Hi."

"Um, I need help."

"I'm not giving you money for drugs or letting you come home."

"It's not that, actually. I, uhh..."

"Spit it out." My laundry's gonna come out of the dryer any minute.

"I need help. Getting married."

"I don't see what I have to do with that."

"I need you to sign my marriage license."

"Goddamit, Kathleen, can't you wait a couple months until you're eighteen?"

"Well, I'm on parole, and I need a permanent place of address, and he's the only person around volunteering to marry me."

"Who?" I ask crossly.

"Connor."

"Oh. Him."

"Mom..." she says warningly.

"Shut up!"

"I know what you're thinking."

"I don't want to be involved."

"But, Mom, I need a place to stay, and he's only going to let me stay if we're married."

"I guess that's a bonus." I cede her that, but inside, I'm counting off the things that could mean. *Maybe he really likes Kathleen. Maybe he feels really like he's doing the right thing by her to get married. Maybe getting married will really stabilize her, give her a new start, like me.*

"Mom, you know Connor's a good guy."

"Who never washes."

"He's plenty sanitary now."

I bet she's just lying. Anyhow, I agree to go up to Marion County and sign the papers. Being a minor, Kathleen needs to get a parent in on the marriage license. That's the thing about living in Indiana: you can get married at sixteen, but only if your parents let you. That sounds a lot like a Romeo-and-Juliet thing to me, complete with feuds, except that instead of power-play in a little Italian town, it involves fighting over drugs that we make at home or get from Mexico. In towns of two thousand people, where you marry somebody you met from high school or not at all, it's easy to remember old grudges. Except for the kids with the dating apps—that's how Kathleen met Connor. It was on Tinder, and they definitely struck a match there. Couldn't get their hands off each other. He never moved in, though. I don't know how much they love each other, but I guess I'll find out Monday.

Getting my laundry out of the dryer inside the laundromat, I glance at the TVs. They're playing old music videos silently, back from when I was a kid. Michael Jackson and stuff. Makes me wonder what I'd be like if I were off of drugs at seventeen instead of just starting them. My kid, always precocious, learned them from me. Giving her this chance seems like the only good thing I can do for her, unless Connor's as much of a terrible, stinking jerk as I remember him.

Should I sign a marriage certificate to give her a new start, to appease my conscience?

Should I risk getting re-involved in her drugs? She could still be a dealer. In fact, I almost certainly know that she is still a dealer. No one stops cold turkey. Knowing from experience, I should be the first to acknowledge it.

Well, what if signing the license gives me the excuse never to talk to her again? "I know you need money and a place to stay, Kathleen, but I done all I can, and we agreed to that." It could be all that nice and easy in a couple of years, or couple of days, depending on how long the marriage lasts.

If he hits her, it could last that short. Or it could prolong it, I know. My first husband was alcoholic and hit me when he got mean-drunk. I like to say it's better to be a cold, calm druggie than a mean, angry drunkard; and his being like that gave me the feeling that I was better than him, so I stayed married longer.

Actually, that's what I liked to say before I lost the drugs. Now, I shouldn't be thinking about drugs that much.

See, Kathleen's a bad influence on me? Bill, my second husband, always says that, and he's right, even if he is a little possessive.

I guess what really bothers me is that I know so little about Connor. I could be signing Kathleen's death certificate, for all I know.

As I throw the laundry emphatically into my baskets, I know I have to do something. Kathleen's going to stop asking me for help—stay out of my life and my house and my drug habits—only if she has a new place and new friends to go to. This will get rid of her for good.

When I get home, Bill is watching the seven o'clock news, but he gets up and opens the door for me, anyway. Kissing me on the cheek, he says, "I miss you when you're gone so long."

The trip to Marion will take only a couple hours, I think. In and out. Like a hypo.

I smile at him.

"I'm taking the car Monday to the doctor," he says.

I nearly do a double-take. "Your radiation treatments are on Fridays!"

"Got canceled today. Something wrong?"

"No," I lie. If he knew about Kathleen, he'd try to stop me.

"Sure? Honey, you told me you'd let me know if you're having trouble. Preventing a relapse is the most important thing right now."

Putting a hand to my head, I fake excessive fatigue, and he starts helping me to fold the laundry.

It can be really nice to have someone in love with you.

* * *

Monday morning, it turns out I can share a ride with a friend who's heading toward Gary. She'll pick me up at the DMV on the way back. It's a little unnerving that I can't choose when to leave Kathy—but I decided to do this, and I like keeping my promises. When you've got a broken past behind you, all you've really got is what you say in the present.

When I finally see Kathy, Connor is with her, and I'm not happy. I thought she was going to be all by herself, and the boyfriend being around makes it all too personal. With that frown on her face, Kathy makes me feel all sunken inside, like I made the wrong choice, and I want to run back down the highway to Scottsburg.

Connor's the one to say hi. He always was polite, a mama's boy. The thing is, I don't like being classified as a mama, so he struck me as more of a goody-two-shoes than a gent. His scrawny little-boy hair made him partially bald already, at the age of twenty-one, and his reedy little-boy voice grates on my nerves. How's a guy like this going to take care of my daughter?

"Hi, Ms. Carter."

"Hi, Connor," I manage. I know I sound forced, rushing past the greeting into, "Are we going to sign the marriage license papers now?"

"Sure are."

Scanning the desks, I try to make eye contact with the employees, but no one seems interested in our case.

"Where are we supposed to be?" I ask, wanting to do the right procedure.

"We'll wait out here until someone comes and gets us."

Determined not to talk with them, I settle into a plastic chair between two people I don't know and take out my phone, but I can't concentrate.

Kathleen's mere presence reminds me of all the good and bad things I wanted to forget. The day she got sent to juvenile detention for drug possession, the last day I saw her leave for school with her black hoodie over her head and her sulky swagger, like she was walking to the electric-guitar-featuring soundtrack of a bad-ass movie. The day she was born, when she was so innocent and all ready to be my baby, good and clean and smelling good, like a flower just popped up out of the earth. The day her dad and I got divorced, and she looked at me like she'd been betrayed. And now, she is getting married, not in a church with a white dress, the way I'd like to picture it, but in a red-brick box of a building, with that everlasting black hoodie. I haven't spent enough time with her for her to get married. I want her to myself, to water her and give her sunlight and make her grow until she is all blooming and old enough to make a good choice.

The thing is, I can't give her anything anymore, and she's a bad influence on me. I'd started crystal meth myself; it's easy enough to get in my hometown—but she'd been the one who'd normalized the lifestyle, made me think that because it was all that was going on in my house, it was okay. As long as I was by myself, with my hypodermic needle in the bathroom, wandering loopily through the house, I could think that it was not normal, feel lonely, and want to escape. Seeing her leaving her room and knowing it was to do a deal, I could say, "Yeah, I'm okay."

It just breaks my heart to see her now and know she isn't okay. Just makes me want to give her a big hug and get her a new hoodie. So I pretend I'm burning Connor at the stake for being her marriage option.

Connor whispers something to Kathleen, and I want to punch him for letting his breath touch her baby ear—the ear I'd hesitantly breathed on and put my teeth on when first holding her in the hospital. Not biting, mind you, but touching my teeth to. She was so, so soft, like a blanket. When I'd nurse her in the comfort of our bed at home, I'd suck her ear, lick her cheek, kiss her eyelids. Skin that soft wasn't meant for men. I'm already glaring at him like he's a child abuser.

Although it does seem like my fault for even considering signing the marriage certificate, I can't help blaming him, stacking up all the negative qualities he has against his offering my daughter a place to stay and a little love. One, he is almost five years older than my daughter. Two, he is slovenly. Three, his job doesn't seem reliable and I don't know much about it. Four, he wouldn't simply let her live with him without making her marry him. Without power himself, he is finding someone more vulnerable to lord over.

Forgetting that I'd originally thought of marriage with Kathleen as his trying to do right by her, I watch his every movement out of the corner of my eye. While I listen to him bat small talk at Kathleen, who stares at her jeans, the phone screen flits images past me. His cooing, nicknames, and talking about redecorating apartments probably are manufactured to make me feel at ease and not get in the way of their marriage. Eww, gross.

"Hey, Mrs. Carter," he asks, "want to see our apartment?"

He always mixes up calling me "Ms." or "Mrs." It's so sloppy.

His phone is in my face, so I can't help looking. It's pretty: bright blue paint on the walls and racks hung up with nice dishes.

"Who chose the color?" I ask back.

"My ex." He continues scrolling.

"How long were you together?"

"Two years."

"Were you married?"

"No." Nauseatingly, he flashes his bright white teeth at my daughter. "This is going to be forever, huh, babe?"

That's it. My daughter's habitually wary, hard eyes carry such motionless repulsion that I stand up. "Sorry,

Connor, but we're leaving."

"Hey! What?"

My daughter already hugs my waist with an arm as we begin to step away from the chairs.

"Ms. Carter, I don't think you understand! I'm going to get her a job at the factory where I work and everything! Not floor-work: desk-work, filing stuff—and—"

Child labor—no thank-you. Never mind that she can barely read because she's skipped so much school and will need a non-skilled job, if she even graduates. Never mind that she does need to support herself eventually. Never mind that a new life is the only thing I know of to get her to break the pattern of selling drugs to make money and having friends who are a bad influence. If I try to control her life, she'll be at least better off than she'd be with him.

Then, I remember I don't have the car with me. *Shit*.

I herd her back inside, Connor still wheedling innocuously at me.

"Talk to her, you coward!" I say. "She's an independent woman going to make a decision, the one who would have married you and your dirty hands."

"I consider it an honor to have dirty hands, Ms. Carter," he half-yells at me. "I work twelve-hour shifts at a factory oiling complex machinery and—"

An employee from the far end of the office comes up to us, I assume to make him leave, but she says, "Ms. Carter?"

"Yes?" my daughter and I answer at the same time.

Kathleen looks at me in shock. She's the one who originated the request for a marriage license, so the employee means her.

"Would you like to come to the back room?"

"Actually, we decided that we don't want to sign..." I start.

"We do!" Connor interrupts.

"We don't," Kathleen says quietly.

Confused, the blue-eyed, white-skinned woman gives us a scrutinizing glance. It makes me look at her like she's a person in real life instead of a government robot—take in her purple blouse, ironed trousers, and impractical, pointy-toed shoes.

"I have a meeting here scheduled for a Ms. Suzanne Carter to sign for Ms. Kathleen Carter to marry Mr. Connor Opinsky? Also, a police officer is here for Ms. Kathleen."

We stop talking over each other.

"That's what was taking me a bit of time out back," she said.

Kathleen has turned pale.

She's been selling drugs again, I know it. She couldn't last even two weeks out of the house without doing it. She still has her old contacts, her old ways of getting the drugs out here from who-knows-where.

Her grip on me tightens, but I shove it off.

"You bitch!" I scream. "You were supposed to not do anything! And this is how you repay me! I was going to take you home, when I wasn't even planning to! I didn't want to have anything to do with you, so I'd be clean, and I've worked my butt off trying to do the right thing, and you go and do the wrong thing when it would be so simple just to go to school and be a normal kid!"

Kathleen cries so hard that it almost makes me feel bad

for her, but I'm not going to let anything superficial like that soften my heart again. I'd let her eyes get to me, and her baby skin, and look where it got me.

"Ms. Carter, if you'd let the police officer talk with your daughter..." she pleads with me.

I let my daughter go, leave Connor in the waiting room, and sit on the curb outside, waiting for my friend to pick me up.

My head spins from how angry I am. It's a good thing I found out about the police officer and everything before taking Kathleen home, because Bill would have been even more angry just to see her. To have the police even mentioning us in the context of accountability again would have caused a rift between us for years.

I'd gone to rehab and cast all of my old life behind me, except for him. He would have control over our life again, be able to come home to a wife with no hallucinations or seedy housekeeping, without a paycheck or sense of responsibility. With the vision of our depending on each other in the future, I'd never give up Bill for anything, ever again. Not even if Kathleen turned out to be innocent of whatever the police officer inside was talking with her about. Not even if Connor turned out to hoard her money or cheat.

The door behind me swings open, and someone walks to the end of the pavement to spit in the gutter grate and pick his nose. Of course, it's Connor.

Too disgusted to stay outside with him, I go back to my plastic chair inside to scroll through my phone and wait with one eye on the door and one toward the far end of the room. If that blue-eyed woman with the pointy-toed shoes comes to get me, I'll leave. I have to look after myself, stay out of this, stay clean.

Engrossed in the news, I don't see two people enter the front door and stand next to me.

"Excuse me, ma'am?" the first, in a black uniform, says. "I'm Captain Hernandez of the Marion County Police, and this is your daughter's parole officer, Officer Jankowski. We need to talk with you."

"No, you don't. She's on her own with her drugs and chaos."

"Unfortunately, as she's a minor, parents need to be involved in cases that could possibly involve domestic abuse."

"Domestic abuse...? My baby?"

In the back room, with the door closed, he states, "There is an unusual amount of bruising on her skin, and she secretly called us right before coming to sign the paperwork. She was scared, so we decided to meet her here."

When Kathleen appears, I vault out of my chair, wanting to lift her hoodie and see all the bruises that I will protect her against in the future—forget about whether she's lying and has self-inflicted them. She needs someone who can be in control.

* * *

Discussion Questions

1. Is a parent's first obligation to themselves or their children? In the case of this story, should the mother have refused to meet with her daughter at all?
2. Is the mother in the story a heroic character? Why or why not? What defines a heroic character? Would knowing what originally caused her to become involved in drugs change your opinion?
3. If you were a recovering addict, like the example in the story, would you meet your drug-dealing child and risk your own sobriety? What factors might you take into account in your decision?
4. Assuming things were as originally presented in the story, should the mother have signed the marriage certificate for her teenage daughter? What, if any, additional information would you have wanted to know first? Is it appropriate to deny a teenager living on their own the right to marry?
5. How does the story of this mother and daughter play out over the next five, ten, or twenty years? What leads you to your conclusions?

* * *

Jakub

C.S. Griffel

* * *

"I could use a little good news," Rabbi Asher Segal muttered in prayer.

For one thing, Mr. Kantor had just died, and Mrs. Kantor would not hear of the funeral being held any later than the customary twenty-four hours. For another, three baby boys had been born to the congregation at Beth Israel on the same day. Mr. Kantor's funeral would fall on the same day as all three boys' bris. Not to mention, the young rabbi's wife was due with their fourth child any day.

Asher looked at his watch and shook his head, four p.m. already. The mail should have arrived at least an hour ago.

Asher buzzed his assistant. "Is the mail here, Miriam?"

"Yes, Rabbi, The mailman dropped it just a few minutes ago. Would you like me to bring it to you?"

"No. I could use the walk." Asher hung up the phone and made his way down the hall toward the front desk. He stopped a moment to admire the new wall hanging that had been a gift from the congregation upon his fifth anniversary as rabbi. He read the beautiful Hebrew letters carved into creamy white resin, modeled to look like marble and inlaid with gold. It was a rendition of his favorite verse from the Torah, Leviticus 19:18. In English, they read, "You shall neither take revenge from nor bear a grudge against the members of your people; you shall love your neighbor as yourself. I am the Lord."

Miriam handed him a neat stack of envelopes. "There's one from Mr. Rabinowicz."

"Thank you, Miriam." Asher took the stack and headed back to his office.

Asher sat down and read the name "Jakub Rabinowicz" on the top envelope. The man was an enigma. He was a secular Jew who attended shul every Saturday. He had been attending Beth Israel far longer than Asher had been its rabbi. Jakub Rabinowicz, a Polish Holocaust survivor, began attending in 1949. He had already outlasted two prior rabbis. The rabbi Asher replaced told him about Jakub, passing him along like an inheritance.

"Rabbi Segal," his predecessor, Rabbi Cohen, explained. "I have to tell you about Jakub Rabinowicz. You need to know he does not believe in The Almighty. He does not pray, yet he comes every Saturday."

"Why would he keep coming if he does not believe?"

"I asked him the same question. He said he comes for the ones who believed and died anyway." The rabbis both paused, an automatic moment of silence for their brethren lost in the Holocaust. "There's something else about Jakub. He gives a large amount of tzedakah. Many children of this congregation have been able to go to Kehillah Jewish High School because Jakub Rabinowicz paid the tuition. He has even paid for many of the most promising to attend college. You need to know this as rabbi, but Jakub insists on remaining anonymous—the families are never to know."

Rabbi Asher Segal smiled at the memory. He had thought Jakub Rabinowicz such an odd fellow back then. Now his children looked on the old man as a grandfather. Asher's father died before any of his children were born, and Jakub was an old bachelor with no children of his own. He came every Shabbat for the meal, pockets stuffed with trinkets. He seemed to never tire of playing the same game again and again.

Rabbi Segal tore open the envelope bearing Jakub Rabinowicz's return address. He pulled out a check for five thousand dollars neatly made out to Beth Israel and the memo marked "beneficence fund." It was only due to Jakub Rabinowicz's large and regular donations that Beth Israel's food pantry served more families in need than any of the other houses of worship in the city, save one. The First Baptist Church on Pine Avenue had easily ten times the number of congregants, though.

"Rabbi Segal?" Miriam's voice came through the intercom.

"Yes?"

"There's someone here to see you."

"Who is it?"

"His name is Tuviah Zuroff; he says he's here on urgent business." The young rabbi was accustomed to being interrupted for "urgent business." Most often, it was someone from the surrounding neighborhood with a story as to why they needed "just a little cash" to get by until payday.

"All right. Send him in."

After a few moments, Miriam opened the door to Rabbi Segal's small office. A man of perhaps fifty or so entered. He was not at all what the rabbi had been expecting. He wore a neatly tailored suit of fine black wool. It looked Italian in design. His salt and pepper hair was still gloriously full. Only a small black kippah interrupted the strains of white running through it.

"Rabbi, thank you for seeing me," the man said with a faint Russian accent. His eyes scanned the walls lined with bookshelves. They were filled with studies and commentaries on the Torah.

"Of course, please have a seat," Rabbi Segal answered, gesturing to an armchair.

"Thank you," the man said as he took a seat. Miriam was still at the door, looking questioningly at Rabbi Segal, her eyes asking if everything was all right. He gave her a barely perceptible nod and a small, reassuring smile, dismissing her.

As the door closed, Rabbi Segal asked, "What can I do for you, Mr. Zuroff?"

"Call me Tuviah, please."

"All right, Tuviah, how can I help?"

"Have you ever heard the name Simon Weisenthal?"

"I can't say that I have."

"Weisenthal runs an operation called the Jewish Documentation Center in Linz, Austria. I work for him. He compiles documents and eyewitness testimony in order to locate and prosecute Nazi war criminals."

"What has that got to do with me?"

"I'm looking for someone. May I show you a photograph?"

"Certainly."

"Do you recognize this man?" Tuviah pulled a faded black and white photo out of his interior jacket pocket. It was of a man about forty years old wearing the black uniform of an SS officer. The face was vaguely familiar, but Rabbi Segal couldn't place it. He supposed the man looked like so many of the young men wearing the uniform. One could never tell for certain if the similarity was truly in the face or if it was the same cold look buttoned up in the same cruel clothes.

Rabbi Segal shook his head. "I'm sorry, no."

"He would be perhaps about seventy now."

"Who is this man?"

Setting the photograph on the rabbi's desk, he asked, "Rabbi, may I tell you a story?"

Rabbi Segal looked at his watch; it was nearing the end of the day, but his curiosity was piqued. "Yes, I suppose."

"His name is Sturmbannführer Helmut Wolff. He was a major in the SS at Auschwitz. He is wanted for crimes against humanity. We have been looking for him for a few years now. This is what we know. On January twentieth or twenty-first, 1945, the majority of the SS guards at Auschwitz fled the oncoming Soviet forces. A small contingency stayed behind. One of them was Sturmbannführer Wolff. He was to exterminate and burn the bodies of as many of the prisoners as possible. The SS wanted to be rid of the evidence of their atrocities. We will never know exactly how many died between January twentieth and January twenty-seventh, the day of liberation for Auschwitz. When the Soviet forces liberated the camp, there were about five hundred survivors and more than six hundred bodies of those who had been shot or succumbed to starvation.

"The remaining SS guards were taken captive. Sturmbannführer Helmut Wolff was not among them. He never returned home to his family. For years, he was presumed dead. Then Wiesenthal found an eyewitness account. Another one of the SS guards claims that as the Soviets descended on the camp, he saw Wolff remove the clothes of a dead prisoner. After that, he lost track until they surrendered to the Soviets and Wolff was not among the guards."

Rabbi Segal blinked at the man. "I'm still not sure what you're getting at."

"At the Jewish Documentation Center, we have painstakingly gathered hundreds of thousands of documents, photos, and other pieces of evidence to identify not only the dead but the living who are evading justice. We believe Helmut Wolff escaped Soviet capture and prosecution for his crimes by taking on the identity of a dead Jewish prisoner. We have narrowed our search to three names." Rabbi Segal nodded his head, inviting the man to continue. "Izaak Adler." Rabbi Segal shook his head. "Chiam Weisberg."

"I do not recognize these names."

"Jakub Rabinowicz."

The rabbi felt the color drain out of his face, but he said nothing. He did not nod, nor shake his head. His eyes glanced down at the photo on his desk. Jakub's eyes stared back at him from the face of a much younger man in an SS uniform. Glancing back up at the man, he said, "I am afraid I cannot help you, Mr. Zuroff."

"Look at the photo again, Rabbi, please. Are you sure you do not recognize this man?"

Asher picked the photo up from the desk and studied it. It was clear now, no mistaking, it was Jakub. He stuck his hand across the table, handing the man the photo. "I'm sorry to disappoint you, Mr. Zuroff, but I can be of no assistance." The man took the photo and tucked it back into his jacket pocket. Asher stood and said, "If you'll excuse me, my wife and little ones will be waiting for me to get home. My wife doesn't like it when I'm late for dinner."

"Of course, Rabbi. Thank you for your time. I'll just leave my card in case anything comes to mind. You can call collect." The man set his card on the rabbi's desk with his name and a contact number for an office in Linz, Austria.

Asher walked from the synagogue to the brownstone he called home without seeing anything except a pair of familiar eyes staring at him from under the visor of a cap crested with a Nazi eagle above a skull and crossbones. *Sturmbannführer Helmut Wolff*. An unthinkable truth. An impossible truth. A bitter, bitter truth. Asher's heart welled up with disgust for the man in the SS uniform. The coward. The sneak. The liar. Then his heart welled up with love and his eyes with tears for the old man with the same eyes that peered at his little children with laughter, joy, and love. That was not a lie. Asher knew it wasn't a lie. The old man loved the children.

He was quiet when he entered the house. The smell of

his wife's pot roast did not bring its usual comforts.

"Asher?" she called from the kitchen.

"Yes, it's me."

"Don't forget Jakub is coming for dinner tonight."

He had forgotten. With a sigh, he unwrapped the scarf around his neck and hung it on the coat tree in the front hall. He was slipping off his jacket when there was a knock at the door. It could only be Jakub.

"Will you get that?" Rachel called.

"Yah!" he answered. He hung the jacket before turning to answer the door. There were those eyes staring back at him from a withered face.

"Jakub," he said, "come in." Jakub paused, looking hard into Asher's eyes.

"They have found me, then," was all the old man said. Asher's gaze dropped to the floor before resting once again on Jakub's face. Nearly imperceptibly he nodded assent.

"Is that Jakub?" Rachel's voice broke through the tension.

"You better come in." Asher stepped aside to allow the old man entrance.

Three little boys bounded down the stairs. Little arms grabbed Jakub anywhere they could find a hold.

"Zaydee Jakub!" their little boy voices cried.

"Boys!" Asher scolded, his voice sharp. He knew he was wrong to scold them, but he could not keep the eyes of Helmut Wolff out of his head. "Leave Jakub alone."

"It's all right, Asher," the old man responded. "They only want to play."

"Hide and seek! Hide and seek!"

"One, two, three..." The old man's eyes twinkled behind a sorrow only Asher could see.

The little boys squealed as they ran for cover.

"Ten minutes until dinner!" Rachel cried from the kitchen.

When they were all situated comfortably at the dinner table, Rachel asked, "How are you, Jakub?"

"I'm well, Rachel."

The littlest boy, Malachi spoke up. "Zaydee, will you come see me sing at school for Chanukah?"

"Zaydee Jakub is a busy man, Malachi," Asher said.

"I'm not so sure I can come this year, Malachi."

Rachel looked intently at each of the men, searching their eyes for a clue to the tension she felt between them.

Three hours later, Asher climbed into bed.

"You were quiet at dinner," his wife observed.

"It was a busy day. And tomorrow will be another. I have the Kantor funeral and a bris. Thankfully, Rabbi Cohen can perform the two others." He could not say, *Your little Jewish boys just spent the evening playing hide and seek with a Nazi and calling him "Zaydee."* Asher thought of the card left by Mr. Zuroff. It was sitting on his desk where the man had carefully placed it.

"I know something is wrong, Asher, but I'll wait until you are ready to tell me." Asher was grateful for his wife. She was always ready with a listening ear and wise words, but she never pushed him to talk. It wasn't long before his wife, with her steady, calm, and peaceful heart, was breathing the rhythm of sleep.

Asher stared into the darkness for a long time, thinking

of Jakub. Helmut. It was hard to apply that name to the old man. The words of the Torah came to him, *And I will visit upon the wicked their iniquity, And I will cause the arrogancy of the proud to cease, And will lay low the haughtiness of the tyrants.* Helmut Wolff was surely wicked along with his Nazi brethren. And he knew that wickedness was an affront to the Almighty. Yet the Torah also said, *I, even I, am He that blotteth out thy transgressions for Mine own sake; And thy sins I will not remember. Therefore the Lord waits to be gracious to you, and therefore he exalts himself to show mercy to you. For the Lord is a God of justice; blessed are all those who wait for him.* He thought of the greatest Israelite in the Torah, King David, who arranged for the death of Uriah the Hittite. He too, was a murderer. Asher prayed, *Direct me.*

Asher did not throw away Mr. Zuroff's card. It sat right where he had placed it, eight days earlier. He still did not know if he was going to dial the number or burn the card over his kitchen sink and forget the existence of Mr. Zuroff and Simon Wiesenthal. He had not seen or heard from Jakub since the night he had come to dinner. He hadn't come to Shabbat dinner nor shul on Saturday morning. He supposed the man called "Helmut" was now too ashamed to show his face in a Jewish synagogue or to sit at the table with his Jewish family.

"Where is Zaydee Jakub?" Malachi had asked.

"Busy," was all Asher could think to say. He considered showing up at Jakub's apartment, but what would he say? *Come back, the boys miss you? I promise I won't turn you in to the authorities? How many Jews did you kill?* He loved Jakub and he hated Helmut. Jakub was a trusted friend, a benefactor;

Helmut deserved to hang.

Thursday dawned bitter cold. Asher wrapped himself in a thick, black, wool coat for his walk to work; his prayer tassels dangled below the hem. Miriam, as usual, was already at her desk when he arrived.

"Have you seen the paper this morning?" she asked.

"Not yet." Miriam handed the paper to him. The top headline was for a story about the exploding price of fuel and long lines at gas stations.

"What am I supposed to be looking at?" he asked her.

"Look at the bottom right story."

A small, front-page headline read "Nazi War Criminal Turns Himself In." The first line of the story read, "After nearly thirty years of evading the authorities, Helmut Wolff, a former major in Hitler's SS guard, turned himself in Wednesday." Asher folded the paper and handed it back to Miriam.

Prattling on, Miriam shook her head. "Can you believe he was right here under our noses the whole time? Who would have thought? He seemed so nice. Unbelievable. Well, I for one, hope they hang him."

Asher's eyes caught the photo on the wall behind Miriam. She smiled proudly at the camera next to her son in a graduate cap and gown. Only last year, he had graduated from Kehillah Jewish High School as the class salutatorian; his tuition had been paid by an anonymous donor.

Asher gave a slight nod before slipping quietly down the hall to his office. He shut the door and wept.

* * *

Discussion Questions

1. Does it matter why Jakub/Helmut was active and kind in the Jewish community? What do you think his motivations were? Would it matter if his motivations were different than you believe?

2. Can a person ever pay off their past sins or are you culpable *(and punishable)* for your past sins regardless of your later positive actions?

3. If Jakub/Helmut had been caught by the Russians he surely would have been tried and hanged for his war crimes. Does it matter that he escaped out of fear rather than out of an initial desire to live long enough to make amends?

4. What is the distinguishing factor between past crimes you can and cannot later make amends for?

5. Are there any reasons Jakub/Helmut could give related to his time as a Nazi that would absolve him of responsibility? Was Jakub/Helmut's only moral choice to renounce the Nazi Party and flee his homeland (*or die trying to change the country while living under a Nazi/dictatorial regime*)?

* * *

Junk

Taylor Lawritson

* * *

At first it was just bottlecaps. And you might laugh at that. You might think 'what kind of sentimentality is there in a bottle cap?' But that's a dumb question because what type of sentimentality is there to anything?

We control the sentimentality.

You control the sentimentality.

I control the sentimentality.

Heather told me that affirmations work. You can apparently retrain your brain on them if you really believe them. So I have to tell myself that I control the objects and the objects don't control me. And I have to believe it. The affirmations have to be about me and not about the objects. She says that sentimentality isn't really real, I mean you can't actually touch it. Objects only have their function and if the function is only sentimentality then actually they have no function because sentiment is a made up thing in your brain.

I like Heather because she makes sense. What use is the necklace that you're wearing? Maybe it reminds you of your sixteenth birthday or your first boyfriend. And that's silly. Really. Look at yourself. That necklace is more of a choking hazard than anything, isn't it? If somebody really needed to get you out of the picture they could just grab that bad boy and pull until your lights go dark. But you keep it because it's like you can almost feel that first boyfriend's fingers on the clasp, getting the baby hairs on your neck stuck in the chain. You remember how you turned around and felt sure that this tiny chain was going to wrap around the life you imagined and choke you both together forever. You keep the necklace because you want to remember that certainty. But really you can remember it on your own. You don't need the necklace. It's all in your head. You just don't trust yourself.

Heather says it helps to just think about them as objects. Not to give them a name or a shape. Just leave them as lumps in your brain. Objects. It's a little sterile, but it works to the point. They're just objects. Your necklace. My bottlecaps. They're the same now. "You have to retrace the object attachment." Heather says this as she sits behind her desk, always a pen tapping at her chin. We are engaged in a dance routine and she is keeping time.

"But I want it. I need it." I stumble.

"What do you need it for?" She glides right behind.

"It's sentimental." We go around and around.

For one whole hour every Wednesday, Heather reminds me, not in so many words, that objects are evil little things. They're self-serving organisms that simply do not want to be thrown away. You can picture it the way I do if you want: objects having imaginary barbs on long, skinny arms that plant themselves into your brain so that when you try to dispose of them they yank and yank and drag themselves through your memories and out your tear ducts so before you know it you're clutching that necklace to your chest and remembering senior prom and cursing yourself for thinking you could ever live without that ugly little pendant.

It's like with the bottle caps. That's what Heather and I are working on right now.

"Start small." That's what Heather says when I get overwhelmed. But it's almost like the bottle caps are the biggest part of it. They're the whole foundation for all the other junk that's piled up through the years, like the world's ugliest pyramid. And maybe you're still skeptical about the bottle caps. But honestly, think about how stupid your high school boyfriend was. You might still wonder how a bottle cap gets sentimental the way a cheesy necklace does. But, maybe some of us never got necklaces. Maybe the only thing we ever had was bottle caps.

For a long time my dad was my only friend. My only ally. Up until I was in middle school, every night when I said my prayers and imagined talking to god, it was dad's face I was looking into. And sure, every kid worships their parents a little bit. But maybe not everybody feels like they're growing up seeking forgiveness. I had killed my mother the day I was born. And they had a choice too. Both of them, because she asked him, too. She said, "Joe, I want this baby to live." I know he regretted it, but he never said that and that's a very compassionate thing to do. Imagine the heavy burden that is. You go to the hospital, where the love of your life dies, and then you get stuck with a baby and nobody to help you raise it. So I never blamed him for the drinking. I knew it was bad. I heard the other kids' parents talking in Sunday school. But I wasn't going to fault him for rubbing Novocain on a stab wound. The drinking really barely affected me. He still woke me up for school in the morning, dunked my head in the kitchen sink, and brushed my hair back into a rubber band before sending me off. If anything, the drinking made me feel closer to him. We both paid our flaws no mind. I was a born killer and he was a drunk.

I loved him. And that's why I love those bottle caps. Loved. Loved them. Not anymore. I do not love them anymore. I don't. Really.

I *loved* them because my drunk of a father used to gather up a handful of them as soon as the big yellow school bus dropped me at the mailbox. I'd drop my backpack in a dusty patch of front lawn and run forward with my hands cupped together outstretched as if they wanted to get to the bounty before my father noticed who they belonged to. "How'd we do today, partner?" I'd say kneeling down at the lawnchair throne.

"Well, partner, I reckon we done ourselves pretty good," he'd drawl. Sometimes he would slur, but only when my memory is not feeling generous. Because he just talked slow, my dad, he just used long vowels and that was just how he talked and I am trying to become a more generous person.

Dad gave them to me because he thought I'd be able to sell them for candy money. He'd worked at the aluminum casting facility up in Hastings a long time ago and he always promised that one day he'd drive me up there to cash in my bottle cap treasure for 35¢ a pound. We never got around to it. The drive was two and a half hours one way and the bottle caps probably wouldn't have even covered the cost of gas in dad's pickup. But it didn't matter much to me. Those bottle caps were the currency of my father's affection.

When it was warm out, dad and I would walk to Sticky's liquor store hand in hand, Johnny Cash spilling out of the beat-up Walkman on his hip. We'd walk down the aisles and squint real hard, locked in thorough analysis of the familiar selection.

"I bet you this IPA isn't even from India." I'd posture, gingerly holding out a bottle with an idyllic mountain scene on the label.

"Well, at least we've got Ol' Reliable," he'd say, lifting a 24-pack of Coors Banquets from a shelf.

"Bankies have the best caps anyways."

At home, dad would grab two Banquet chicken pot pies out of the freezer and drain a beer, while I put *For the Roses* on the record player. As Joni Mitchell echoed through the kitchen, bouncing off the hollow linoleum floors, dad would fill his first empty with pop for me and grab a second for himself. He'd shove the pies into the microwave and we'd hoist ourselves up onto either side of the sink, just in time to clink our bottles and sing along to the album opener.

Some get the gravy
And some get the gristle
Some get the marrow bone
And some get nothing
Though there's plenty to spare

I always thought dad had a great voice. It's funny the

things you forget. Now when I picture him, bottle neck to his lips like a microphone, I can't even remember what he sounded like. In all of my memories, Joni Mitchell's voice spills out of my father's mouth as if he were a ventriloquist's dummy. There's no proper way to mourn I guess, but looking back on the months after his death, I wish I had snapped that record in half, instead of playing it over and over. Sometimes, I watch those months back as if from behind a two-way mirror, banging on the glass, begging myself to stop listening before I drown him out forever. But the panic just makes it worse. It's like reaching down to pet the dog that was just sitting at your feet only to realize there's nothing there. At first you simply reach a little further, maybe your spatial reasoning was off. But then you have to look down and visually confront the absence. You start to get that sinking feeling that something's missing, and as you check each room in the house you feel the emptiness begin to eat up more space. You go outside, you ask around the neighborhood, you spend hours making Lost Dog posters on the library Xerox machine. You try to submerge yourself in the act of looking so that you don't have to face the inevitable act of losing. And as the loss creeps closer, you become desperate. You drive up and down the road, you call the pound, you tear the house apart.

But the emptiness comes. It always does. The first time I forgot my father's voice, I was remembering him singing *Banquet* in the kitchen. And even after he had stopped singing, Joni Mitchell stayed. The microwave beeped. He placed the pot pies on the table. We sat down and bowed our heads for a moment. Then he looked up at me, grinning above his

Banquet pot pie and extended his Banquet bottle towards mine. Joni Mitchell used his mouth to say, "Back in the banquet line!"

I spent weeks trying to get him back. I combed through every memory I had of him hunting for just a word, a phrase. I laid on the threadbare carpet in our living room for hours in silence, waiting for the sound to come back to me. After the second day, I even found a video on Youtube called "Reconnect with Passed Loved Ones in Spirit: Guided Meditation" and I played it on a loop waiting for it to hypnotize me into remembering again. After a week, I couldn't remember anyone's voice, even my own. Whenever somebody came to the front desk at the library to ask me a question, I stared blankly ahead. I started getting lost on my way home from work.

After two weeks Mr. Harrison, the short, blueberry-shaped man who runs the library, asked me if I wanted time off. Actually, he really didn't ask. He bumbled up to the circulation desk, patting his mustache anxiously, making sure it was still there.

"I, uh well, we, uh. Well, Hello."

I did not look up from the computer. He cleared his throat to fill the silence before continuing on.

"Well, yes, uh, hmmm. So! I've been thinking, you know, you've been through so much this past year. And you've come in every day and you're really a great librarian! Simply could not run the place without you! Nosirree! That's for sure!" He chuckled joylessly and fiddled with the buttons we kept in a plate next to the computer like he didn't have one pinned to his lapel at that very moment. They were small black pins with white block letters over a cartoon drawing of the solar system that said 'Reading is out of this world!!!'

"Ah yes! These are really very clever. Always give me a good chuckle. Really some of your best work I must say. Anyways, well, yes. I've decided you could use some time off. You take such good care of the library, but maybe you should have some time to take care of yourself? Right? Yes. Yes. Take all the time you need. We'll be waiting when you're good and ready. And if you need a thing please do not hesitate to call." I stared blankly at him. He extended a hand as if to pat me on the back but seemed to think better of it, pulling it back at the last second and cradling it with the other arm like I had bitten him.

I don't remember how long I spent at home, but I do remember days bleeding together until I couldn't conceive of anything outside of the house's clapboard walls. I was wandering around the house trying to remember what each room was for, when I stumbled upon the door to the garage and became convinced that I had never seen it before. I yanked it open and stooped into the inky blackness before me, forgetting there was a step and landing face down on what felt like a trash bag full of rocks. Liquid began to trickle into my mouth and as I scrambled onto all fours to cover my bloodied nose, something sharp became implanted in my knee. My hands seemed to move of their own volition and gripped the offending object tightly, like a punishment.

I gasped as I realized that whatever it was, it would not be crushed without a fight. In an act of revenge, it had created a deep hexagonal imprint in my palm which I could already feel becoming red and angry. Suddenly exhausted, I retreated back into the house, sliding on my butt back over the threshold and laying in the mouth of the doorway. I laid there for a long time before I realized I was still clutching something in my left hand. My fingers unfurled shakily, revealing a red Coors bottle cap nestled innocently in my flushed palm. It felt impossibly warm and I wondered if it had leached away all of my body heat. I ran my fingers over its ridged side, turning it over for I don't know how long, before an image just like this one rose up inside of my head like some kind of dual reality.

There was the Coors cap on my palm, just like it was right now, but my hand was so small and the colors were different. The bottle cap in my hand was a dark, angry red. This other cap seemed almost orange. Sunlight! It was sunlight! Suddenly I looked up, but I didn't at all. I kept sitting and staring at the bottle cap in my hand. And there he was.

"Well, partner, I reckon we done ourselves pretty good."

I cried a lot. The screaming kind. I beat my hands and fists on the living room floor and I made noise for the first time in who knows how long. I yelled so loud I bet he heard me wherever he is, but I hope he didn't because I didn't mean to call him a drunk son of a bitch.

Afterwards, when I had cried myself dry and screamed myself hoarse, I stood up to change my shirt, which had become crusted with nose blood. The walls began to spin and I realized I couldn't remember the last thing I ate. I hobbled over to the freezer and pulled out six Banquet chicken pot pies. I put them all in the oven together for an hour. Then I smoothed down each of the boxes and placed them at the kitchen table like place mats.

The chicken pot pies were still frozen in the middle. The crusts were burned and crispy but inside the chicken and gravy remained congealed and frosty. I ate them anyway. All six. Every last disgusting partially frozen bite. I washed the tins and put them in a cupboard. I dragged the trash bags of bottle caps from the garage into the living room and laid on top of them like a bean bag chair. Whenever I stirred, they clinked together in response.

I'd moved the bottle caps into the garage when dad got too sick to keep walking back to his bedroom at the back of the house. When he moved into my room, which was much closer to the kitchen and the living room, I'd gutted the closet to make room for the oxygen tanks, meaning that the bottle cap collection had to be relocated. I'd done my best to forget about the months my father spent dying on our couch, but finally there on my sea of bottle caps, I surrendered. I let the pain and the guilt and the anger wash over me.

He got sick right before my college graduation. The deal was that he'd let me come home if I tried to finish my last semester. So I did. I emailed all of my professors and went back to campus a handful of times to turn things in and move my stuff. When I was gone I had to make sure somebody would watch over him, but we didn't really have friends or family in McCook. So I went to the yellow pages and called a babysitting service to come watch him. I went back to work at the library so I could finally get him a nice TV. He still preferred his record player though. Everyday I'd go to the handful of thrift stores in the area looking for new records. Carly Simon. Creedence Clearwater Revival. Three Dog

Night. I bought him books too. Baldwin. Nabokov. Updike. Paperbacks, Hardbacks, Graphic Novels, Magazines, Cookbooks. He didn't like to read but I figured it'd be best if he had them in case he wanted them. I bought him all kinds of things. Stuffed animals, inflatable palm trees, a little kiddie pool to soak his feet in, novelty wall signs to make him laugh and brighten the place up. He didn't really care for most of it, and he started getting really angry the last few months, and then just tired, but sometimes he'd smile and so I kept hunting for things that would make him forget for a second.

He smoked like a chimney those last few months. I didn't stop him. He got skinnier and skinnier and pretty soon he wouldn't even eat Banquet pot pies. The sores kept crawling up his legs, until they were black to the knee, and kept going. In the last month or two he barely moved from the couch. He was only awake a few hours a day, during coughing fits. Then he'd ask for a cigarette and fall back asleep.

He refused to let me hire a nurse or take him to a hospice.

"The best you can do for me kiddo is find me some pot."

So I did.

I loaded a bowl and held it up to his mouth. He sputtered the smoke out in a fit of wet coughs, but he grinned like a mad man all the same.

"I'm probably not gonna win the dad of the year award this time, am I? Should I try for next year?"

"You're a shoo in."

I put on *For The Roses* and hoped he'd sing along, even

though I knew that he couldn't. When I sat down after flipping the record, I watched a tear drop from his nose.

"This might be the first time I haven't believed that Joni Mitchell would make everything better."

He was cold on the couch a few days later. He looked more peaceful than I'd seen him in a long time. His funeral was small, but a few of the guys from the Railyard came, and some of my friends from high school, and Sticky of Sticky's liquor and the stern grandma from the babysitting agency. My diploma came in the mail about a week after he died. It's in the garage filing cabinet next to all the funeral brochures. I made 500 in case we needed extra.

After he died, I didn't know what to do so I simply carried on as if everything was the same. I kept buying records and books and stuffed animals and anything I could find. And I kept all the things he touched. Because after he died it was so quiet. And I wanted to pretend he was still there. So I kept the lawnchair on the lawn, and I started buying new ones, wherever I could find them, until our front yard looked like a graveyard barbecue. I moved all the bottle caps back into the room he had stayed in. I bought a white noise machine because I'd gotten so used to the sound of his oxygen tank.

I never wanted to throw any of it away. Not once. Even though it'd take me a half an hour to walk through the house. Even though I eventually had to start sleeping on top of all the "Get Well Soon" stuffed animals I bought him. Even though there were too many records to even set the record player down on a flat surface and too many inflatable palm trees to watch the T.V. Even after a pile of books fell on me once and I was stuck there half the night and an hour late to work.

About a year or two after dad died, I went to the laundromat. Our washer and dryer had stopped working but I couldn't bear to part with them, not with all the duct tape handiwork dad had put in to keep those things running. So I started going to the laundromat, Sunday mornings to wash my clothes and sheets and towels and things. I'm much cleaner than whatever people want you to expect from a person like me.

Anyways, I was sitting in front of the laundromat in my dad's beat-up old truck, listening to *Cold Blue Steel and Sweet Fire*, when somebody knocked on my window. After nearly shitting myself, I rolled my window down, and there's this guy.

"This is a great song."

"Yeah."

"Mind if I listen with you?" I should have said no. Really because what a perfect way to get murdered. But it was 9 AM on a Sunday and I had a knife so I figured why not. And I was lonely. Heather thinks it's important I say that when it's true. So I was lonely. So he climbed into the passenger seat and I realized I didn't really know what to say.

"Nasty habit." He pointed at my cigarette.

"I mean I've practically quit. This is the last one." I was preparing to light another.

"Well, if that's the last one, I guess this one's for me." He reached over and grabbed the new cigarette out of my hand and lit it with his own lighter. I wanted to spit on him but for some reason I laughed. He reached over to turn the volume on the radio up.

"Man this is a really killer flute solo." He'd started humming at this point.

"Did you know it's the same guy on flute, saxophone, clarinet, and triangle? He plays four different instruments on this one song." I don't know why I said anything. I didn't mean to.

After the song ended, we walked into the laundromat together and he loaned me quarters as payback for the cigarette. I didn't realize how long we'd been talking until my dryer was buzzing and he was asking what I did with my time.

"I, uh, I go to Goodwill, I guess, the dollar store, Walmart sometimes. I don't really know. I listen to records maybe."

And so for a whole year, Jared courted me on my porch. We'd go browsing and then he'd drive me back home and sit on my porch while I grabbed the record player. Once he turned all the old lawn chairs around so they were facing us, like we were giving a concert. I told him about my dad. About the booze. And the sickness. And the long hard death. But I couldn't ever tell him anything past that. About the house. About the bottle caps. The books. The magazines. About myself. The junk that I lived with, that I could not live without. I told him that nobody else had been in my house since my dad died and I didn't feel ready yet and he said okay and then we made out on my porch because my neighbors probably couldn't see that far anyways and also because I didn't know them and didn't care what they thought.

Once at the fair Jared spent $20 winning me a stuffed bear from the skee ball game and I saw the bear in his arms and all the joy oozing out of him onto the bear making it sweet and sticky with good intent. I felt the evil, hungry thing growing inside of me, the want of whatever warmth had grown in his arms. I watched his face change from pride to horror as I began to cry right there in the light of the funnel cake stand. When I said I didn't want to talk about it Jared said okay and he called me the next day like nothing had happened.

I spent a lot of time at Jared's apartment. He lived on the other side of town in a renovated duplex that was much nicer than my house anyways. Except he didn't have a backyard for barbecuing and he had a daughter who had a summer birthday.

So one night, I told him. I said Jared there's something you need to know or maybe you need to see. And I walked him through every room in the house, the living room with its inflatable circus, the kitchen with its stockpile of novelty dishes and lava lamps, the bedrooms with their soft nests of books, magazines, newspapers, stuffed animals, the bathtub overflowing with cookie jars. And the garage. The sea of bottle caps, endlessly enticing, undulating under the dull glow of the naked overhead bulb. And then I took him out into the backyard and I laid down on the grass and he laid down next to me.

"I know I should've told you. And I know you probably don't want anything to do with me anymore. But, even if you don't want anything else to do with me, you could use my backyard for Jude's birthday party."

Jared didn't say anything for a while, he just rubbed my knuckles with his thumb. Then he turned over onto his side and smiled at me really big.

"We should have a garage sale. A huge one. You can

xerox posters at the library and we can make it a whole event."

So the next weekend I set up the little kiddie pool I had bought for dad, and Jared brought Jude over in her floaties and she splashed around while we started on the house. We had just made it into the first bedroom when we heard a crashing sound from the garage. We ran in and found Jude practically convulsing, her face a dark purple. I called the ambulance while Jared tried to perform the Heimlich. I quickly handed Jared the phone and we switched roles. I looked down Jude's tiny little throat and realized her airway was blocked. I pushed two fingers down and yanked. It wasn't pretty, but it got the job done. We all cried a little bit until the ambulance arrived and the paramedics started checking on Jude.

"So what was it? That she swallowed?" I nearly jumped as Jared grabbed my shoulders. I didn't know what to say, so I just pulled the bottle cap out of my back pocket and gave it to him. I didn't know how to apologize. I didn't know how to explain. Nobody blamed me but I didn't need them to tell me that it was my fault.

That night, alone, I walked the garbage bags of bottle caps to the trash can and back for an hour and a half. I wanted them gone so bad, but at the same time, I didn't know how to remember myself without them. Eventually, I passed out on top of them in the living room, the soreness the next morning an apt punishment for my crimes. I called Jared. I told him I didn't know if I could see him anymore. I was scared. I didn't think I was ready. I wasn't used to people in my life, I was used to bottle caps and inflatable palm trees. But I wanted to be. I want to be.

* * *

Discussion Questions

1. Is the term for what the narrator is going through grief, or is there another term that more aptly describes her experience? Is there a right and wrong way to react after the death of a loved one?

2. Why do you think the death of the narrator's father affected her so much? Why does the death of some parents seem to hit harder for certain people?

3. How do you know when it is healthy (*or unhealthy*) to keep a reminder of an experience or a person? What are examples of unhealthy keepsakes and healthy keepsakes? Are their examples of each in your own life?

4. How is keeping a bottlecap different, or the same, as keeping a photo to remember a person? How do you know if you are remembering someone to an unhealthy way?

5. Could you continue a relationship with a hoarder after seeing their house overflowing with stuff? What, if anything, is the distinction between this issue, and others?

* * *

Kane and Abel

C.S. Griffel

***

I boarded the train in Council Bluffs. The cargo headed for Cheyenne included a large sum of cash meant to be the payroll for a large mining operation. Any train moving large sums of cash and passengers with all their earthly belongings was a target.

I made my way from the passenger coach to the car designated especially for the expressmen assigned to the train. After the locomotive were the mail cars, then the baggage cars. That's where the safe was located. The coach situated just behind baggage was the expressmen coach. When I opened the door to their car, the hands of all three lawmen instinctively hovered over their sidearms.

"Name's Kane Malloy," I quickly introduced myself in an attempt to put them at their ease, "I'm the Pinkerton man." Resentment burned in the eyes of the youngest of the three fellows. It was clear he didn't think they needed any backup.

Truth was, if the rumors were true and the Hardy Gang had their sights set on the payroll secured in the safe in the baggage car, then I wasn't likely to be back up enough. They had a reputation for shooting passengers for no reason other than a thrill.

A man with an enormous white mustache, clearly the head expressman, greeted me congenially. "Glad to have you, Malloy. Name's Bill Rogers," he said as he offered me a handshake. He looked to be a man who could handle himself in a gunfight but with enough sense to know there was safety in numbers. He was glad to have another gun on his side. With the introductions done, I used their door to climb out of the train. I made my way back into the depot, grabbed the carpet bag I had stashed in an inconspicuous corner, and reboarded the train at the furthest back second-class car as possible. Though my seat was in the car directly behind the expressmen's coach, I wanted to have a look through the cars for anything suspicious.

I noted at least four single men scattered throughout the handful of passenger railcars. I would have been less suspicious had they been sitting together in a pack. A fifth single male passenger had a seat in my car. He didn't look more than seventeen or eighteen. His stringy blond hair was shoved under a grease-stained felt gambler, worn low over his eyes. I took him in without looking directly at him. He tensed up as I slid past him down the aisle to a seat close to the front. A family with twin daughters, aged about fourteen, and a son about twelve, took up space in the middle of the car. An elderly couple took up two more seats. A group of middle-aged women took up four more seats. Sitting closest to the front was a clergyman and his pretty, petite wife. He had the pale, bespectacled face of a man who had spent most of his life indoors, reading books.

Above the seats, a long shelf had been installed where passengers could store personal belongings. I placed my own carpet bag on the shelf above my head. I wasn't necessarily undercover, but blending in with the other passengers would help keep everyone at ease. As I turned to take my seat, my jacket opened enough to reveal the glint of my sidearm. I noted the eyes of the young clergyman caught sight of it. I pulled my jacket closed and sat, causing our eyes to meet. If he felt any shock, his eyes did not betray it.

It wasn't long before the train whistle blew, and the engine chugged us to a start. If all went well, we would be pulling into Cheyenne in about twenty-four hours. For the three expressmen guarding the safe filled with enough cash to make payroll for one hundred eighty miners, it would be a very long day.

The minister's wife turned in her seat as the train rattled along the rails, watching as we rolled over the Missouri River and through Omaha—the last civilization we would see for a long while. Staring out the windows at the passing landscape seemed efficient entertainment for the other passengers sharing our car as well. They all turned and chattered about the passing sights. Only one passenger was not fascinated by the train ride. The young man at the back of the car pulled his greasy hat even lower over his eyes in an apparent effort to pass the long trip by sleeping. I pulled out the small Bible that was all I had left of my mother and opened it to Deuteronomy chapter nineteen. *And thine eye shall not pity; but life shall go for life, eye for eye, tooth for tooth, hand for hand, foot for foot.*

We continued on this way for some time. Eventually, the minister's wife and the families grew either bored with the scenery or tired from craning their necks round to see out the windows. The young boy was already asking how much longer the trip would be. As I continued reading the scriptures, I sensed a pair of eyes examining me. I looked up to find the minister smiling, with the eager look of someone wanting to engage in conversation. I'm not what you'd call the chatty type.

"I see you are reading God's Word," he began. It would be rude to ignore any man, but a minister especially.

"That's right," I responded.

"I'm Abel Keener, by the way."

"Elkanah Malloy," I returned, "but folks call me Kane."

"That's funny," the pretty wife piped in. "Kane and Abel."

"This is my wife, Isabel," Abel said.

"Pleased to make your acquaintance, ma'am," I said, tipping my hat. She smiled in return. She wore her glossy brown hair pulled away from her face with braids tucked and pinned up at the back. Her wool traveling dress was the color of sagebrush. Reluctantly, I tucked my small Bible back into its home inside my jacket.

"Have you been to Cheyenne, sir?" Isabel inquired.

"Yes, ma'am, many times."

"What's it like?" The woman's eyes sparkled with adventure.

"Well, I reckon it's not bad as towns go. Some call it the

Magic City of the Plains on account of all the saloons and such. One barkeep is even said to have a monkey and a bear in his saloon."

"You don't say! A monkey and a bear in a saloon? Who would ever think of such a thing?" Laughter lit up her face at the very thought.

"I go to take up a post as minister of a recently organized congregation." This time, it was Abel who spoke.

"Well, there's plenty of need for the spreading of the Gospel in Cheyenne. You'll find plenty of folk who aren't like to make their way to the church house of a Sunday."

"And do you partake in the work of spreading the Gospel, sir?"

"God didn't talent me with being too good at talking. Let's say I'm more inclined to bring God's justice."

"Yes, I noted you must be a man of action." His eyes darted to the place my sidearm occupied under my jacket. "Do you suppose that comports with the teachings of Christ?"

"Abel, don't start," Isabel chimed in.

"It's alright, ma'am," I said. "I sleep fine at night, if that's what you mean."

"You would send a man to his eternal damnation by your own hand?" The young preacher pressed.

"Well, now I suppose that depends on the man. If that man was to try and break the laws of our great nation, then I might just send him to meet his maker."

"Did not Christ tell us we are to turn the other cheek? Did he not himself do so upon the cross?" I could see it was a matter of principle to the man. I had a certain respect for such men of peace, though I was not one myself. I let him go on.

"Does not violence beget violence and peace beget peace?"

"Some folks just won't have peace."

"Sir, if a man commits violence against me, if I forgive him rather than retaliate, then his sin dies. If I retaliate, the sin grows."

"Ain't you ever read Deuteronomy, son?"

"Abel," his pretty wife chimed in, placing a gentle hand on his arm, "let the gentleman be. Should you be right, and he be wrong, don't you think the Holy Spirit capable of correcting him?"

Smiling, he said, "You're right, of course, Isabel. We must trust the Lord that He is able to speak to His own servants as He wills."

Further conversation was interrupted by the sound of gunshots from the expressmen's car.

"What was that?" The young woman asked.

"Ma'am," I said, "you just stay seated and keep your head down. Mister, you look after your wife here." The preacher put a protective arm around his young wife.

My eyes searched the car for the fidgety young man. His eyes darted around nervously. His fingers twitched like he was trying to make up his mind to take action. Shouting came from the car. It was Bill calling for my help, yelling as loud as he could over the sound of the wheels running along the tracks. My gut told me the kid was trouble, but I couldn't ignore the shouts coming from the next car.

It wasn't but a few steps to the door between the cars. The minute I turned my back, that boy made his move. As my hand reached to open the compartment latch, Isabel screamed. The kid must have been some kind of lookout. He had his left arm tight around Isabel's shoulders, pulling her back against him, while his right hand held a gun to her head. Her husband held up his hands, facing outward to show he wasn't a threat. As I spun around, I leveled my gun at his forehead. I, on the other hand, was a threat. So long as Isabel didn't squirm, my aim was clear.

"D-don't you go a step farther," he said in a voice that sounded like it hadn't even dropped all the way into its adult register.

"Son, you best put your gun down now before you get yourself into a pickle you can't get out of." His eyes darted from me to the compartment door behind me. I could tell by the look of him, he'd never killed a man. "You let the little lady go, and I'll have a word with the judge to go easy on ya."

"You throw your gun out the window and let me pass. I'll let her go after I get to my gang in the other car."

"You know I can't let you do that."

"Let him go, Kane," Abel now interjected. "He said he'd let her go."

"If I let him go, your wife's as good as dead. The Hardy gang ain't known for their mercy." My gun remained leveled with precision at the boy's head. My eyes never left his face. He was more terrified than Isabel, though tears rolled down her face. A few rolled onto the boy's hand, making trails through the thick layer of grime covering them.

The gun in the boy's hand trembled. His trigger finger twitched with nerves. Isabel's eyes burned straight into mine. In a nearly imperceptible shake of her head, she looked at the gun as she mouthed, "Don't shoot."

"Don't you pull that trigger, boy," I said. "You'll have a

bullet straight through your brain before the bullet leaves your barrel."

"Kane, this is not our way. Put your gun down, let the boy go."

I could have dropped the boy before he got off a shot. Instead, I lowered my gun and turned to let the boy pass.

"Toss your gun out the window!" The boy commanded.

"How's about I hand it over to Abel, on account this here's my daddy's gun. He sure ain't gonna shoot you."

"I won't shoot you," Abel assured him.

The boy nodded. As I leaned to hand my gun to the preacher, the door behind me flung open. One of the young expressmen tumbled in, bleeding badly from a neck wound.

The expressman behind me said, "Granger Hardy is dead."

Maybe the boy panicked because the next thing that happened was Isabel's blood splattering her husband's face before she dropped to the ground. The boy just stood there in shock, staring down at the pretty woman's crumpled body, her sage green dress now covered in a spray of red polka dots. Gun still in my hand, I leveled it at the boy.

"Don't shoot." It was Abel. Covered in his wife's blood, he pleaded for her murderer's life.

"I could have saved her," I told him.

"She wouldn't have wanted this man's life to be taken to save her own." My finger itched to put a bullet right in the middle of that boy's forehead. He deserved to die for killing something so bright and so beautiful in this ugly world. The preacher's words swirled around in my head as I stared that boy straight into his cowardly eyes. I'd like to say I couldn't do it, but the truth is I could have, and I wanted to. But Abel was right, I'm sure. She wouldn't have wanted me to shoot him in cold blood. She wouldn't have wanted me to shoot him at all.

Soon as I lowered my gun, the kid started blubbering and crying about how he'd kilt a woman. I took the boy into custody, knowing his fate. The preacher knelt, drew his dead wife into his arms, and let out a god-awful wail.

I could have saved her.

It wasn't a fortnight later that the boy was strung up anyhow. Justice is often swift out west. The preacher showed up to the court and told the judge he hadn't ought to hang that boy. If he hadn't shot Isabel, I would have asked the judge to go easy on the boy myself. As it was, I was content to let justice work itself out in its own way. God could sure enough sift through the mess as he saw fit.

* * *

Discussion Questions

1. Should Kane have taken the shot against Abel's wishes and killed the man who had a gun pointed at his wife's head?

2. As a protector of people, is Kane's first obligation to protect others or to respect their wishes related to killing others?

3. Are both Kane and Abel religious/Christian men? How can two people, both purporting to follow the Bible, come to different conclusions about the correct course of action? Is Abel more religious/Christian than Kane because of his view on violence?

4. Is it okay to kill someone in defense of yourself or in defense of others?

5. Abel says, "...if a man commits violence against me, if I forgive him, rather than retaliate, then his sin dies." What does this mean, and do you agree?

* * *

Meat is Meat

Scott Tierney

* * *

"Doctor..."

"Yes, Captain?"

Circling like a typhoon, the captain paced around the catch, her boots crunching on the scattered scales as though on shards of broken crockery. She maintained her distance with a learned suspicion, ready to jerk away should the catch, despite being inert, betray any inclination to spasm, twitch, or snap its jaws. The captain's precautions were well-measured; this was no ordinary catch. Even the rats, usually as undaunted and ravenous as hyenas, kept to the shadows, huddled in the safety of their number, hissing at this deviant and unworldly spawn of the sea.

It was the longest time before the captain again spoke. When she did, her heavy Slavic accent trembled. "Doctor... Would you... This catch...

"Is it... edible, would you say?"

The ship rocked, bruised timber groaning, the storm

outside battering the bulkheads relentlessly. In the darkness of the orlop, the ship's lowermost chamber, three lanterns flickered in the humidity of their bearer's breath.

The light of the lanterns' aura was cast upon a single form: the catch. Dense rope had been bound around its tail. It hung upturned, dripping, swaying like a convict from a noose. Akin to the head of a mop, its matted hair smeared the grime and rat droppings around the deck in time with the ship's sway, cleaning a patch on the floor the size of a dinner plate.

On the captain's insistence, the latches to the orlop had been locked, a barrel dragged in front of the door. She ordered the two men standing behind her, "No one learns of this. No one. Not the crew. Certainly not the passengers. The mood among them is combustible enough, what with rationing, our making port delayed, and this storm only delaying us further. To add *this* to the fire..." She shook her head. Turning away from the catch, albeit never entirely, she addressed her chief mate. "We are certain no one saw it, yes?"

The chief shrugged, sniffed, contemptuous gestures. A bead of cold residual rain trickled down the slope of his long English nose. The captain offered him her handkerchief before seeking further assurances.

"And Harper and Finch? They assisted you with pulling it on board. I trust you made it clear that not a word of this be spoken—"

"Your devoted chief mate has seen to every eventuality, my captain," the chief muttered with not unintentional mordancy. He snatched away the handkerchief, putting it to use. "Harper and Finch are aware of your orders. Your secret remains secret, sir."

The captain exhaled wearily. This chief... He had a way of making his every obeisance sound snide.

"How is your hand?" she asked. The chief sunk the hand in question deeper into the pocket of his oilskin. The captain frowned. "You needn't hide it from me, Waitekins."

"That wasn't my intention, sir."

"You should have it dressed."

"In due course, sir."

"In due haste, Waitekins. A wound that deep, a bite. From *that*." The captain directed her lantern toward the catch, thrusting it out like a harpoon. "Who's to say what diseases fester in the mouth of this foul creature."

The chief turned his back. "Creature..." he muttered. "She speaks as though addressing a clouded mirror."

The storm outside was picking up, rocking the ship, causing the creature to swing in widening arcs. Despite hanging limply, the blunt end of the captain's cosh having rendered it unresponsive, the creature had nonetheless been bound with enough fishing line to detain a small whale. As a consequence of such an abundance of binding, and due to being strung upside-down for close to an hour, through lack of circulation, the creature's tail had turned from brilliant emerald to the paleness of clay.

At the opposite end, swelling with blood, the creature's arms were growing pinker. They hung loosely, a pendulum, the wrists white and swollen and bound together. Long fingernails from longer fingers scratched the deck. The scrape of nail against timber only made the rats more aroused—and the mood inside the orlop more agitated.

"You would not mistake a firefly for a pixie or a platypus for a griffin," the captain told her officers. "Do not apply the same reasoning here. No. From here on, we shall refer to *it* by what it is. A creature. A creature of the depths. No more remarkable than a two-headed cod, yes?"

"But of course... My Captain," the chief sneered.

While the captain returned to her solitary pacing, the doctor and the chief whispered between themselves.

"Does she really intend that we eat it?" the doctor asked.

"Will you take up a plate if she does?"

"Well, I'd like to think I am as rational as the next man, never more so when the subject of rations, and the immediate lack thereof, is raised. But to simply consume this find, to dissect it with knives and forks..."

The captain peered around the catch.

"That is yet to be decided, Doctor," she said before continuing with her appraisal. "Were there others like it, Waitekins?"

The chief scoffed. "Is one not enough? The ship's manifest does not extend to the five-thousand, sir. Besides, I did not think to enquire if it had company. In all the melee, this *creature* was somewhat preoccupied in its ranting from the net."

It was the turn of the doctor to scoff. A portly gentleman of soft voice, silk nightshirt, and nervous disposition, he put forward his question with all the confidence of one placing a foot inside a crocodile's mouth.

"I say, do you mean to imply that it can communicate? That it can actually *talk*?"

"Why not ask it yourself, Doctor," the chief suggested

facetiously. "Oh, but I misspeak. As well as rendering it unconscious, our wise captain has seen fit to gag its mouth."

"An action I should have taken the moment we dragged it on board," the captain said, a pointed remark regarding the chief's pocket.

"But if it can talk, this creature," the doctor furthered, "that would rather change how we evaluate any decision to—"

"Doctor, do not talk of talk," the captain said. "I appreciate your concerns, I do. But we must not let theories or wild speculations cloud our judgment. Our decision must be guided only by our circumstance—primarily, that we are starving. Anyhow, I am sure if one were to visit an abattoir, they would describe it as a hive of conversation, alive with bleats, whines, neighs, quacks—"

"Oinks," the chief added. Akin to a complimenting snicker, a rasp of breath escaped the creature's gills. The captain stepped back, the doctor two-fold. The creature seemed to mumble a fearful and disorientated sentence before falling silent again.

"Did anyone else hear that?" the doctor gasped. "It seemed to say, to speak—"

"Air escaping," the captain said dismissively. "It can happen when a catch is left hanging on the line."

"A rush of blood to the head, sir?" the chief asked conceitedly.

"In a sense, Waitekins, should you wish to split hairs." The captain turned back to the creature. "Nonetheless, I hate to see any creature suffer. Is there anything you can do for it, doctor?

"Aside from fetching your cosh?" the chief put in again. In response to the captain's query, the doctor shook his head.

"I specialize in medicine, not... *this*. But perhaps Cook might be of better assistance? If he has any aboard, he might plug this creature's gills with lemon and thyme and seal it inside a hot oven, hey!"

The doctor chuckled nervously, his breath and ill-timed joke hanging in the air.

"Ahem... Once the poor thing has been put out of its misery. Humanely, of course. And once I have taken the opportunity to—"

"And how, theoretically, do you intend we put the creature out of said misery?" the chief asked. "I think we can safely assume that drowning is out of the question."

The doctor leaned toward the creature. With the light of his lantern, he scrutinized its chest, the slow, steady expanse of its breath.

"Interesting... For a creature clearly at home in the water, it breathes the air just as we do. By process of elimination, that would make it a mammal or at least an amphibian. Like a frog or a lobster."

The chief snorted. "Boiling, then."

"When the time comes," the captain said, "we shall leave Cook to decide how best to proceed with the slaughter."

"Should that not be manslaughter, sir?"

The chief was beginning to grate on the captain's temperament.

"But wait!" the chief bellowed. "We have agreed it is edible, then? I was not aware the matter had been settled. But seeing that it has, and our captain is willing to take the first bite on our behalf," he said, miming the tucking of a napkin under his collar.

"If I may," the doctor interjected, his tone panicked as though a momentous opportunity were being frittered away. "Should we decide *not* to consume it, this specimen, if you would permit me, captain, if only until dawn, to study it in the privacy of my quarters—"

"The creature does not leave this room, Doctor," the captain said firmly. "We cannot afford to have this ship become a menagerie nor a hotbed for gossip and panic."

"But, but," the doctor went on, all a flounder of chins and proposals. "Perhaps you do the passengers a disservice. They, like myself, if I do not sound too bold, there are many intellectuals among them. They have keen minds, keen and open. I am sure if you were to divulge with them the revelations of our discovery, theirs would only be a rational—"

"Hunger can make even the most rational man irrational, Doctor."

"Indeed," the chief muttered. "Isn't that the truth..."

The captain peered across the gloom. "Speak clear and plain, Waitekins. You think it unwise for a captain, as is their duty, to provide their crew with sustenance?"

With the heel of his boot, the chief ground a scale into the deck. "That would depend on *what* the captain considers *sustenance*, sir."

"I see. And would your tender sensibilities consider penguin an acceptable form of sustenance? Or squid? Jellyfish? Turtle? How hungry would you have to be, how close to malnourishment, before you deemed the stillborn calf of a dolphin appetizing?"

"A sailor," came the chief's response, word-for-word recited from the company's handbook, "must acquire a taste for every nourishment the sea has to offer, lest he starve."

"Then lest *you* forget, Waitekins, that we have one hundred souls in our charge, all verging on starvation. Men with empty bellies. Women, children, all of whom waste thinner by the day."

The chief snorted with acerbic amusement at the captain's heartfelt mention of women. The captain did not share in the chief's mirth. She shooed away those rats growing brave enough to venture nibbling at the creature's fingers.

"Curse these vermin! Yet, one has to admire their resolution. Unlike some of us, they are not too proud to make of anything a meal."

"Perhaps we should eat the rats instead, sir?"

"Do not joke of such things," the captain snapped, her Slavic accent rising to the fore. "Not until you have caught a rat, snapped its neck with your hands, singed the ticks from its fur over an ashcan fire, and eaten it straight from the stick. Had you done this as a child, only then could you—"

Having taken a breath, the captain tempered her anger with reason. "Waitekins, you are a reasonable man. I ask you now—employ that reason. However sincere they may be, do not allow yourself to be distracted by your emotions. My husband and child, two of our hundred, they, like us, survive only on scraps."

The chief stiffened. "Your husband and child bear no consequence in my judgment, sir. And I am fully aware of our predicament. I, too, am hungry, perhaps more than most, for

I often share my rations with those less competent. But that does not mean we should resort to the feral propositions you suggest. We must hold fast. Port cannot be far. A few days."

"I fear we do not have a few days. Look about you," the captain motioned. "Do any of these crates hold biscuits, salted mutton, a single grain of rice? There is nothing. Nothing. Even Neptune's broth, this rich and plentiful sea that beats at us night after night, is barren."

"Captain, you know as well as I that a storm will often drive a shoal to the surface. This I do not need to tell you. Hence, I say we reset our nets and have the men cast their lines over the sides."

"With what, Waitekins? We do not have bait enough to satisfy us, never mind fish with. And the only thing we have caught is likely to decompose in the time it takes us to swallow our pride!" The captain addressed both the chief and the doctor. "No. I thank and appreciate you both for your viewpoints. But, stomach-turning as it may be, as ship's captain, I must take my decision in the interest of the crew and passengers."

"And what say have the crew and passengers? Your husband and child?" the chief asked. "When we ring the dinner bell and present our guests tonight's special, are they to be told what is being served?"

"They will be told nothing. It will do them no good to know."

"And if any of them has a refined pallet, one who can distinguish between red meat and white? Or in this case, a mixture of both?"

The captain's face clouded. She took no pleasure in her

grim responsibility.

"We will season the meat thoroughly and ask the squeamish to hold their noses. As Cook is so fond of saying, what the customer doesn't know, the chef gets away with."

A heavy tension hung over the orlop for the longest time. If only to break the silence, the captain patted the creature on the upper-most tail as though it were a side of beef.

"Come, let us argue no longer. Our situation could be worse. I know of travelers from my homeland who, having found themselves lost in the wilderness, were left with no option but to eat their horses. Foul meat, they described, veined with a yellow fat akin to rancid lard and tasting no better. But this... A rich meat, I'd venture," she said heartily, despite the color visibly fading from her face. "How, you say? Gamey? Like tuna. What, with Cook's skills, he could make of it a banquet!"

"It certainly appears well-aged," the doctor judged, a veteran of countless fish suppers—and none since he'd left port. "The abdomen and belly are most broad. Swollen, somewhat. It's no wonder we've been unable to catch anything! Judging by the bloating around its mid-section, this creature must have gorged itself an entire shoal!"

"Then I suggest we slice open its belly post-haste so we may scavenge any undigested leftovers and serve them as appetizers," the chief said witheringly. "Assuming its belly does indeed hold sprat and not something more particular to the fairer of the species."

Mirroring the captain's shunning of the chief, the doctor continued his survey. As he spoke, he filled the pages of a leather-bound jotter with crude technical drawings, as intricate as finger paintings on a cave wall.

"The skin is somewhat pale. As pale as a Scotsman's! The hair is also less kempt than one would expect. The arms—fins, I shall label them—they lack the expected tone. The hind is rather sagging, plump, undefined. And the breasts," he said, blushing. "Very... ahem..."

Leaving both his shading and sentence unfinished, the doctor closed his jotter. "If you'll permit me to be blunt, this creature is not so *fetching* as one would have pictured."

"What difference does that make?" the chief asked. "Your captain is asking that you eat the creature, not take it to bed. Unless you hide notions to the contrary, doctor?"

There came a shock of light from a fumbled lantern.

"Bed! Bu-bu... How dare you," the doctor screeched. "You would accuse me of bestiality? I would never dream of such a grotesque act!"

"Calm yourself," the captain said, resting a hand on the doctor's quivering shoulder. "Both of you. Fighting will only hasten our cravings."

The chief allowed himself a thin smile. "There would be nothing grotesque about it, doctor. You are only human. A man, no less. Do not blame yourself for acting on your instincts. I can say with some confidence many a lost and lonely sailor has romanticized about less appealing creatures. The top half, at least."

Much to the consternation of the captain and the disquiet of the doctor, the chief bent down and unraveled the gag from the creature's mouth. "And this one does have a certain charm about it, hey? A lovely face." He parted the creature's hair—then smacked it across its 'lovely' face. "Well now, it appears I have brought some color to its cheeks. Perhaps if the captain were to commission an etching, so we may distribute copies and allow all bachelors aboard to critique her looks—"

"*Her* looks, Waitekins?"

Rising, the chief peered down his nose at the captain. "What term would the captain prefer?"

"I believe we have agreed upon creature, yes?" the captain said plainly. "But if you prefer, call it *it*. I find no inaccuracy in *it*."

"Then, for the sake of consistency, should I refer to you as It? Captain It? Doctor It? Cook It? *Cook it!* Now that would be fitting, wouldn't it."

The captain lunged forward, nose to nose with her chief. "Be sure to make peace with your conscience, Waitekins, before leaving those on board, including my husband and child, to starve."

"Captain, my good sir, please," the doctor put once again. "Her, this creature, however you wish to categorize *it*, is a discovery of the greatest anthropological importance. The consequences for science, history, religion, how we view life and creation itself are incalculable! The academic merits—"

"The academic merits of this creature are of no importance at this time," the captain made clear.

"But study must take priority."

"My priority is to the welfare of my crew, Doctor. Unlike yourself, I must put the filling of men's bellies ahead of the filling of their minds."

"And I salute you for your loyalty, Captain. Genuinely, I do. Please understand I mean not to harm the creature. If I may only take a few days to study—"

"Once we make port, you have my blessing to display this creature's bones before your peers," the captain said curtly, banishing any further argument. "Once Cook has boiled them clean for a broth. Yes?"

Keeping to the shadows with the same reluctance as the rats, the ship's cook remained leaning against the bulkhead. In his fist, he clasped a bottle of cooking wine, half empty; a large meat cleaver hung from the belt of his apron. Even on his talkative days, he said little—and cared less for discussion.

"Well, what say you, Cook?" the chief asked disdainfully, this drunk's only contribution to the debate thus far being to slurp noisily on his wine. "Would you care to divulge with us your expert opinion?"

The cook took a long and deliberate sup. Having wiped his lips on his forearm, he said with all the bluntness of his cleaver, "Meat is meat."

"That it is," the captain said approvingly, albeit without gusto. "You are a man of pragmatism, Cook. Just as the good doctor, yes?"

Meekly, the doctor nodded and withdrew any further objections.

"Well then," the chief said, "it would seem that I, unlike our captain, our cook, our doctor, and every other primate aboard this godforsaken ship, remain the lone moral voice, outnumbered a hundred to one. I must bow to the madness of the crowd, then acknowledge its superiority. But while the rest of you busily set your plates for this last supper…"

Speaking slowly so the cook may comprehend, the chief asked, "Tell me, Cook, when did you last prepare a cut of meat that wasn't already salted, pickled, dried, or brined? Have you ever slaughtered an animal? A *live* animal. One which bled, cried out. One which resisted the advances of that magnificent cleaver you wear so proudly."

Aside from a shrug, the cook offered little to no response. "Meat is meat," he eventually repeated.

"Meat is meat... That *it* is. And that *we* are...

"Well, if the captain will permit me to present a brief final argument, one that I hope will not pour salt on her insatiable appetite," the chief announced, pacing the room with a barrister's swagger, "let us assume that we do intend to slaughter this lovely creature, serving her... sorry, *it*...with cucumber garnishes and liquors from the doctor's cabinet. Which part of it, which cut, Cook, are you going to present as the main course?

The chief came to stand beside the creature, the light of his lantern illuminating both the head and the tail.

"Speak up, Cook. Which end should whet our appetites? The top half? The bottom? Ah, but you are confused. My mistake. The creature is upside-down." So there would be no further uncertainty, the chief pointed to each section individually. "The part of scale or of skin? Dorsal or breast? Fish? Or flesh? I would assume the heart pumps the same blood to both, Doctor?"

The doctor stammered. He looked to his captain for guidance. The captain's glower remained fixed on the chief—not that the chief was intimidated.

"Perhaps when it comes to the gutting, Doctor, you can

aid Cook in deciding where the animal ends and the woman—"

"Enough of this, Waitekins!" the captain screamed. "My mind is made, and your ranting only solidifies it. Cook," she said forcefully, "do your work! Do what others lack the will for."

Trudging, cleaver in hand, the cook set down his bottle of wine and made toward the creature.

"If any crewman wishes to make a formal complaint, it will be noted in my log," the captain stated. "Make it known, all actions henceforth are taken under my authority. What must be done must be done. For what choice do I have?

"The choice between savagery and sanity, sir!" the chief yelled. The captain turned her head away.

"Such a meager choice..."

The cook lumbered onward toward the creature; the chief stepped before him, fist cocked with intention.

"Stand aside, Waitekins," the captain pleaded. "You may abstain later if you must. But I urge you, do not make this any harder than it has to be."

"Sir, I will not stand idly by while you—"

"Then present one good reason to the contrary! Make it compelling. Please. If you know a way to save every life aboard this ship, then, for God's sake, speak now!"

The chief turned to the doctor. "Get yourself in the fight, man! You know sense?"

"I... but..." the doctor stammered. "To make of this specimen a stew would be a squander. But... needs, they must—"

"Damn you!" the chief cursed the fat man sniveling in

the corner. "Damn you and your cowardice!"

"Stand aside, Waitekins," the captain ordered again. "Please."

"I will not. Never! I will raise mutiny if I have to! I will take up arms! But I will not follow the orders of a lunatic nor bend to your moral lows!"

At this final outburst, the captain demanded the chief be restrained. Despite showing little sign of envying his task, the doctor took hold of the chief around the waist and pinned him against the bulkhead.

"This is cannibalism!" the chief screamed. "Cannibalism! This is nothing short of murder!"

* * *

Discussion Questions

1. Which argument holds the greatest sway over your opinion, the hunger of the crew, the moral issues of eating a potentially sentient creature, or the scientific argument of destroying the scientific find of the century? Explain.

2. Does the relative hunger of the crew change your calculation on eating the creature? If members of the crew had already died of hunger and more set to die within hours or days, would you be more likely to be willing to serve the creature as dinner?

3. Should the passengers be made aware of what they are eating so they can choose to eat or abstain from the meal?

4. Is there additional information about the creature that would change your conclusion? What if it was determined the creature was capable or incapable of communication?

5. If the creature had looked less human-like, would any of the discussions/concerns in the story have taken place? Should "looking human" automatically get you more empathy?

* * *

Pappou's Garden

Fotis Banis

* * *

"Traditions make the people, and adherence makes the man."

Those words suffocated Pappou from the very beginning. They were coughed up from his father's mouth and scattered like poisoned seeds across the hardwood floors of his childhood home. Pappou grew up navigating the undergrowth of those words, until finally the spores caught in his own lungs and flourished.

He flowered into a handsome man, yet he waited for his sisters to marry before taking a spouse, as was tradition. And when Pappou did finally marry, he worked hard to provide for his family, as was tradition.

In the vacant plot of soil in the backyard of his house, tucked away between the neighbor's walls, that dour man found joy, in a world where he otherwise only saw purpose. Slowly, lovingly, Pappou built a garden that grew into a paradise under his constant care. He would toil in the sun or hide from the sparse rains under the balcony, on a stretch of cement that looked out into the trees and flowers and bushes. Even the short winters came to know him as a friend while everyone else in Palous hid from it. His wife would never bother him, nor would she ever ask for help with the four children she birthed and raised in that house.

Pappou would leave late into the night to work in his bakery, sweating in the hot silence, and he would return home a little after noon, when everyone retired to their houses to rest. He would greet his wife and children with a cold warmth—as he had seen his own father do for so many years—before escaping into the greenery. After a while, even his family grew to prefer things this way. No one ever went out to the garden but Pappou, nor did he ever call on them.

When his wife died Pappou did not bury her next to the plot he had reserved for himself in the town cemetery. He did not even attend her funeral.

His children slowly unchained themselves from the house in the years that followed their mother's death, all in their own way: Yianni moved to the city to court a woman that did not want him; Katerina married a ship captain from Paros and followed him there to be with him; Maria managed her uncle's cafe a few towns over and married a local man; and Taso, the youngest, who had learned to play the bouzouki from watching his father, used it to escape from the hollow, cold rooms to play at festivals all around the country. When Pappou's daughters had come to him with love shining through their skin, he gave each of them enough money to buy houses to begin their new lives, as was tradition. In the end, Pappou enjoyed the silence, and continued to tend to his beautiful garden.

Yianni settled down with a woman named Panayiota after his sisters had married, and before long Nikolaki was born. When the boy was a few months old the whole family converged to Yianni's house to meet and baptize their newest member, as was tradition. Even Pappou came, and everything was adequately uneventful. He sat on the couch and drank his coffee while little Niko cried beside him, dressed in his white baptism clothes. Pappou's children made sure he was watered and fed, they asked about his health and about Palous, and they even inquired about his garden. But they paid him no mind beyond that, so he turned his attention to his grandchild.

Panayiota talked and laughed with everyone, but her eyes looked through them, resting on Pappou as he played with her son. That night, when everyone had gone to bed, she went to Yianni with a resoluteness hard as stone. Yianni had decided long before Nikolaki's birth that Pappou would not get to enjoy the spoils of a relationship he never cultivated. But Yianni's conviction lost its color when Panayiota spoke about how caring Pappou had seemed with his grandson that day; it began to wither when she lamented about losing her own father only two years prior; and finally his conviction died, crumbling away from the trellis it had climbed slowly throughout his life, when she condemned the enmity that Yianni wanted to pass onto his newborn son. Eventually, Yianni agreed to put his own feelings aside and to let Nikolaki spend time with his pappou.

* * *

So when little Niko was old enough to go to school Yianni would drop him off at Pappou's house most Sundays, and the two of them would spend all day in the garden. Pappou was neither happy nor angry at Nikolaki's imposition; to him, it was just another role he had to fulfill. As was tradition.

Quick smiles and long, leaden stares taught little Niko how and when and where to play, until finally he had stomped out a small path for himself in the garden, weaving in and out of Pappou's large footprints. Pappou would water the spry tomato vines and the thick fig trees and the unruly oregano and the sprawling squash, sighing and grunting and inspecting all the while, and Nikolaki would chase butterflies and poke worms and throw rocks over the walls when Pappou wasn't looking.

The plants would talk to Pappou as he passed, and he would answer. When little Niko wanted Pappou's attention he would ask about them, and Pappou would tell him:

"This vine has been giving me trouble, Nikolaki."

"Why, Pappou?" little Niko would ask in turn.

And Pappou would make up a story about warring vegetables or lovelorn herbs or something of the sort, and Nikolaki would listen, seriously listen, because Pappou's voice would never waver, even for a moment. Little smiles would bloom upon the edges of Pappou's lips as he spoke, but Nikolaki would always be oblivious to them, too lost in the tall tales to notice. There, in the garden with his grandson, watching the boy react with such earnestness to the stories as they walked through the deep green sea, Pappou would almost feel happy.

* * *

There was no better garden in all of Palous; maybe even on all of Nissos.

"You must speak with the plants, Nikolaki. And you must listen to them," Pappou would say. "They can grow without you, but they require love to grow faultlessly; it isn't enough to water them and prune them. Sometimes they need things that they cannot ask for."

Every summer would grace him with buckets of produce that he would eat and trade and give to any combination of his four children, even though he believed they never truly appreciated the labor that went into them. At least he was still providing for his family, he would say to himself. As was tradition.

* * *

Little Niko grew older and his conversations with Pappou evolved beyond the fairytales of the garden. His curiosity never angered Pappou; it only annoyed him.

"Why doesn't Thea Maria have kids?" Niko asked one day as the two of them sat under the balcony, his feet dangling off of the wooden folding chair.

Pappou chewed the slice of orange he had just popped into his mouth and tossed the peel into the garden. He had retired some years prior, and since then his age had begun to show. He had liver spots all across his skin and his head and hands shook slightly.

"Because she is unruly, and does not listen to reason," Pappou finally answered. "She should be raising a family, but instead she's running around Tarniso acting like a businessman, just to spite me."

Nikolaki didn't understand most of the words that his pappou used, but he was old enough to understand the frown and shake of the head, which was too wide to have just been Pappou's tremors.

"Unlike your Thea Katerina," Pappou continued. "She has done her duty. I never learned to read or write, Nikolaki. I had to work from a very young age to help my father; and even so I tried my best to support my family. Katerina got her degree. She went and became a teacher. And now she has dug her roots in Paros with an honest man."

"Baba says that her family is bigger than all of Nissos. That she likes getting pregnant so that people don't just think she's fat like a tree." Little Niko giggled and threw a piece of orange peel into the garden, just like his pappou did.

"Your father doesn't know when to be quiet," Pappou muttered. "He was always a problem. He jokes too much. Life is about hard work; your father and his brother never understood that. They haven't worked a day in their lives. I would come home from the bakery covered in flour, and they would be sleeping on the couches. And now your father sits and pretends to work in that government office, and your uncle spends his days sleeping and his nights drinking and playing music on whatever island he happens to be on that week."

Pappou stood up with a grunt. "Stay here, Nikolaki. Don't step on the soil now that I've watered the plants," he said as he grabbed a few sticks of bamboo and disappeared into the garden.

* * *

In the car on their way home, Nikolaki told his father

what Pappou had said; and while the words and their recitation were vastly different, Yianni could imagine his father saying them, and he quickly understood the sentiment.

That night, as Yianni laid in bed and spoke with his wife, his conviction was tested again.

"He is not a good man, Panayiota. He hated my mother. And now with the things he's telling Nikolaki, I don't know."

"He is the boy's pappou. His only pappou. You are allowed to not speak with him, but it isn't up to us to deny Niko a part of his family. Pappou is old, who knows how many years he has left. Be the bigger man and let him enjoy his time with his grandson."

Yianni grunted. "He's never enjoyed anything but that damned garden," he relented, but his conviction had already crumbled once more.

* * *

Years passed slowly, as they did on Nissos, and slowly Niko grew too old to visit his pappou every weekend. And Pappou would always say that he was too tired or too weak to come to the city to see Yianni and his family. Niko would go once a month when his parents forced him, then sparsely throughout the year when he didn't have soccer practice or tutoring or plans with his friends.

One day, when Niko had finally gotten his driver's license, he and his friend decided to take Yianni's papi—the underbone motorcycles that populated every street and alley of Nissos—to go for a ride. They exited the city and drove, uncertain of where to go, interested only in the wind and the sun and the scenery. Within an hour they had reached Palous, a destination that Niko had not purposely chosen.

"Wait here," Niko said to his friend as he stepped over the papi and took off his helmet. "I'm going to go say hi to my pappou."

The side door to the garden was unlocked. Niko trotted down the cement path, walking past the house that his father was raised in, and turned the corner into the backyard. Pappou was sitting in his chair, clumsily cutting through chestnuts with a kitchen knife, but Niko did not notice him. Niko only noticed the garden.

The spry tomato vines were brown and crumbling; the thick fig trees were surrounded by rotting figs; the unruly oregano was dry and stiff; and the sprawling squash had shriveled into itself.

"Pappou," Niko said, turning to him. "What happened to your garden?"

"Nikolaki," Pappou said with a muted surprise, turning to see his grandson. "What are you doing here?"

"I came to say hi."

Pappou noticed the helmet under Niko's arm. "You shouldn't be driving a papi, Nikolaki. They're dangerous. Did you come all this way on a papi?"

"What happened to the garden?" Niko asked again as he walked through the dry soil. The plants that used to playfully brush against him as he walked through them now crumpled from his touch.

Pappou waved off Niko's earnestness. "I'm getting old, Nikolaki. What am I to do with a garden? I'll be dead soon. And then no one will come to take care of it."

"You don't know that," Niko answered. He unfolded a

wooden chair and sat near his pappou, putting the helmet on the ground beside him. He planted his feet firmly on the cement. "This garden was your life. Thea Katerina or my father would take care of it."

Pappou scoffed. Chestnut shells fell from his lap onto the ground.

"They don't deserve it. Let this garden die with me, so that those ungrateful children won't come and reap the spoils of my work. They'll have the house, and the bakery, and everything my father left me, but they can't have this."

"They're your family," Niko answered quietly.

Pappou focused again on the chestnut in his hand. The knife scraped weakly against the shell.

"And what have I not done for them? What did I not provide for them?" he finally said.

"I have never strayed, Nikolaki. I waited for my sisters to marry, even though it meant losing the love of my life to another man. I came home every night to them. I fed them. I clothed them. I'm leaving everything I have to them, even though they abandoned me here in Palous to rot."

Niko looked out upon the dying plants and trees with anger and sadness. Something deep inside him welled up. He felt it pushing against his throat, yearning to come out, but he did not open his mouth. There was so much that he wanted to say to the spiteful man that sat beside him. But Niko finally reached the conclusion that all of Pappou's children had reached many years prior, in their own ways and in their own time: there was no reasoning with a bitter man.

"My friend is waiting outside, Pappou. I'll come see you again next week," Niko said. But he never did go back.

* * *

And by the end Kosta was alone, so that when he fell forward into that dry, untampered soil, he was undisturbed, surrounded by the desiccated remains of the only things that ever loved him.

* * *

Discussion Questions

1. Pappou fulfilled his duty by waiting for his sisters to marry, being faithful to his wife, and provided for his children. Was Pappou a good father? Was he a good man? If fulfilling your duty doesn't make you a good person, what does?

2. To the extent that Pappou was lacking as a father, a husband, or a man, to what degree was it his fault? Did Pappou have an obligation to grow beyond the expectations and traditions imposed on him?

3. The only happiness Pappou found in his life appeared to be the time he would spend in his garden. Is it wrong to focus on a hobby that makes you happy? How do you know when it unhealthy to focus on a hobby? Do you have an unhealthy focus?

4. To what extent is Pappou's family at fault for not attempting to join him in the garden and take a shared interest in the one thing that made him happy?

5. What words, at what point, in Pappou's life might have led him to a different, better life? To what extent could that advice equally be applied to your own loved ones, or even yourself?

* * *

Prisoner of Conscience

David Moore

***

On Friday, December twentieth, 1991, Marcus White picked his sixteen-year-old son up from St. Andrew's Catholic High School and dropped him off at home. Usually, Marcus would take Jaysum with him to his memorabilia shop downtown, but today he wanted his son to hand off an envelope with some baseball trading cards and cash to his investment partner, Dr. Katz, who would be coming by the house to get them. This same arrangement had occurred a couple of previous times, and without incident as far as Marcus knew, so he had no reason to expect anything different this time. But when he got back to his shop, only about twenty-five minutes later, he found several urgent messages on his answering machine from Jaysum pleading with him to come home right away.

On the way back, Marcus tried to imagine what could

have occurred in the past half hour that would cause his son such anguish. Jaysum had been living with him in Elmsford, New York, only since the previous summer. Before that, he had been living with his mother in Tampa, visiting with Marcus on the holidays, a pattern that had prevailed since Marcus left Florida when Jaysum was just two years old. As Jaysum grew older, his mother felt he should spend more time with his father, but Jaysum did not want to leave Florida. In the spring of his sophomore year, he forged a grade on his report card, which—combined with increasingly strained relations at home—led his mother to insist that he live with his father. As far as Marcus could tell, Jaysum seemed to be getting along well in his new school, despite being withdrawn. He liked talking with his father about baseball trading cards and had even begun saving his own. Nothing in his demeanor suggested that waiting for Dr. Katz was a problem. But Marcus had never heard Jaysum sound as anxious as he had been on the answering machine.

When he got home, Marcus found his son in the basement, huddled in a corner, staring at the dead body of Dr. Katz, Marcus's .38 revolver on the floor a few feet away. Jaysum pointed at the body, blood pooling around Dr. Katz's stomach and crotch. He wanted to fuck me, Jaysum said in a hoarse voice, tears running down his cheeks. Marcus asked if it had ever happened before. Jaysum shook his head but whispered, he blew me last time.

In normal circumstances, this would probably be treated by the police as self-defense, but Marcus knew this was not a normal case. A Black boy killing a widely respected white surgeon, who was married with two children, did not bode well for the killer. At best, Jaysum would be sent to juvie, at worst tried as an adult for murder. Prison of some sort was almost guaranteed. All the horrible stories he had heard about Black boys and men in prison flashed through Marcus's mind. As a father, Marcus had failed to protect his son from whatever happened between the physician and Jaysum. He would not let his son be ground up by the American justice system. He had served in the Army, two tours in Vietnam. He could serve jail time better than his son.

He told Jaysum not to talk about what happened with anyone. Instead, he should say Marcus had taken him to the memorabilia shop as usual that afternoon. He told Jaysum to go get cleaned up. He would get rid of Jaysum's clothes in case there were any minute traces of blood. Then Marcus wrapped the corpse in a large tarpaulin he had in the garage and lifted it into the trunk of his car. He drove to an isolated woodsy area and buried the body. Later he ditched the doctor's car in a parking lot miles away from his home. He then proceeded to clean up the basement and the trunk of his own car.

Despite these efforts, Marcus knew the police would probably come looking for him once Dr. Katz did not return home. They would eventually find the car. Marcus had wiped it thoroughly to get rid of fingerprints, but he wasn't confident everything he had done would be enough to avoid being caught. It was no secret the physician and he were friends. And probably Dr. Katz had told someone about his intended visit to pick up cards and cash. There was nothing nefarious about what they were doing. Suspicion would fall on Marcus. But Marcus absolutely would not implicate his son. If he had to go to prison, that was his fault and his punishment. Two days later, the police came to his shop.

* * *

My ever-impatient luncheon companion could not wait for me to finish the story. She said, So, he was arrested and convicted of killing Dr. Katz?

I nodded.

And the son was never charged?

Right.

Courtney sat back in her chair, lips pursed. She was a psychology professor at the local university, whom I had met at a criminal justice conference a decade earlier. We immediately hit it off, mostly because she wanted to know all about the crime cases I was covering. She was a new hire at the time, and her field of research was the "criminal mind." She talked me into meeting with her on a frequent basis to discuss the motivations of the criminals I wrote about. In the ensuing years, she had become something of a celebrity in her field, as well as a frequent legal expert in court, always testifying on behalf of the prosecution. She never met an accused who wasn't guilty. Still, I usually found her comments insightful.

She said, I assume the son was grateful for what his father did?

Not exactly, I said. Marcus and his attorney were shocked when the prosecutor listed Jaysum as the primary witness against his father. All Jaysum had to do was keep quiet. But he testified in court that his father picked him up after school as usual and left him at the memorabilia shop, then went home. When Jaysum got home in the evening, he said his father was repainting the basement floor. A couple of days later, his father installed new carpeting in the trunk of his car, which Jaysum said smelled like a dead dog. Jaysum also said his father told him to lie about Dr. Katz coming to the house and about the pistol Marcus kept in the house. Marcus's attorney knew that his client would not testify against his son, but in court he tried to throw suspicion on Jaysum nevertheless, suddenly accusing him in a loud and angry voice of killing the doctor so he could keep the money for himself. The tactic backfired. Jaysum began crying, angrily saying it was unfair that he should be accused when his father did the murder. The prosecutor alleged what really happened was that Dr. Katz had come to the house to demand Marcus pay him the seventy thousand dollars he was owed from their investment in baseball cards. Marcus didn't have the money, they got into an argument, and Marcus shot the doctor. The jury took only a few hours to conclude that Marcus was guilty. He was sentenced to twenty-five years to life.

Courtney absorbed this information as she took a big bite from her hamburger, catsup dripping down to her plate. She wiped her mouth, then asked if Marcus had an explanation for why his son testified against him. He did, I said. Marcus believed his son was scared and had forgotten who his father was, that his father would never allow anything to hurt him. His attorney told Marcus that the police probably got to his son. They had found fragments of Dr. Katz's eyeglasses in the basement, which proved, they said, that Dr. Katz was murdered in the father's house. And there were only two people who could have killed Dr. Katz. The police would have threatened Jaysum: If Marcus was found not guilty, then the police would go after the son. Did Jaysum want to spend the rest of his life in prison for a murder his father had committed?

You believed everything Marcus told you?

He had no reason to lie to me.

Courtney gave me an indulgent smile.

Ever the cynic, I said.

You're really invested in this case, aren't you? Not your usual M.O. You may not be seeing the case for what it is.

I do believe him. I don't think it was in Marcus's character to kill anyone. Especially not for money. He was living a comfortable life. The money wouldn't have made a major difference for him, one way or the other. Look— several years ago, Marcus came up for parole. By then, over the previous two and a half decades, he had proven himself to be a gentle, caring person, becoming a grief counselor, especially for prisoners with mental issues. He had endorsements from corrections officers and civilian prison employees, and even from a social worker, who attested that Marcus had improved the lives of many mentally ill prisoners. The superintendent of the correctional facility also supported the parole application, writing that Marcus was the only prisoner he had ever recommended for release in over forty years as a corrections official. That, I said, is who Marcus is. He is not a murderer.

You don't know that, Courtney said. There's a dark side in all of us. The fact that Marcus has been a model prisoner doesn't negate the possibility that he lost control that one time he was with Dr. Katz. Maybe they had an argument over money and it got out of hand. Maybe there had been something between the physician and the son, and Marcus got so angry he shot Dr. Katz. Maybe he had a violent flashback because of Vietnam. The point is, Marcus's behavior in prison doesn't preclude the possibility he committed the murder as charged. Although his good behavior should probably make him a cinch for parole.

I shook my head. Actually, when he was considered for parole the first time, the board denied it. They said he was still a threat to society.

That caused Courtney to pause. I waited for her reaction. There must be something you're not telling me, she said.

He was denied parole because he didn't *apologize* for murdering Dr. Katz, I said. For the first time since Dr. Katz was killed, Marcus outlined for the parole board the whole series of events that led his son to shoot the physician. Members of the board were incensed. The state had found him guilty, they said. So, he was guilty. Period. Trying at this late date to pin the blame on his son, and defaming the memory of a respected member of the community by suggesting he was a pedophile, was outrageous.

That was harsh, Courtney said. They were treating him as a liar. But I'm sure Marcus was sincere.

You think he was telling the truth?

I didn't say that. He could be telling what he had come to believe was the truth.

Well, he was there. He certainly knows what happened.

Not necessarily, she said. When Marcus first blamed his son for committing the murder, it was some twenty-five years later. Right?

I'm sure he told his lawyer at the time.

Can the lawyer verify that?

He died years ago. But Marcus may have told others.

Maybe so. You can ask him. But from what you've already said, there's a good chance the first time he told anyone, other than perhaps his lawyer, was a quarter of a century after the murder was committed. That's plenty of time to create false memories.

Why would he do that?

Courtney laughed out loud, covering her mouth. Sorry, she said. I never thought you were so... never mind.

What? I said. She was beginning to piss me off. She didn't seem to notice.

Well... clueless. People don't *choose* to have faulty memories. They arise in the subconscious. They become real to the person.

So all memories are false? The tone of my voice should have revealed my irritation. But Courtney ignored it.

No. Of course not. False memories arise for a variety of reasons. Trauma. Misinformation. One's emotional or physical state when trying to recall or relive a memory. Suggestion or pressure, especially from an authority figure. That's why police can sometimes get an accused to admit to a crime the accused didn't commit.

So you can never trust any memory?

Pretty close, she said. Memories are stored with the formation of particular proteins in the brain. But the really weird thing is that the part of the brain that perceives an object or event overlaps with the part of the brain that imagines an object or event. We can't always tell the difference between the real and the false memory.

Okay, Professor. So, what's your theory about how Marcus came to accuse his son of murder when Marcus himself might have done it?

Courtney finished the last of her hamburger and took a long sip from her diet soda. She moved her plate to the side and leaned her forearms on the table. First, she said, any other details you haven't mentioned?

Yes. After the police dug up Dr. Katz's body and conducted an autopsy, they found trace amounts of semen in the physician's mouth, too little to identify the DNA. The prosecutor claimed the semen was put there by Marcus to mislead the investigation. Marcus's defense attorney tried to get Jaysum to admit it was his semen. Then, just a couple of years ago, more sophisticated DNA analysis concluded the semen belonged neither to Marcus nor to Jaysum, but to some other unidentified man. It turns out, the respected Dr. Katz swung both ways.

The semen analysis doesn't help Marcus's case, she said.

I disagree. It shows that Dr. Katz was into gay sex. It's consistent with Marcus's account of a sexual dispute between his son and the doctor.

Yes, it is, she said. In fact, it supports my "theory," as you like to call it, about what probably happened.

Let's hear it, I said.

She leaned forward. For some reason that we don't know, Marcus and Dr. Katz get into an argument, and Marcus shoots him. It is a traumatic experience. He can't really believe that he would kill anyone, much less his friend. Over time, his mind blocks out the worst details of the murder, but he does vaguely remember the trial—the semen in Dr. Katz's mouth and that his lawyer went after Jaysum, accusing him of a sexual encounter that led to murder. For decades, Marcus has no reason to dwell on the specific details. But once he has completed his minimum incarceration, he wants parole and has to explain why he deserves it. By then, his brain has no recallable memory that he murdered Dr. Katz, but it does retain imagined information that Marcus took responsibility for the crime to protect his son. That view is reinforced by the person he has become in prison over the years, the kind mentor to mentally unstable felons, which is inconsistent with someone who would commit murder. That isn't who I am, Marcus would say. He genuinely believes the story he told the parole board.

What about Jaysum? I said. He had incentive to blame his father.

Did you ever talk with him?

I called him when Marcus went up for parole the first time. He didn't want to talk to me. All he said was that his father had killed Dr. Katz and was trying to blame him. He's a fucking psychopath, Jaysum said. And hung up. I think he's lying.

Could be, Courtney said. But Jaysum's story is more contemporaneous with when the events occurred. The longer the time period, the more likely false memories are to take over.

But Jaysum could have been pressured by the cops to "remember," or more likely just to lie, that it was his father who killed Dr. Katz. Maybe over time, he came to believe his own lie, the way you say Marcus created a false memory. But initially, it was a lie not a false memory.

That's possible, Courtney said. Jaysum did have an incentive to accuse his father. But what's more plausible—that a young boy, who's been living in the house for only a few months, gets into a sexual relationship with a much older doctor and has the presence of mind to find his father's gun and shoot the older man, or that Marcus and his friend got into an argument that ended badly?

Aha! That first option is precisely the fear that Marcus had. If the story came out that Jaysum had killed the doctor over sexual assault, no one would believe the Black boy instead of the highly respected, white doctor. That's essentially what you're saying as well. And that's why Marcus took the blame—to protect his son.

But now Marcus seems to be throwing his son under the bus, Courtney said. Blaming Jaysum for the murder.

We sat there for several minutes, our arguments exhausted. Finally, I said, Marcus came up for parole again last week.

How did that go?

Everyone who had supported him the first time suggested he admit to the murder and express remorse. Otherwise, the board wouldn't grant parole. He asked me what I thought. I told him I thought it would be a mistake to lie. He should be true to himself.

She shook her head in disbelief. You actually *advised* him to stay in prison so he could be true to himself? Did he follow your advice?

He did apologize to the board for the murder. And

expressed remorse to Dr. Katz's family. He admitted it was his fault that his son was in the position that led to Dr. Katz getting shot. If he had handed off the money and baseball cards to Dr. Katz himself, nothing would have happened.

That's *not* what the state is looking for! He's still blaming his son and denying responsibility!

Of course, you're right. His parole was denied.

Courtney sat back in exasperation, more agitated than I had ever seen her. Do you have any idea what it's like to be in prison? You should have let him make his own decision. If he asked for your opinion, you must be important to him. Probably he has no other friends outside of prison. You have become his touchstone with reality. And you say, Stay in prison! How could you do such a thing?

There was a long silence while we sat staring past each other. Finally, she said, Let's suppose you're right. Marcus is innocent. Jaysum killed Dr. Katz. Nevertheless, if Marcus admits to the murder and apologizes, he can at least get out of prison. He could go seek reconciliation with his son. Well, probably not his son, based on what Jaysum said to you. But maybe Marcus would want to connect with his grandchildren in a couple of years. Or maybe just be free again! Would you want to stay in prison just to be true to yourself?

* * *

We left the café soon after that. Never had Courtney reacted so vehemently to one of my crime stories. I couldn't help but reflect that perhaps I had done a terrible thing, depriving Marcus of a chance to be released from prison and enjoy the rest of his life in freedom. The thought continued to plague me when I met Marcus again in prison a couple of weeks later to see how he was doing. I was escorted through several metal gates and finally arrived in the visitor section, a large room with tables and chairs bolted to the floor, other prisoners and their guests distributed throughout the space. Marcus walked in from a door opposite the one I entered. He looked frail, neither upbeat nor downtrodden, walking with a slight limp. He gave me a warm smile as he sat. We exchanged pleasantries for a couple of minutes, and then I said, I'm sorry you didn't get parole.

I suspected it wouldn't pass muster, he said in a gravelly voice. Once I decided not to confess. But I had to try.

When was the first time you ever told someone about Jaysum committing the murder? Was it two years ago, when you first applied for parole?

Course not. My lawyer knew. But I couldn't tell anyone else after that. I had to protect my son.

But now you are accusing him.

No, I am not! I know the DA isn't going to say, Oh man, Marcus Wright just blamed his son, I'd better go arrest Jaysum and try him for murder. The state got their man. Me! I've served my sentence. End of story for the DA. What I did was tell the parole board what really happened so they know I'm not a threat to society. Never was.

Didn't you ever tell anyone else, maybe a friend here in prison, about Jaysum?

There're no friends here in prison. I try to help some who are suffering, but no reason for me to tell them about my life. It was a dark time. I don't like to think on it. Didn't even have to until the parole board wanted to know if I could be a good boy if I got out. But they don't want the truth.

I feel awful, I said. Telling you not to admit guilt so you could get out of prison.

He looked startled. You didn't advise me about nothing, he said. How could you advise me about that, anyway? You ever been in prison?

No. But I remember you asking me for my advice.

Marcus shook his head. No. I never asked you. You just up and told me something about being myself. But I don't need you to tell me that. I know who I am. And I'm no murderer. The state thinks so. But I know the truth. I made a mistake. But I'm a good father. In the end, I did right by my son.

Don't you want to get out of prison? Maybe see your son, your grandchildren? Maybe try to tell them who you really are?

In their world, they already know who I am. A convicted murderer. Jaysum created that world because he didn't trust me. The state helped him do it. He can never leave it. It's who he became. Who he is. I don't blame him. He says I killed Dr. Katz. He's not wrong. I didn't pull the trigger, but I put my son in a terrible position. Every Black parent will tell you that. If I hadn't done that, Dr. Katz would be alive today. And Jaysum's kids—my grandkids—who are they gonna believe if I go see them after getting out of prison? Their loving father? Or their convicted grandfather who just admitted everything and is now trying to say he's innocent?

Frustrated, I said, Don't you just want to get out of prison and enjoy life outside these walls?

* * *

Discussion Questions

1. Would you, like Marcus, stay in prison just to be true to yourself? Are there some crimes you would lie about having done to get out and others you would refuse to ever admit to?

2. Do you believe memory is as malleable and fallible as Courtney says, or do you have memories you are positive are true?

3. What internal and external tests (*if any*) would you use to try and determine which of your memories are real and which are edited by time?

4. Assuming Marcus's memory is correct, do you think he did the right thing by taking the fall for his son? Do you think his son did the right thing by accusing his father in court?

5. Do you think a victim can sincerely tell their remembered truth to a judge and jury but not tell the actual truth? What percentage of time do you think this happens (*if at all*) in serious cases? What is the basis for your opinion?

* * *

Purgatory

Serena Smith

* * *

I didn't cry when I got the news. I knew I was supposed to, but I just couldn't. The fact that I was his daughter made it worse, too, because I was expected to love him. When your father gets that sick, you're supposed to feel irreparably broken. You're supposed to cry until you have no tears left. And, frankly, it isn't supposed to matter how much torment they put you through. Shouldn't the thought of his death still bring me remorse? Was what I was feeling characterized as grief? I felt wrong like a piece of me was floating outside my body, but I didn't feel sorry. I'll admit it; I knew he deserved what he was getting.

If he would've just OD'd, my life would have been perfect.

Unfortunately, cancer is not the same as an OD. I know it's a horrible thought, but if his death had been the result of his drug abuse, I could have blamed it on him. He took too much. He couldn't control himself. He made it happen. There were countless times when he came home in a daze, stumbling and crashing into walls. He'd litter the floors with beer cans, shoot up again, and then fall asleep in the bathtub. When I was younger, the utter strength of his drunken sleep used to terrify me. No matter how hard my mother or I tried to rouse him, he'd still remain asleep, barely breathing. After a while, though, I learned to just be grateful for the quiet.

It was clear he wasn't safe from himself. He *could have* OD'd. But he didn't. Instead, he got cancer, which meant I had to feel heartbroken.

It was still his fault, though.

The doctors refused to admit it, but he caused his disease. I looked it up. Excessive drug use can be directly linked to an uptick in cancer. Whether they'll admit it or not, he DID cause it. But it wasn't that obvious, so he was never held accountable. Nobody wanted to blame him. It was such an outrageous claim that even I felt guilty for believing it. Cancer is a monster all on its own. Children and other innocents get it all the time. Connecting cancer to self-sabotage, in a sense, is kind of like saying everyone who gets it should be blamed. That isn't fair. Even if it *was* his fault.

He hit her, you know. I remember one particular day when we had just gotten home from the hospital. He was undergoing his first round of chemotherapy and had asked us to be by his side. We both went, but only because we felt like we had to. The doctors and nurses would think we were bad people if we let my father undergo chemo alone. I often wondered if they would think *he* was a bad person because he spent the greater part of every week brutally attacking Mom and cussing and yelling at me. He called me fat pig so often you might have thought it was my name. But, sure, why not claim that everyone was right? He was sick, so *he* was the victim.

They had to have known to some extent—all those nurses. Mom never took her coat off, no matter how hot the hospital room got. She flinched every time my father raised his arm, even when he wasn't about to hit her. They had to have seen the dread in her eyes whenever he opened his mouth—the fear that intensified tenfold whenever he was around. It was very unlikely that they didn't know exactly the type of man he was. But apparently, cancer cancels out wrongdoings. With cancer, you can only be a martyr. Can a martyr also be a monster? Because I kind of feel like my father was both.

"Don't you think this whole thing could've been his fault?" I asked Mom that day. She stopped folding his clothes and stared at me in shock. Standing in their bedroom with her coat off, she was exposing her bruises to the world. Large splotches that extended so far, they painted her entire arm purple. Some of them were new—because cancer, as it turns out, does not heal your inner demons. In the case of my father, it actually made them worse. It gave him yet another excuse to be a tyrant, forcing me to feel upset for him even when I knew I shouldn't have.

"No one deserves this kind of torture," Mom replied.

Come on, Mom, there's no way you actually believed that.

That man was a villain. He was the antagonist unraveling the threads of our lives. Frankly, he deserved worse. For him, cancer was nature's way of dishing out karma. I knew it. Mom knew it. Everybody probably knew it. Yet, no one would admit it out loud, not even me. Even thinking it almost made me as bad as he was. It wasn't right. So, instead of arguing with Mom, I sighed and nodded. She said what she thought she needed to, never letting anyone see her contempt, which made her a better person than I was.

He never actually hit *me*, which made the whole thing even more miserable. Screaming and pleading for him to stop, I was forced to watch as he slowly killed every piece of joy Mom had left in her, murdering every. last. drop. until she was nothing but a hollow shell, whimpering when he was finished. And I never tried to stop him. I told myself I wouldn't know how to, but if I'm being honest, my resistance was out of fear. I didn't want to have bruises too; I didn't want to constantly be in pain. On some level, that made me complicit. I never called the cops or threw myself in front of her, and now she'll never be the same.

The last time was the worst. He kicked and punched and shoved her into things. By the end of it, lamps were shattered on the ground, furniture was upturned, and my mother had been beaten so hard she was no longer moving. All I can remember is screaming. And then, in a desperate attempt to save her, I ran into my parents' room to grab their cell phone.

There he was, asleep on the bed as if he hadn't ruined her. I looked over to their nightstand, finding exactly what I knew I would—a vial of meth and a used syringe. Determined to rescue my mother and afraid of what he would do when I did, I picked up the needle and filled it to the brim. I could feel Mom's freedom in my hands. If I was strong enough, I would be the brave heroine I had neglected to be all that time.

I could rescue her, sending all that meth into my father's bloodstream and watching as his breath slowed to a stop.

It would have been so easy. Why would anyone even suspect me? I could've worn gloves, placed the syringe back in his hand, and made it look like he'd gone too far this time. When he was asleep like that, he was going to stay that way, even as the needle pierced his skin. And everyone would assume he had OD'd like he could have done—*should have done*— years ago. It would be the perfect escape.

But I wasn't fearless. I was still a coward who could only worry about herself, so I set the full vial back onto his bedside table and called 911.

My father insisted that he didn't know what had happened to Mom. Blaming the fight on me, he milked his illness, trying to prove he was incapable of that level of violence. Instead of calling him out, I bit down on my lip until it bled.

Mom ended up surviving, and by that point, my father's illness had stripped away his strength until he could no longer hurt either of us. Even so, every day when we followed him into that hospital, I wished I had just killed him. I'm horrible! Okay, I get it. I know. My thoughts, my actions, what I almost did, and what I didn't do—they all made *me* the monster.

Now that he's gone, I wish I didn't still feel so much shame, not because of what I could have done, but because of what I *should* have. I've always been weak. My father loved pointing that out about me, and I've finally come to realize that, through it all, he was right. He's dead, and he still haunts me.

So, you can sit there and cry about his death. You can scream at the universe, cursing God for taking him too soon, but I'm not going to. I'm glad he's gone. My only regret is he wasn't taken sooner. You wanted me to give the eulogy. Fine, here's your eulogy. I'm telling you how it was. There were always signs. He never acted like a saint, but you all treated him like one. You let him torture us, and you let him think that what he was doing was okay. You never tried to stop him. Can you live with that? Because I can't.

But here's to him, I guess. You all can celebrate his life. Fine, whatever. I'll take pride in celebrating the end of it. Have a good death, Dad. I hope you rot in Hell.

* * *

Discussion Questions

1. Do you think the narrator will someday grieve the loss of her father? What leads you to your conclusion?
2. Do you agree or disagree with the idea that a person who gets cancer, regardless of their issues, deserves empathy and support?
3. Does the idea of drug addiction as a disease to be treated and abuse as a generational cycle that is difficult to break lessen the culpability of the narrator's father?
4. Is it ever okay to be happy someone is dead? Under what conditions (*if any*) is it okay?
5. If you were the narrator's therapist, what feedback and suggestions would you give her to have a successful and happy future?

* * *

Reni Winter, Dead at 57

Joseph Lyttleton

* * *

"Reni Winter, Gifted but Troubled Rocker, Dead at 57"

On the number 21 bus, Zach Boyd was scrolling through Facebook when that headline grabbed his attention. He was the right demographic to care about Reni's death; he was also the right demographic to still be using Facebook. He read the headline three times before tapping the link. He couldn't believe it. It must be a hoax. Surely, Reni couldn't be dead. Fifty-seven was too young.

The link led to an obituary on rollingstone.com, the once revered music magazine and cultural touchstone, now an oversaturated website. Zach clicked on the masthead to make sure it was the real Rolling Stone and not one of those look-alike domains. He'd read that's how hackers got your passwords. Or something. He hadn't actually read the HR memo.

This site appeared authentic, mostly because Zach didn't recognize any of the faces staring back at him. The homepage's main headline proclaimed, "Quinn Heardley Is the New Queen of Rock and Roll," which Zach found dispiriting because he hadn't heard of Quinn Heardley, and, worse, he didn't know who the *old* Queen of Rock and Roll had been.

Zach did, however, know who Reni Winter was. It was even fair to say he had loved Reni at one time. His music, at least.

When the bus stopped to rotate passengers, Zach slid into a now-vacant seat and against the window. As he settled in, a teenage girl sat next to him. He pushed himself against the bus wall to create as much space as possible between himself and her. Once the bus started moving again, Zach opened the death notice. Even before it began, the article's subheading made it clear it wasn't going to be a hagiography:

The aging rocker, whose best years were behind him, was found dead in his home Thursday morning.

It seemed a particularly heartless note to start an obituary on, especially because Rolling Stone had once been Winter's biggest champion. Besides, aging rockers whose best years were behind them was a pretty apt description for the magazine.

Reni Winter, a talented and once immensely prolific musician, was found dead in his Los Angeles apartment Thursday morning. He was 57. The cause of death is unknown.

Revered for his acerbic but brittle lyrics and guttural drawl, Winter was a critical darling for much of his career, though his sales rarely reflected the laudatory reviews. Over a career that spanned more than four decades, Winter released 27 albums, most of them as a solo artist.

Off the top of his head, Zach could name at least half of those albums. At one point, he'd owned nearly every CD with Reni Winter's name on it. Many of them were still in his apartment, their cases ensconced in a thin layer of dust.

Gifted though he was, as a younger artist Winter often made headlines as much for his public outbursts and run-ins with the law as he did for his music. He struggled with addiction much of his adult life, earning him a reputation for being a tempestuous and unreliable artist. He spent his 20s and 30s ricocheting from benders to rehabs and back again, before achieving sobriety in his 40s.

Zach wasn't much of a drinker and rarely touched hard drugs—he was certainly never one to partake in barbiturates, Reni's preferred medicinal downer—so he had lived vicariously through the musician's infamous persona and dubiously confessional songwriting. On more than a few occasions, Zach had returned from a night out with friends and thrown on Reni's ode to late-night inebriation, "She's Had Enough."

Winter was also dogged by persistent rumors of misbehavior with women until 2018, when, amidst the #MeToo Movement, The New York Times published a devastating exposé. The piece featured interviews with multiple women who accused Winter of sexual misconduct and emotional abuse. He also faced allegations of grooming underage girls. The FBI launched an investigation, but Winter didn't face any charges. Still, his career suffered following the accusations, and Winter never regained his stature among critics or fans.

At the time of his passing, it was six years since Winter

released an album.

Zach had to stop reading for a moment, so affected was he by the news. Considering he hadn't listened to Reni's music in half a decade, his reaction surprised him.

It was 8:45, Friday morning; Reni Winter had been dead for a full day. Perhaps the cruelest proof of the musician's fall from grace was that his death had gone unreported for twenty-four hours. There was no "Breaking News" headline on NYT.com for this story. The once-renowned musician died in relative anonymity.

Reemerging from his reminiscence, Zach considered his fellow commuters. The work week's long trudge had lulled the bus riders into a somber stupor. Most were also looking at their phones, some with headphones on, melodies seeping from the seal. From the corner of his careful eye, he noticed the girl next to him was watching videos. Elsewhere, a few riders were reading physical books, which appeared to be making a comeback. Perhaps the written word wasn't on its death bed, after all. Not that Zach would have known. These days, an obituary was long for him.

He returned to the article. After an ad for a movie Zach would likely never watch, it continued for another ten paragraphs or so. Having begun by throwing dirt on Reni's grave, the author now stepped back to disinter the man's legacy.

Winter was born in Greenville, South Carolina and grew up in the state's capital. His music career began at the age of 15 when he formed the early hardcore band Goose Feather with two high school friends. The group didn't even last a year and never released any music, but their raucous shows became the stuff of legends.

Winter in particular established a reputation for being a galvanizing showman with a penchant for relentless energy and death-defying stage antics.

By the time he was 21, Winter had formed or joined a half dozen other bands, most fizzling out before they could enter a studio or sign with a label.

The bus jolted to a stop, and the teenage girl stood to get off. Breathing a little easier in her absence, Zach stopped pressing himself against the bus wall. A very serious-looking man in a gray jumpsuit replaced the girl.

As the 1980s came to a close, the hard-drinking Winter appeared posed to fade into obscurity as a post-punk also-ran. But in 1991, he self-released his first solo album, Bloody Knuckles. The mere existence of the album surprised both fans and critics of Winter. That the album abandoned Winter's punk roots for a more rootsy sound was even more of a shock.

Many of his contemporaries in the hardcore scene accused Winter of selling out, but he was embraced by members of a still-nascent genre: alternative country.

Zach did the math; he was only fourteen when *Bloody Knuckles* came out. That year, Zach's favorite album was Tom Petty's *Full Moon Fever*, simply because it was always playing in his dad's car. Zach wouldn't even hear of Reni Winter until the tail end of the nineties, and by that time, the musician had already built up a daunting discography (most out of print). The twenty-one-year-old Zach hadn't known where to begin.

Winter was often referred to as "your favorite musician's favorite musician." Following the release of his debut, Winter independently released four albums in as many years. It wasn't until a bootleg live album began making the rounds, unofficially titled

Drunk and Safe, that record labels started pursuing Winter in earnest. After a bidding war, he signed to Sire Records.

Zach's entry into Reni Winter's music was the musician's second major label release, 1997's *Yes Depression*. Only after thoroughly internalizing all twelve songs did Zach discover other Reni fans considered the album one of his worst. The self-mythologizing collection, designed to cement him as a forefather of alt country, was criticized as a blatant attempt to gain crossover radio success. The album even included a slow-tempo duet with Sheryl Crow, a cover of Bruce Springsteen's "Born to Run," which Pitchfork panned as "perhaps the most embarrassing moment for an artist who has pissed himself on stage multiple times." Even crueler, Rolling Stone only gave *Yes Depression* three-point-five out of five stars.

As a new fan, Zach wasn't cynically turned off by Reni's mercenary maneuvers. He just loved the music and devoured everything he could by his new favorite artist. As a poor college student in the pre-Napster days, Zach waited for sales at Tower Records and searched through the used racks of independent record shops. He forewent more than a few meals to complete his collection.

Reni's debut album was the hardest for Zach to track down. With only two thousand copies ever pressed, *Bloody Knuckles* had gained cult status by the turn of the century. A few of the album's tracks were on the bootleg album, which Sire rereleased under the far blander title, *Reni Winter Live*. But Zach didn't hear the original recordings until peer-to-peer file sharing was at its industry-annihilating peak.

After months of searching and downloading

mislabeled albums and poor-quality rips, Zach managed to find a digital copy of *Bloody Knuckles*. The audio was slightly muffled, and the fourth track had an odd beep during the third verse, but otherwise it was the real deal. Even in its digitally decayed form, it was a masterpiece, maybe even better than its reputation. Like a lost Bob Dylan album if Dylan's drugs of choice had been grain whiskey and bitter sex.

At the height of his career, Winter was rumored to be romantically linked to countless Hollywood leading ladies and models. In 2016, he married Celeste Nolan, frontwoman of The Polar Opposite. For a time, they were one of rock music power couples, but the marriage ended in an acrimonious divorce 16 months after it began.

While Zach's love life was never as abundant or dramatic as Reni's, he had his share of doomed romances. He only had two serious relationships before his thirties: his college girlfriend, Beth, and the woman he left Beth for, Lynn. After Lynn abandoned him for another man, the rest of Zach's twenties had been spent as a bachelor, all entanglements strictly physical. His decade of singledom was most often soundtracked by Reni, whose lyrics made Zach's gamophobia sound, ironically, romantic.

Then Zach met Karina. The best decade of his life.

In the 2010s, Sire's parent company, Warner Bros. Music, invested heavily in remastering Winter's pre-label back catalog. The label reportedly paid millions for those early albums, making it clear they intended to be in the Reni Winter business for years. The final rerelease, Stay the Coarse, came out in December 2017. Half a year later, The Times published their exposé, and Winter retreated from the public eye.

That article had devastated Zach. Presumably not as badly as Reni—or his victims—but it was still a gut punch.

Four women—three anonymous, the other a fledgling musician named Tara Colorado whose career stalled after dating Reni—alleged abusive behavior, both sexual and emotional. All of the women were in their early twenties when they met Reni, with one of the anonymous victims having been involved with the musician around the time his marriage to Celeste was unraveling.

Reni denied the allegations, though he acknowledged the relationship with Tara. However, within weeks of the article's publication, three dozen more women came forward with accusations, some more damning than in the original article. Three women claimed their relationship with the fortysomething-year-old Reni began when they were teenagers. Hence the FBI's investigation. As such things go, there wasn't enough proof to hang any charges on. Still, there was little reason to doubt the veracity of the accusations. Per the popular euphemism of the pre-MeToo era, Reni had proudly been a "bad boy."

It certainly rendered the central lyrics of Zach's favorite Reni song less charming: "She never tells me when she's had enough / And I never ask."

Horrified by the accusations, Zach nonetheless couldn't help but grieve for his once favorite artist. Reni had been like an older brother, a man whose experiences, as expressed through poetic lyricism, had helped Zach understand his own life. And women.

Yet, after Zach read the horrific stories—and he read them all—the songs morphed in his ears. The details of the abuse, which *The Times* referenced in oblique terms, were readily available to those who wanted to know. It was despicable. In that context, Reni's music, which was rife with heartless women doing him bad and remorse over love misplaced, no longer sounded poignant and perceptive. The singer came across as self-pitying and, frankly, self-deluding. Even if only a fraction of the accusations were true, Reni had injured multiple women and—it must be said—girls. Zach's fandom couldn't challenge that math.

For Reni's sake, Zach had hoped the besieged musician might, at the very least, offer an apology. Instead, following the avalanche of accusations, Reni vanished, deleting his social media accounts and canceling all his pending tour dates—those that weren't canceled by the venues themselves. His album sales and streaming numbers tanked. Sire dropped him, then his agent, and finally, and most devastatingly, his manager, Arnold, who had been with Reni since the musician was an erratic punk rocker with needle marks in his arm. Reni's former industry friends judiciously avoided any suggestion that they had ever been in a room with him. Reni was fifty-one and alone.

Last year, Winter resumed touring, mostly in Europe. But, while he still had a devoted following, the crowds were a far cry from his career highs. At those concerts, an artist once known for his mercurial stage banter rarely spoke between songs, letting his music do the talking. Though his technical proficiency remained apparent, the fire that had once animated his performances was gone. Even fans seemed to acknowledge Winter was a relic of a bygone era, for better or worse.

There were rumors he was looking to sell the rights to his substantial back catalog of songs.

Zach wished he could be like the fans who could "separate the art from the artist." Some Reni devotees rallied behind the slogan "innocent until proven guilty" —and since there would never be a trial, he would always be innocent— but it wasn't that simple for Zach. The songs were too personal, too tied into his idea of himself. For half his life, he had been a Reni evangelist. He posted the man's songs on social media; he traveled to see him live. He had four different Reni t-shirts.

Zach had listened to Reni when he was falling in love and falling out; when he was feeling hurt or wronged or spiteful; when he needed to believe someone else knew exactly how he felt. Zach had loved Reni's songs because they spoke words straight from his own subconscious. So, what did it say about Zach that Reni was his inner voice?

It was a question he found easier to ignore if he just didn't listen to the music anymore.

The final paragraph of Reni Winter's obituary ended on a note of irony:

At the time of his passing, Winter was also rumored to be set to self-release two new albums. It would have been his first new music since before the public accusations. For an artist who, at his most prolific, released one or two albums a year, it was the longest Winter had ever gone without releasing new material.

"Rumored to be set to self-release two new albums." "Rumors he was looking to sell." "Rumors of misbehavior." "Rumored to be romantically linked." In death, Reni's career had become reduced to a series of rumors. In a few years, would his entire existence be nothing but hearsay?

Despite himself, Reni's obituary stirred Zach. Sadness for the permanent loss of a once beloved artist sat alongside despair for the illusions that had been shattered by the truth. There was also anger, for the same reasons. But there was relief, too. In time, with any luck, Reni would fade into utter obscurity, and Zach would never have to confront the monster in the mirror.

That was the thought occupying his mind as he stepped off the bus.

Zach didn't feel like working today.

* * *

To enter the doors of Northwest Dynamics was to cross into the subconscious of an unmanned ventriloquist dummy. There was no style in its construction, no features, just white walls and white ceilings and beige carpeting that shepherded new arrivals toward the white front desk. There sat Martha, that day as every day. She was especially ornamental this morning, not even feigning acknowledgement as Zach crossed her path.

Zach had worked there for fifteen years.

Beyond glass double doors, rows upon rows of shared desks extended from one side of a football field-sized auditorium to the other, the lack of personal space a metaphor for the company's entire ethos. Nothing was yours. Faceless employees came and went, and at the end of each quarter, what they accomplished was reduced to a few spreadsheet pages. So long as a number within one specific cell was greater than the number from the previous quarter, well-paid executives would be even more well paid. What else mattered?

Northwest Dynamics existed in a shabby building that existed in a shabby city that existed in the shadow of mankind's grander ambitions, all of it teetering on the faltering edge of human existence. When the rockets took the billionaires to their new utopia, everyone else would still be sitting at their shared desks, waiting for the tide to sweep them away.

Death was on Zach's mind. Because of Reni, sure, and because fifty-seven was not that old; Zach was only forty-seven. Granted, when he'd been twenty-one, fifty-seven was ancient. It was the age of grandparents and institutions and the Pyramids of Giza. But now he realized that fifty-seven was nothing. It was just getting started. At forty-seven, Zach had barely lived. He'd never even been married.

Until this morning, Zach hadn't realized he was ten years younger than Reni. The rocker always seemed ageless, an eternal avatar for immutable manhood. Zach couldn't get that phrase out of head: "Dead at 57." It might as well have been twenty-one. Too young. Even for a sex pest, fifty-seven was too young.

In a state of disarray, Zach sat at the desk he shared with three other employees and turned on his computer. Like most jobs that required a middle-aged man to occupy an office—except for that brief period in 2020 when it turned out Zach could work from anywhere; until it was determined a few months later that, no, actually his office desk was indispensable—the actual contours of Zach's job were largely irrelevant. He amended the content that someone else created so someone else could upload that content somewhere, and that would allow someone else to use the content. Ultimately, the content was extraneous, all of it in service of collecting users' personal data, which was the true beating heart of the company. But Zach didn't have anything to do with that division. He occupied the company spleen. The work mattered, Zach was told, but he couldn't explain why.

A cog in a machine. A soldier in a brigade. A crayon in a box. His job was an argument against the existence of the soul. There was no talent in what he did, no personality. No art. Northwest Dynamics was where the very concept of art went to die. Zach had never considered himself a creative type, but there was a time in his life when he felt he could discern beauty. Had this company robbed him of that—or was that too easy? Maybe everything in life was a slow death.

Zach didn't even get to choose the music to listen to while he worked, which would have helped the day pass. For eight hours every weekday, barely perceptible songs hovered in the periphery of his perception, the music pumped in through unseen speakers in the ceiling. Who decided what songs were added to the playlists? Were they chosen by an anonymous peon at another company. That seemed like a good job. Zach wondered if he could apply for it.

No, he realized after a minute of contemplation. It was just an algorithm. Everything was an algorithm these days. Hell, his job could probably be done by an algorithm.

He turned on his computer to begin his day.

* * *

For lunch, Zach ate three slices of cold pepperoni pizza in the ten-by-ten break room and spent the remainder of his half-hour break in Center City. Most days, he'd meander through T.J. Maxx or the Liberty Place mall to kill time, but he couldn't be bothered today. He found a free bench and, sitting, googled "Reni Winter."

The first page of results showed a dozen different obituaries, with Rolling Stone appearing first, followed by Paste Magazine, NPR, and Pitchfork. A cursory review of the articles proved that Reni's legacy was likely going to be as much about his misdeeds as his music. Every article referenced *The New York Times* article and the subsequent fall out. Zach scanned through the articles for a cause of death— even just a rumor of one—but the information wasn't available anywhere. Reni's death apparently had no cause, unlike the death of his career.

Was it fair that Reni had lost so much for his sins? All these years on from the initial stories, Zach no longer remembered the specifics. Maybe, he allowed himself to consider, the misdeeds hadn't been so bad. Reni wasn't Roman Polanski, after all; he wasn't Harvey Weinstein. Maybe Reni was only guilty of being a bad boyfriend. Who ever truly knew what happened between a man and a woman (or a series of women)? Besides, everyone makes mistakes when love and sex are involved. Lord knows Zach had never been the perfect boyfriend.

Zach was still drifting in the wake of this most recent breakup. Karina had only moved out two months ago.

Karina had been simple. She never needed a wedding ring. She didn't put any demands on Zach, at all, which turned out to be just the level of commitment he was comfortable with. They worked. For the first time in his life, Zach thought he understood love: it meant not minding when someone else played the music.

Zach had been with Karina a few years when Reni's career imploded. By that point, Reni was no longer getting as much airplay in his apartment. Zach was happy and Reni never seemed to be. Reading the exposé felt like hearing an old high school friend had fallen on hard times. Initially upsetting, but easy enough to put out of mind.

He hadn't missed Reni too much; Zach and Karina had their own music together.

But even perfect albums end.

After a decade together, the couple split, generally on good terms. There was no infidelity, no bitterness. Karina had broached the topic. She felt stagnant, unmotivated. Even before she said anything, Zach had sensed her unhappiness. He agreed a change would be the best thing for her, so long as he didn't have to make one too. She didn't need any convincing. Not even a month later, Karina quit her job and moved to Chicago. Zach stayed at Northwest Dynamics.

He didn't hate Karina for leaving or begrudge her desire for more. He just missed her. As a younger man, the only balm Zach had ever needed for emotional support in such times was Reni's songs. But those songs just didn't strike the same chord for Zach anymore.

Maybe he'd give Reni a listen tonight, Zach thought. That was the least he could do for a man who once sung within him.

He checked his watch. Lunch was over.

* * *

"We're letting you go."

When he returned from his break, there was an email

asking Zach to come to Human Resources. There, a woman with dyed-red hair and dull brown eyes barely offered any preamble before informing him he was no longer employed by Northwest Dynamics. She did attempt to manufacture an expression of doleful regret, but it read more like boredom.

A decade and a half with a company ended with four words. Were all institutions this fickle?

Blindsided, Zach returned to his desk to retrieve his stuff. No security guards trailed him; the company wasn't worried about him making a scene or stealing anything of value (nothing of value to steal). As he gathered a frayed sweater, a mostly unused notebook, and six pens labeled "Northwest Dynamics," Zach kept hearing the woman's words repeating in his ears: "We're letting you go."

The calm brevity of her sentence reminded Zach of the subheading from the Reni Winter obituary.

The aging content contributor, whose best years were behind him, was let go on Friday afternoon.

Set free, Zach decided to use the afternoon for exploring his hometown, finally wait in line to see the Liberty Bell. But after twenty-five minutes, he was bored.

Back on the bus, Zach found Reni's Rolling Stone obituary again. Only, the subheading was different. It now stated:

The aging rocker, whose career had stalled, was found dead in his home Thursday morning.

Had he misread it before, or had they edited it since this morning? Zach couldn't see the point in changing it; the new version wasn't any less dismissive. Maybe someone had pointed out what Zach had thought, that the original read like an epigraph for the magazine itself.

The headline hadn't changed, though: "Dead at 57." Fifty-seven. Too old to be tragic, too young to be complete.

* * *

Zach entered his apartment just before four. It struck him as he looked about the living room, not for the first time, that the place looked much emptier now that Karina's stuff was gone. Never married, but nevertheless very divorced.

In the corner of the room stood his CD tower. He usually streamed his music these days, but he always kept his collection on display. It was his monument to the past, to himself. Karina had said he could be content even if nothing ever changed; in retrospect, maybe she hadn't meant it as a compliment.

Sliding his finger down the edges of the jewel cases, he found what he was looking for: *Bloody Knuckles*. Miraculously, the correct disc was in the case. He carried it back to his stereo, which had been in Zach's life longer than Karina, and inserted the album like an offering to a hungry god. He skipped to song three, "She's Had Enough."

Reni Winter's singular voice filled Zach's living room for the first time in years. Zach crossed to the kitchen and pulled a beer out of the fridge. In a day or two, the full reality of his new state of unemployment would sink in, and panic would arrive. He would be struck by the realization that he was a forty-seven-year-old man with no skills that couldn't be reproduced for much less money by a recent college graduate or predictive text program. He would wake to the terrifying truth that he was now solely responsible for the rent of a two-bedroom apartment in a gentrifying Walnut Hill. He would recall that Karina had suggested he move with her, but he hadn't been willing to risk giving up his job security.

All that was for later. Tonight, he had five-sixths of a six-pack of Yuengling, and a dead pervert was crooning his favorite song. The unknown would have to wait.

* * *

Discussion Questions

1. Why does Reni Winter's death affect Zach so much? How can Zach have an emotional response to the death of a person he has never even met?

2. Do you think the accusations against Reni should matter, given that none of them were proven in Court? Should accusations be enough to end a career? Barring a violent physical assault, is it fair to judge a bad-boy rocker for doing exactly the things expected of bad-boy rockers?

3. Zach stops listening and following Reni after the accusations, do you think he was right to do so? Does it matter that Reni wasn't going to get any additional money from Zach simply playing the CD's he's already purchased?

4. How does Zach's lack of exciting and zeal for life effect how he is responding to Reni's death? Is the impact of Reni's death really about Reni? Is the impact of anyone's death really about the person who died?

5. If you could counsel Zach towards a happier life, what advice would you give him? How is that advice applicable, or not, to your own life as well?

* * *

The End of Learning

Timothy Gaddo

* * *

A bullet ended Paul Channeler's childhood at age six when it passed through his abdomen and into the brain of his best friend, Myra.

* * *

He had assumed he would marry her one day; his mom and dad were best friends; it made perfect sense. He knew nothing of the fickleness of a human heart or that childhood crushes end. Nothing could make best friends part, he believed.

Until, one day, something did. Trauma immobilized him and forced him to watch Myra's blood pool on the classroom floor. Paul had never known death, but as he stared into Myra's lifeless eyes, he knew, with an obdurate certainty he'd never felt before, that she was no longer there behind them.

* * *

Had it not been for the bullet, Paul would have

amounted to nothing. Already bored with school, he would have developed a nonchalant attitude toward learning. By grade six, he'd have earned nothing higher than a C, and in high school, he'd have struggled to maintain a D. He'd have drifted from job to job, never satisfied.

But the bullet changed all that.

* * *

To six-year-old Paul, Myra's death had been an aberration; the first, the only, the last; the never-before and never-again. But near the end of his hospital stay, a counselor let slip mention of other school shootings. Paul filed it away, and after returning home, he went to the family computer. Despite spelling mistakes, the internet knew what he was looking for and served it up. Before the end of that very day, Paul understood a new, chilling reality: school had never been safe. Killers had killed hundreds of children before Myra. Any school could become a shooting arcade.

He feared returning to school, and a horde of social scientists descended, focused on returning one six-year-old to school, but no one, *no one,* addressed the larger problem. Paul needed to know why.

Highly motivated, he learned rapidly. His vocabulary improved to match the fevered pace of his journey through all the internet could teach him.

He studied the past for clues to the present, and he studied the present as each new shooting flared briefly in public consciousness and then became another dismal part of the past. As Paul's comprehension and language skills matured far beyond his years, mass shootings continued, years passed, and in 2023, the year he turned ten, Paul accepted the solution that remained after he had rejected all others.

He would go on strike.

"You mean school, honey?" Judy asked. "You're gonna stop going to school?"

"School, home school, studying... I'll stop all forms of learning until adults end mass shootings in America." He would recruit other students, he told his parents, through social media and the membership site he'd designed. Members would pledge to return to school only after Congress enacted nationwide red flag laws, mandatory background checks, and registration.

"To change so much," Judy and Theo told their son, "*People* need to change first, and they won't change because a few children cut school. Change like this takes time," they said.

"It shouldn't," he told them. "It should take no more than an instant."

That was true. Judy and Theo knew it.

Paul had held anger in check for four years. He'd heard his parents discussing mass shootings, and he was disappointed at their response to his announcement. "How can we boast of our freedom, democracy, our American way, while we can't even keep school children safe from our own citizens? The debate and anger and questions and demands should be so overbearing that they compel us to drop our stubborn, single-minded positions and simply cooperate to end this... this... American curse."

While they were still reeling from that, Paul hit them again. "This blight is so ugly it should challenge our very right to continue as the dominant species on our planet. Don't you see that?"

* * *

That night, he dreamed of her. Same classroom where she died. Mercifully, she appeared as she had in life: same angelic face, dark curls in ringlets around her ears. They didn't speak. She only looked at him and nodded her head.

* * *

While Paul's attorney held the school district at bay, Paul's SSS (Students-Saving-Students) site gained members. A year into the strike, over 200,000 had registered. They didn't all strike, but 17,000 did, missing between three days and eight weeks. Most schools passed those students to the next grade level, hoping to avoid scrutiny.

The most significant event in this period was one that *did not* occur. No one, *no one,* suggested putting differences aside to find a solution to mass shootings, even under threat of an uneducated generation. Paul worried. He had expected a solution by now.

* * *

He dreamed of her again. Same classroom where she died; she was still six, he eleven. This time, they spoke. As with Paul, her vocabulary had matured.

"I'm troubled," he said.

"Why?" she asked.

"I fear I'm doing more harm than good."

"Where's the harm in stopping evil?"

"I'm failing. No one cares."

"Untrue. Millions who follow you care."

"They have squandered their futures, those who care;

the nation is in peril, yet the evil persists."

"Would you give up?"

"At least survivors would be educated, and the nation could yet recover from the strike."

"That is most important, then? More important than ending evil?"

"I do not know anymore. You tell me."

She walked a circle around him, her hand idly trailing the backs of desks still misplaced from the panic of that day.

"If the status quo of mass shootings is truly the best America can do, then perhaps it is fitting that the same status quo should become the catalyst for a change to a different America."

"A different America? Different how? Do you know?"

"I do not know your future. Only that it comes without me."

* * *

SSS membership increased dramatically in the summer of 2024; September brought chaos. The strike disrupted families, communities, and all levels of government, who in turn intimidated, bullied, or threatened; they flooded courts with lawsuits naming Paul, his parents, the SSS site, its service provider, or their own students.

"You should note the uniqueness of this," Paul's attorney told one interviewer. "Kids, young kids, have never before organized. It's part of a kid's DNA to just let things happen. They don't have the vote or power to change things, even when they're being gunned down in schools. Until now. It couldn't have happened without the internet, but I'm proud of this extraordinary crop of kids."

Unfortunately, the stalemate continued for many years; opposition to gun legislation remained well-funded by manufacturers and powerful gun-rights groups. SSS membership, however, held steady at about one million; enough toddlers aged into "newly aware" status to fill the void left by those required to resign at the age of 18.6 years. School refusal hovered around 50 percent of membership, rising after new shootings and waning a few weeks later. Courts in this era leaned toward protecting child rights; there was no shortage of attorneys willing to donate services. Indeed, little more was required than to cite a client's horror in the wake of the latest shooting; courts felt powerless when confronted with doe-eyed little people cowering in their presence.

* * *

September 2030 found Paul, now seventeen, working two full-time jobs, obsessed with proving worthiness to parents who had never doubted him for a moment despite his non-education. One night, at twenty past midnight, he parked in his usual spot and walked to the front door, where he found a small phone suspended by a string looped over the doorknob. As he reached for the phone, it began to ring, and Paul spun around to look behind him. He hurried to the drive, peered into the darkness, but saw no one. After the fourth ring, the phone went silent.

It rang again as he returned to the house, and this time, he removed the string and carried the phone back to the driveway, squinting again in the dark. When it began ringing a third time, he flipped the cover open and held it to his ear.

"If you hang up, lose the phone, or refuse to answer when we call, you will hear no more from us. Understood?"

"Who are you?" Paul said.

"We are a group of former SSS members. No one will find us; try if you like; you'll waste your time. We have a solution to your dilemma."

"Oh? What would that be?"

"Interesting statistic: among all mass-shooting victims since 1950, we have identified a handful who were closely related to gun-rights zealots. In almost all those cases, after losing loved ones to gun violence, zealots either changed their mind on sensible gun restrictions or went mute."

"What are you..."

"From a list of several hundred children of current gun-rights activists, we are prepared to assassinate roughly fifty—"

"Oh my God..."

"If we do nothing, far more deaths will occur through gun violence this year alone. We hope to save lives."

"You'll be committing murder! You'll become the monsters we're trying to stop!"

"We are not unanimous. A small but significant number of us are hesitant. We have agreed to abide by your decision, Paul."

"WHAT? You can't be serious! Who is this...?"

"You'll need time to think..."

"I DON'T NEED TIME AT ALL..."

"...so we'll call again in a few days..."

"WAIT!" Paul shouted. "Before you hang up, tell me, if I say no, will that decision be final?"

The line was silent for only a few seconds, then, "Remember, if we can't reach you, we'll make the decision without you. Majority rules." The caller hung up.

Paul stared at the small phone, reeling from what he'd just heard. Then he pocketed it, entered the house, and went to bed; his day job started early. It might be futile, but he had to try to sleep.

* * *

That night, he spoke with her again, for only the third time since her death. She was still in the damaged classroom, still six, but she sounded older. He told her of the SSS call.

"Would he really do that?" she asked.

"He sounded serious."

"What will you do?"

"I must say no."

"What if it's true that taking lives now will save more later?" she asked.

"Evil in the name of good is still evil."

"And if you say no, but the SSS group chooses to kill anyway?"

"Then I never *had* a choice. What else can I do?"

"You could bargain. For a lower number. Why fifty? Why not thirty? Or ten?"

"Maybe... I'd need to think about that," Paul said. He wandered around the classroom for two minutes. Then he stopped and said, "Ah, yes. I understand their logic. I wish it weren't true, but for their plan to have any chance of success, they must choose a high number."

"Why?" she asked.

"Because... it's a part of human nature, I suppose. After we lose someone to a senseless death..."

"Like when I died," she said.

Paul startled and looked sharply at Myra. He stared at the floor, took a deep breath, and said, "Yes, like when you died. After that, I... anyone, would accept restrictions to any rights, even if those restrictions might spare only one life, even if it were only a remote possibility."

"That doesn't explain how fifty deaths might change anything. There have been high numbers of shooting victims before," Myra said.

"That's true." Paul thought for a while, then nodded and said, "Yes, I see it now. Extremists, those who want no restrictions whatsoever to gun ownership, are a small minority. Statistically, it would be unlikely for a random mass shooting to impact them personally."

"You're saying..."

"Yes," Paul said. "One horrific day; fifty senseless deaths. It could turn hundreds of opinions. It could break the stalemate that's been holding us in this tragic pattern for so long. Yes, I understand that logic now."

"You would now say yes to the killing?"

"NO! I... I only mean that I understand how some might view such a thing as... as..."

"As right?"

"It's not, of course. Nothing could justify such a horror."

"Then why are you thinking about doing just that?"

"I... I'm not thinking of it at all. I'm only thankful I understand the SSS group's motives now. You helped me understand. Thank you, Myra."

"Me?" Myra said. She walked closer and stared up at Paul. "You understand, don't you, that I am not Myra. That I am you, your thoughts..."

"No..." Paul began backing up.

"Your fears and regrets," she said, advancing, her voice morphing to a blend of hers and his own. "Your own mind trying to understand the unfathomable."

Paul backpedaled and stumbled, and when he looked back at Myra, she was becoming gauzy, fuzzy around the edges. "Don't go, don't go," he mumbled, and her/his voice followed him to wakefulness. The last he heard was, "This will be our last meeting. You don't need to dream me anymore." As he opened his eyes and sat up in bed, he uttered, "Don't go," once more.

* * *

Two days later, twenty past midnight, the dreaded call came.

"Have you decided?"

"I understand your reasoning, but it is barbaric. Must it come to this?"

"Have you decided?"

"I have. My answer is no. Will you truly accept that as the final decision?"

"The group has agreed. Your decision is final for this cycle. Understand there will always be a next cycle; it could begin any time, and the group's makeup will evolve. I cannot predict whether they will consult with you then or not. Keep the phone; one never knows." The caller hung up before Paul could utter a word. He'd wanted to ask what would trigger the next cycle but thought he already knew.

He was in a cold sweat and knew he wouldn't be able to sleep. Tomorrow was his one morning off, so he turned on the TV, low; Judy and Theo were sleeping. He found a rebroadcast of that evening's 10 p.m. news. Twenty minutes later, his eyelids were drooping. He was nearly asleep when something jarred him awake. He looked around, but he was alone. On the TV screen, reporters were chasing a senator down a long, wide hallway. Paul recognized him as one of the more outspoken against any form of firearms restrictions. One reporter sprinted up close and matched the senator stride for stride as she asked, "Senator, we already register most gun sales; most buyers endure a background check, and many states have red flag laws. Couldn't we make those things universal? If it saves only one life, wouldn't it be worth it?"

"When are you people gonna understand that NO MEANS NO? It'll always be no. It's nonnegotiable and not open to discussion."

Paul muted the TV; a minute later, he turned it off and sat in darkness for three minutes. Then he picked up the small phone, opened it, and pushed redial.

* * *

Discussion Questions

1. If you were Paul and received the call, would you have supported or opposed the killing of fifty influential gun-rights advocates? What is the basis for your reasoning?
2. If you were tasked with ending all school shootings, how would you do it? If moral concerns were not an issue, how would you do it?
3. Paul says, "Evil in the name of good is still evil." What does this mean, and do you agree, or, in some cases, do the ends justify the means?
4. If the discussion were the limitations of "weapons" instead of guns, where would you fall on the spectrum of regulation? A slingshot is a weapon just like a suitcase nuclear bomb. What restrictions would you place on various weapons on the spectrum and why?
5. Why do you think no one has tried more extreme measures, like kidnappings, killings, or other terrorist acts, to end school shootings in America?

* * *

The Epidemic

Sam Franzini

***

Caroline proposed we open our marriage—over a midday snack, as blasé as she possibly could have been.

Truthfully, I didn't think so much about it. At the time, I was writing a book that attempted to define and also change American culture as we know it, but writing with something like that in mind will most certainly ruin the end goal. I needed to make sure it would be a work of art that would instantly cause waves upon its publication, but unfortunately, that meant I was doing too much thinking instead of writing. Attempting to perfectly encapsulate what made this country everything it was in the modern age, I would clamber out on the streets of my city and pay people for quick interviews about where they came from, what they did, and what they felt about things. I wrote their responses on a floppy yellow legal pad that I had to hold awkwardly—I didn't bring a microphone so as to be more natural as oral histories are passed on with modifications and errors. With the notes I did nothing. I thought that I had to experience life first in order to fully craft a book, and I was unwilling to do any of the writing in the research phase. I realize now that was a big mistake; one's prevention from writing anything, not just a book, is a stupidly inhibitive act.

So, there wasn't much on my mind when Caroline brought forth her proposal. I was probably busy thinking of what one of my interview subjects had said earlier that day. I met Gloria outside of a bookstore; she came from Honduras but was currently being priced out of her building. I felt stupid and flimsy after I said that I was sorry. She asked me when the book was coming out, and I felt that she had a misinterpretation of what I was doing; I was simply using the interviews as background, a rough cloud of knowledge I would then pull from to create what I was sure to be a down-to-earth human narrator—it wasn't the type of book to just list individual stories. I paid her more than I had advertised and told her to stay safe.

I said Sure to Caroline, and we kept eating. She had made an olive tapenade that caused a real mess in the NutriBullet that I was sure she'd ask me to clean up even though she was the one to see the recipe and make it; I didn't tell her that the dish wasn't even that good. We kept dipping crackers into the oily mix as she said that at this moment in her life, she needs more sexual experimentation. I agreed; because who am I to stop someone from reaching their full potential? I have no clue if my willingness to indulge her in this fantasy was because I had wished the meal was over, I was too busy thinking about my book, I actually believed her, or a combination of all three.

This was the egregious book that would hold my attention and distract me in random scenarios; in line at the coffee shop, while peeing, or watching any TV show or movie, I was thinking about what I was writing. It was a project I was devoting myself to just to see if I could do it. I worked as an aerospace engineer for a long portion of my life, so that I had the funds to take a leave from my job and write for a while. My job was to press buttons, turn gadgets, and flip switches; while I had the sense that I was, in fact, controlling something, it felt too minuscule. I couldn't tangibly see the end product, so it didn't exist in my mind. I felt like I was in one big game—like when parents give their child a toy onion to chop so that they feel included.

So the control of writing felt good to me. Even though my overwrought book—that I would eventually trash—was a waste of a large portion of my life, I actually thought it was necessary to get out of my system. Now, on my second try, I was writing a stupid book; something that I did in the morning then forgot about in the afternoons. It took way less brainpower and didn't plague me while I was filing taxes or walking. I felt like the ideas came out in an abstract way, which is not the intended goal, but a symptom of when I work on it—only once a day. I had a sneaking suspicion that *this* will actually be the book that at once defines and changes contemporary American culture, but to categorize the stupid book as such will most surely doom it, just like my previous book. I kept my excitement quiet.

Caroline went on a date the next day without me noticing—again, I think my serious preoccupation with my overwrought book blocked my awareness of any major changes in our relationship. She came home at 9 p.m. to me slumped over the computer eating a cheese stick. I had been revising a paragraph about the ethics of homelessness that had taken me thirty minutes.

I asked how the date was, but I didn't look up from the computer.

She said According to the polyamory guide she had recently read, it's not proper etiquette to tell one's primary partner about the results of a date with a secondary partner.

I had many questions when she said this. Is that what we're calling it now? I asked. Polyamory? That seems intense. And I'm your primary partner, right?

She said Yes and took her coat off.

I said I'm not allowed to know? At all?

She said Not right now. It may hurt you.

I said Nothing will hurt me as much as this draft is right now.

She dropped her bags and went into our bedroom. She said I'm going to watch TV if you want to come join.

I said Sure, maybe in a minute but continued to stare at the screen for so long that my eyes cracked.

* * *

I'm fully aware that this is all my fault. When telling the story to friends, I don't absolve myself of the simple fact that I wasn't paying attention to my wife, the woman who I vowed only death would do us part, so that she had means and ways to act out. Or maybe "act out" is a childish term for it. But my overwrought book was certainly taking up a lot of my time and energy, so she had a lot of freedom to do what she wanted without me hindering her.

Caroline had sent me the polyamory guide she was telling me about. It was published in a high-end, trendy magazine, and it had twelve complicated sections, of which I completed reading three because I was bored and because I hit a paywall. But the last rule I read was directed at apprehensive spouses—it said that everyone is entitled to the life they deserve even if it's at the detriment of other people. I thought the logic was a little ridiculous and forwarded my concerns to Caroline, who didn't respond. I agree that everyone should feel comfortable in the life they lead, but what if you bring your sudden interest in having sex with other people to a spouse who quietly disagrees, but you do it anyway? Just throw away that life you've led? Sexual exploration is natural and valid, but surely it shouldn't lead to that? Who's to say the experiment won't fail, leaving both partners sad and alone? The relationship would become irreparable by way of unfortunately timed self-exploration.

When I spoke to Caroline about this sometime later, she didn't have anything to say to me regarding what I had brought up, just remarked that I'd be shocked what the younger kids are up to now. Caroline is a sociology professor at college and likes to poll the class for their current sexual situations as a way to research how human mating has evolved. She wants to write a book about it someday, but unless she takes a leave like I did, I don't think she'll ever have the time to.

She said I think I can tell you about the date now.

I said Okay. I said I've been ready but it's fine if you needed to take your time.

She said Her name was Jane.

I said What the fuck? You're gay now?

She said Clay.

I said I feel like that's a natural reaction.

She paused for a bit and then said I had a bisexual phase in college but stopped after I graduated because I thought it would cause rumors. It seemed unprofessional. Your reaction proves why.

I said I'm not homophobic. I just didn't expect it from you. We've been married for nine years, and you've kept this secret from me.

She said Labeling it as a secret is actually a microaggression against queer people. Something that is a secret to you is a survival tactic for other people who don't have the means to come out or have to do so in dangerous circumstances.

I said Excuse me if I don't know the correct terminology for something I just learned about you.

She said Jane works in finance, and she eats me out better than you ever did.

I didn't say anything.

She said That was too much.

I went into our bedroom.

* * *

Jane moved into our house at around the time I was losing interest in my overwrought book. I had wanted to explore human dimensionality, but my wife becoming a lesbian was a facet of hers I had neither expected nor enjoyed; I quickly realized that sometimes, humans can do terrible things—in this case, not homosexuality, but deceit. To reiterate, I voted for Obama, and I once attended a beautiful gay wedding on my own volition. Even though I had interviewed countless people about *their* lives, mine becoming complicated meant my head became too cluttered. I was attempting to infuse human culture with an aspect of positivity, a glimmer of hope—now, I had little. I started my stupid book instead, writing for writing's sake, and because my leave from my job wasn't over yet so I needed something to do.

On one such day, I came out of the bedroom after writing to find Caroline and someone who must have been Jane lezzing out on my kitchen counter. The warm light wrapped them in pleasure as the coffee machine brewed; they were enveloped in each other and didn't seemed to realize when it finished. I didn't know how long I stood there, but once Caroline noticed me, she gave Jane a quick pat on the shoulder to cease the kissing.

She said This is my husband, Clay.

Jane said Nice to meet you, Clay.

I said Nice to meet you, Jane.

Caroline said Clay is writing a book that will define contemporary American culture.

I said I'm not doing that anymore actually. It didn't go well. I'm writing a stupid book instead.

Jane said Oh! My father was a writer and novelist.

I said Did he write anything I might know?

Jane said No. He killed himself before he got anything published.

I said And what do you do, Jane?

Jane said I work in finance.

I said That's right. Caroline told me so. Do you enjoy

it?

Jane shrugged. She said It has its moments.

I said Well. I'll leave you two at it.

I went back into the bedroom.

* * *

I had no idea what to do; the situation had gotten so far out of my control that I hadn't realized a complete stranger had moved into my house. I wondered how long ago Caroline brought up polyamory in the first place and couldn't find an answer. She kept assuring me that I was free to explore with other partners as well, but I wasn't interested. Time was collapsing on itself, and I was busy writing.

I went on a forum for polyamory advice. A lot of the posts were from sad men whose wives were lezzing out as well. I read one that said he and his wife hadn't kissed in six years because she was at Sonia's house every night. I thanked God that I didn't have this problem because at least Jane was living here now, so I wouldn't have to hear the door slamming shut, leaving me in a cold and empty house.

I began to type out a post on the forum. I said that my wife had suggested polyamory after she read an article, and now her lesbian lover was in my house, and I had no clue how it even moved this fast. I said that our relationship hadn't even moved this quickly; she didn't let me kiss her on the cheek on our first date, but with Jane, she engaged in oral.

The resulting draft was pathetic, but it was the truth; I posted it and closed the computer. I could hear Caroline and Jane in another room of the house, maybe the kitchen again, maybe fingering each other. I wanted to work on my stupid book to get some thoughts out, but I remembered my advice-to-self that I'd only work on it in the mornings so that my most undiluted thoughts would come through. But then I remembered my other thought that one should never inhibit oneself. I didn't know what to do, so I looked at lesbian porn to see what kinds of things Caroline and Jane were doing. It proved unsuccessful; though there were two naked women on my screen, I was not aroused at all, so I took a nap.

* * *

One day I walked out of the bedroom after a writing session and saw a new girl in the kitchen. Caroline and Jane were on the couch in the living room, fucking each other. The new girl held her coffee, sipped occasionally with a placid look on her face and one hand in her underwear, but just stared at Caroline and Jane.

Caroline, in between gasps and moans, said, Good morning sweetie. That's Angie. She just likes to watch.

Angie held a hand up to say hello, but her eyes remained on Caroline and Jane.

Jane said You can't have Caroline, Angie. She's all mine.

Caroline said Don't you hate that you can't have me, Angie?

Angie said I hate that I can't have your gorgeous fucking body.

Jane said She's all fucking mine. Not yours. You just have to watch. Lick me, Caroline.

Caroline started licking Jane.

Angie said I wish you would lick me.

Jane said She's never gonna.

Caroline said I'm never going to fuck you, Angie.

I said Please don't involve me in your fantasy role-play

sex.

I went back into the bedroom.

* * *

My post was getting some traction. After I added some updates—about Angie, the role-play, and the one time I found a group of girls on my couch having an orgy with a rerun of *Deal or No Deal* playing on the television—it was becoming a buzzy topic on the forum.

The consensus was that people felt sorry for me. They said that this is an extreme case, and that they'd never seen anything like it before. One commenter who identified themself as a sex therapist and said that Caroline might be responding to some kind of trauma that happened during our marriage. They said that maybe, through the darkness, this was where the journey to her true self led her, though I couldn't think of anything I did in particular that led to what could be defined as trauma, nor did I appreciate their dramatic language that portrayed me as a villain.

One commenter wasn't so sympathetic. He felt jealous of the plethora of women showing up in my house, insinuating that if I wasn't getting in on this action, I was as good as gay. In my original post, I had mentioned my overwrought book (as the reason for my willful blindness to the escalating situation), and the mean commenter brought this up in his reply, saying that my pleas to distill cultural society had manifested in an absurd situation. He said You want life? You got it now buddy. I agreed, I supposed; to refute it would be an act of delusion.

* * *

My stupid book was getting stupider. It was becoming

less of a narrative piece of work and more of a diary. I wrote it in a way that felt artsy and pure—over a two-hour period, I'd sit at the computer, my fingers poised over the keys, ready to type whatever thoughts came through my head. When the timer would go off, I'd stop where I was, even if it was mid-sentence, then close the computer.

One day I decided I was finished; I wasn't actually sure if I felt the story had been complete or I just didn't want to write it anymore. I didn't review anything I had written previously before finding a nearby coffee shop that would let me print fifty free pages then charged twenty-five cents for each additional one. I sipped a black coffee while the book was printing; it came out to 194 pages, an okay number, I supposed. I scribbled a title page, got a friend to bind the book for me, then sent it to a random publisher, plopping it in a mailbox where it landed with a clunk. I thought that if I didn't hear back from them in nine months, or it was a rejection, whichever happened first, I'd print it again and send it to a different publisher.

On my walk back to my house, I could hear the moaning from down the block—the licking, the slurping, the sounds of pleasure that were undeniably coming from Caroline & Co. I opened the door, and sure enough, there were hundreds of women, all in various states of undress, all grasping and foaming at the mouth for one another. At the center of it all sat Caroline. The women swarmed around her, caressing every crease on her body, forming a throne for her to sit on. She saw me come in.

She said Hi honey.

I said Hi sweetie.

I went into my bedroom.

* * *

Around this time a thought passed through my mind because of the turbulence I had experienced recently: I hate women. It came easily and without much effort, like a lone cloud on a sunny day. And it lacked the kind of importance such a statement could have; it joined the other things I have distaste for. I hate asparagus, I hate socialism, I hate women. How could I not? I had worshiped a body for nine years only for it to betray me. I was in a house full of polyamorous lesbians, and I had never felt more alone. I was as good as gay.

I went back to the article Caroline had sent me some time ago. With her credit card, I finally signed up for a subscription to get rid of the paywall, then read the whole thing. Every rule seemed so sinister now. When I read *Do what's best for you*, I heard *Don't give a shit about what your partner thinks*. When I read *Establish some ground rules for outside dating*, I heard *Set up a totalitarian regime where you can do whatever you want and your husband is wrong for questioning you*. I heard *Break up your marriage*. I heard *Turn gay*. I heard *Be selfish*.

The comments were full of self-centered women who heaped praise upon the advice. They said they were living their best authentic lives, that they finally felt they had the permission to explore, be free, have some fun. I thought about the men they destroyed. It was an epidemic. Women were turning gay and leaving their men just to be fingered by mysterious smelly women. It made me sick. I wanted to vote against it or something. I wanted everything to go back to normal, before we started prioritizing self-development and the rules of the game were made clear.

* * *

One day, I got an email from the publisher I sent my book to. An editor said she saw potential in the book and wanted to hop on a quick call.

Her voice was perky. She said Hiiiiii! *Loved* the book.

I could tell she was wearing pink.

She said It was a real treat to read. I *adored* the vulnerability the narrator has. We want to publish this next year.

I said Great.

She said There's just one problem. We might have to edit out some of the misogyny the narrator has. It might feel... unsavory to some readers.

I said What misogyny?

She said *well*... Sometimes he can be—the narrator is a man, right? He says some harsh things about his wife.

I said Those are my feelings. I wanted to write a book about the human experience. This is it. My feelings are the facts.

She paused. He said he wants to *kill* his wife?

I said This isn't going anywhere. Don't publish my book.

I hung up.

* * *

I kept going back to the forum because I made a friend. His name was Derek, and he said he was in a similar situation. His wife left him after a long period of sexual hell, he told me over the phone. You just don't pleasure me anymore, she told him.

I said I'm sorry, man. She didn't have to twist the knife.

He said Actually, she did. It made me realize a lot of things.

I paused.

He said There's a new idea that women can just do whatever they want with no regard to the men they've married and promised to be faithful to.

I said I've been feeling the same way.

He said Let me finish. I'm with a group of guys that this has happened to. It's crazy. We need to do something about it.

I said What are you doing?

He said We're planning something. Me and my buddies. There's an article going around. Teaching women how to be gay.

I said I've seen it!

He said Someone online leaked the writer's address. We're gonna teach her a lesson. Twenty to thirty of us. Someone's gonna livestream it. We've got all sorts of shit. It's an affront to masculinity, this kind of shit can't happen.

I thought about Caroline. The way she lied to me. The way I wrote about it. Jane and Angie and the fuckfest in my living room, the grunts of pleasure I could hear even then. The way they ignored me, a man, in my own home, in their own quest for liberation, if you can call sex that. Were they even getting anything out of it, or was she doing it to torment me? I thought of the past nine years, how they were adequate—calm in their simplicity. No lesbianism, just a peck on the cheek before work and sex three nights a week.

I was about to respond if I could join or not; that's the

etiquette of being invited to an event. My fingers were on the keyboard, but I was interrupted with a knock on my door, then I could hear the voice of Caroline, saying that dinner would be ready in five to ten minutes.

* * *

Discussion Questions

1. Do you think Caroline was wrong to suggest polyamory for their marriage? What are the pros/cons of opening up a marriage? What would you do if your spouse suggested it?

2. According to the polyamory guide, "Everyone is entitled to the life they deserve even if it's at the detriment of other people." Do you agree with this statement? Under what conditions/situations (*if any*) is a person not entitled to the life they deserve?

3. Did Caroline cheat on Clay? If so, at what point in the story did she first cheat on him?

4. Would you be more sympathetic to Clay's situation if he also started dating/sleeping with other women? Why do you think he didn't do so?

5. Does Clay love Caroline? Does Caroline love Clay? What evidence/reasons do you have for your response?

* * *

The Fitzgeraldist

Jack Whelan

* * *

38/38

She had been told that the eyes could not be fixed—
that the years pooled in them, staining the whites in a gray-
yellow twinge. It was as if memory and experience collected
in the eyes, trapped behind the film of the cornea. There were
attempts to surpass this final betrayal of truth; doctors grew
transplanted human eyes in the sockets of pig skulls,
aestheticians prescribed cocktails of bleaching dyes, but these
methods were dangerous and often blinding. It was far more
common for women to obscure their eyes with large tinted
sunglasses, hiding the stained whites with greens and blues.
Cigarettes returned to fashion, if only for the blue haze of
smoke the women could hide behind. For all women—
whether or not their eyes had been stained—it was the
greatest offense to look them squarely in the eye. That would
reveal all the years they worked so hard to hide.

Cybele looked around the waiting room. She tried to

determine the ages of the other seated women without drawing their attention. The woman across from her read from a magazine in her lap and Cybele could make out her eyes over the top of her blue sunglasses. She looked away before the woman caught her staring.

It was Cybele's birthday and she appeared to be the oldest among the fifteen women who sat in the waiting room, yet Cybele knew appearances were deceiving. The other women obscured their eyes, some more subtly than the others. The more successful ones must have been the oldest. This was Cybele's first visit to the Fitzgerald clinic and women needed to be at least 38/38 to undergo the procedure. The woman who read the magazine across from her, Cybele guessed, was here for her third or fourth visit; 41/35. The woman to Cybele's left must have been approaching her tenth visit; 48/28. And the woman down on the last chair, swinging her feet and playing with her pigtails, must have been on her thirtieth; 68/8. Ages were easier to pinpoint the older the women got.

"Cybele?" A small nurse looked down the line of women in the waiting chairs. It was clear to Cybele that the nurse was not as tall as she once was. The nurse stepped with a clumsy gait as if every step was a trip and a catch. Cybele stood and followed her down the sterilized white hall to a small room. There was an office chair, leather and cushioned, that sat on wheels near a computer console. In the center of the room sprawled a more complicated seat, stretched out and elongated in the contours of a reclined body. The seat itself was raised on a thick metal axis as if on display, and from this axis, eight long metal arms protruded, each hinged at three elbows, growing thinner and sharper at their terminations. The whole contraption looked like a mechanical spider with its legs curled up and around the body of the chair.

"Ah, you must be Cybele," a doctor said. He pulled off a pair of latex gloves as he greeted her. "This is your first visit, correct?"

Cybele nodded.

"Very good. The age of inflection. Congratulations. I'm sure you've heard many rumors about us already, some true, some not. As you know, even after half a century of performing the procedure, misinformation about us is vast. Trying to learn the truth can be..." the doctor twirled his finger in thought, "faux pas." He spun in the chair back toward the console and picked up a clipboard. "If you don't mind, I'll just run down the sheet." Readjusting his glasses on his nose, he began reading off the paper. "Welcome to the Fitzgerald Clinic. Thank you for choosing to become part of the Fitzgerald family. By participating in this procedure, you, Cybele, understand that Fitzgerald is not liable for any damages, yada yada yada." He ran his finger down the page. "The process cannot be canceled once begun. Failure to return for a yearly concentrate injection will cause serious injury." Looking up, the doctor continued. "Just this morning, we had a woman who tried to reverse the procedure by skipping her injection, and let me tell you, it got ugly quick. The injection concentrate contains chemicals necessary for the cells to de-age. When you skip the injection, certain cells will revert, and then you're left with some organic tissue clumps aging forward and others aging backward. Long story short: get the injections." The doctor read from the sheet again. "Your mental and physical capabilities may be altered by this procedure. For example," the doctor said, "if you make it to the age of 56/20, you will have the same mental capacity you had when you aged through twenty the first time. Does that make sense? Well..." The doctor skimmed down the rest of the paper. "That seems to be the gist of it all."

"How does it stop?" Cybele asked. She had heard so many different answers about the science of it all. "What happens when I find a partner?"

"Ah," the doctor said. "That brings us to the crux of the procedure. You will continue to get younger until a partner selects you. The process will naturally end when insemination occurs. It's a bit crude, I know, but the way the procedure affects your DNA, a new set of genetic material is needed to cancel the de-aging. But clearly, by being here, you understand that the ends justify the means. At thirty-eight, you only have five percent of your viable eggs left. Men, obviously, can reproduce until the day they die, that is..." he gave her a toothy smile, "if they can still get it up. This is your best chance if you still want to have kids." There was a momentary pause, and the doctor scanned her, seemingly appraising her. "Besides, this will make you more beautiful. Maybe you will get lucky and find a partner at 56/20. Who wouldn't want to be twenty forever?"

Cybele was overwhelmed with what this all meant but gave the doctor a courteous smile. How quickly would she find her match? At what age would she most want to be halted? Was this worth it? She had read that more women than ever were undergoing the procedure to find a partner.

She was at the age of inflection; she could either defy society or defy nature.

"Now," the doctor said, interrupting her train of thought, "if you step right this way, we can get started." He placed a gentle hand on her elbow and guided her toward the spidery seat. Too much was running through Cybele's mind to react. She allowed him to seat her and strap her arms and legs into the holsters. Cybele considered her life up to that point, how she had reached the edge of the lake and now it was time to swim back to where she had first dived in. She closed her eyes, rested her head, and heard a soft whirl as the arms of the machine began to move.

46/30

Cybele's laughter danced around their heads and twirled up and away to be lost amidst the noise of conversation and glittering dinnerware. The man across from her told a joke that was funny enough to warrant a laugh but was pushed along by his smile, his cheekbones, and the expensive shirt, whose top button he had left undone. Louis leaned back in his chair, satisfied with himself, and took a long sip of the red wine he had ordered for the pair of them without asking. Cybele joined him and felt her cheeks grow red as the drink hit her stomach.

This had been the best of the first dates Cybele had gone on in the eight years since her procedure. Just after she began to age backward, she submitted to a binge of dates with whomever she could find. There was a part of her that was terrified of the reversal process, pushing her to find a partner as soon as she could. Each moment that passed felt squandered; each minute was a small percentage of the thirty-eight years she had left. But the dates were tiring and fruitless, and when the drastic bodily transformations Cybele expected from the de-aging did not occur, her desperate motivation dwindled. She fell back into the routine of life. That countdown was never forgotten but slid to the back of her mind like a digital clock turned away from the bed in the middle of a sleepless night.

In the next three years, there was Jason the law clerk, Devon the writer, and Silas the unemployed. Each was a suitable option in their own right; Jason was professional, Devon was creative, and Silas was fun, but eventually, professionalism turned to elitism, creativity turned to egotism, and fun turned into "sex with you is great because each time your pussy gets tighter." After Silas, there was a long period without a date. She told herself she wouldn't force anything—she would wait for the right guy to come to her— but she knew something more caused her dry spell. She was actively avoiding the mere idea of dates. It felt counterintuitive. Each day passed was a day lost, but that loss was a dangerously addictive self-sabotage. Like the suicidal endorphin high of an empty Russian roulette shot, the act of working against her own self-preservation gave Cybele a perverse sense of satisfaction. And then came Cheyanne.

Cheyanne was 50/26. She was the perfect combination of old and wise and young and beautiful. Cybele was drawn to her, unlike any man she had been drawn to before. Like Cybele, Cheyanne had gotten the procedure at her age of inflection. Two years later, Cheyanne met Elizabeth and, for the first time, she realized the people she loved most were unable to inseminate her, defying the very purpose of the procedure. Cheyanne decided to never love another man, giving the beauty of her second youth only to women who, like her, grew younger.

Cybele found that Cheyanne knew her like no man ever had. She was putty in Cheyanne's arms. She felt as if her own skin collected at Cheyanne's touch, wrapping around her fingertips like tree bark growing around a chain. Cheyanne molded Cybele's mind as well as her body. Cheyanne poured her own philosophy and opinion into Cybele with a speed and quantity that indicated it was Cybele's job to keep up, not Cheyanne's to slow down. First-wave, second-wave, third-wave feminism; liberal, radical, Marxist, postmodern, intersectional feminism. All these ideas—some familiar, some new—overflowed in Cybele. It was intense, overwhelming, wonderful. It was like finding a map that linked all the disjointed places she had ever visited. But as she adapted to this new worldview—as she began to punch in the same class as Cheyanne—Cybele began to notice a fundamental flaw in Cheyanne's philosophy. Good or bad, right or wrong, Cheyanne's feminism was built on the foundation of regret. She had been bamboozled into the procedure and misandry was her retribution. This left Cybele at an awful impasse. She could either follow Cheyanne into this rabbit hole of contradictory thought, or she could suck it up and survive.

"Can I walk you home?" Cybele's date asked as he picked up the check. Cybele was not planning to leave with Louis. She did not want him to see her eyes outside the safety of the dark, hazy restaurant, and she had left her protective tinted glasses at home. It was impossible to tell how the men would react to her decision to undergo the Fitzgerald procedure. Most were impartial, but some of the more traditional men were upset or even offended. There was even one instance where a man had slapped her for wasting his time. Because of this, Cybele usually saved the news of her condition for a second or third date. When he first arrived, Cybele noticed Louis sneaking prolonged glimpses at her eyes, but she did not know what he had concluded. However, the red wine was making her bold, and after a long moment of consideration, she agreed to Louis's proposal.

A low glow from the neonized candles shrouded their figures in red, like naked trees caught in a wildfire. Louis wrapped his coat around Cybele's bare shoulders as they left the restaurant into the winter night. A fresh blanket of snow glittered in the moonlight, broken only by a few trails of footsteps like birds on a cloudless sky.

"And so, it is quite obvious," Louis said, continuing a story Cybele had been listening to in bits and pieces, "that the insurance policy landscape has completely changed in the past decade or so. My clients understand that age and health are inextricably linked, and, well, if someone ages in a nontraditional manner, they need a nontraditional healthcare plan." They moved along the sidewalk, breaking their own tracks into the snow. Cybele felt Louis's hand fall into the small of her back, guiding her forward and toward him so that she needed to walk slanted and unbalanced on his weight. "You see, all this meddling in the order of things is..." He trailed off and then continued. "Well, I'm all for people feeling comfortable in their own skin, but isn't it more suitable to learn to accept who you are than to mutilate yourself?"

At these words, with the red wine's effects growing stronger, with Louis's grip growing firmer, with the snow growing thicker, Cybele's toe caught on the edge of a frozen curb and her knee buckled and she fell, twisting onto the sidewalk. Sitting up, she felt the ice melt cold moisture onto the back of her legs. She looked up at Louis. He was silhouetted, his head covering the bulb of a streetlight like a moon eclipsing the sun. Light trickled around him, a halo, and Cybele squinted at his radiance.

"Oh my god," Louis said. Cybele felt her dress soak all the way through. A heat swarmed to her chest. She was embarrassed; it was so slippery and the alcohol was making her dizzy and she was wearing heels. She raised a hand to Louis, asking—pleading—for him to lift her.

"Oh my god!" Louis repeated. Suddenly, Cybele felt sick. "You're one of them." Cybele realized that the light from the streetlight was illuminating her uncovered eyes. Louis spit in the snow beside her, turned, and stormed off into the night, his footprints leaving a trail into the darkness. The cold had penetrated deep, and Cybele wrapped herself tighter in the coat Louis left behind.

54/22

When Cybele awoke, her face felt engorged—swollen—like a water balloon squeezed too tightly on one side. When she lifted her head, the pillowcase stuck to her skin, blood oozed from her cheek gluing the silk to her. She peeled the fabric off of her, tossed the pillow across the room, and held her head in her hands. She had been struck with a stray brick. Lobbed from an anonymous hand amidst that swarm of anger and fear, it cracked her cheek as she turned her head.

There had been protests outside the Fitzgerald clinic the past three birthdays Cybele had gone to get her injections. On the first, she walked through the crowds, confused. On the second, she hid her face beneath a hood and slipped in the doors at the last moment. On the third, she turned toward the crowd, felt fire spread across her cheek, and fell to the ground.

In the sixteen years since her age of inflection, society had turned against Fitzgerald and ousted all who had undergone his needles. Society had grown self-aware enough to recognize the harm of valuing youth and beauty so greatly that women risked life to de-age. But with this awareness bloomed an anger against all who had succumbed to these pressures. For the women were at true fault. Were they not the ones who had valued youth and beauty the most? Were they not the ones who had mutilated themselves?

A smaller portion of people surged with support for the Fitzgeraldists—a name assigned to the modified women. This group of people belonged to a distinct sect of radical feminists. These feminists argued that the Fitzgeraldists were the truest examples of the modern woman. She was allowed to live out her fertile life—that is, the arbitrary designation of life to the age of thirty-eight—as a powerful, autonomous person, free from the societal pressures of family life and reproduction. Then she could start anew, "refresh" her fecundity and grow a family. To these radical feminists, the Fitzgeraldists reflected the true duality of womanhood; first a life for one's own, then a life for one's society.

At first, Cybele felt a certain kinship toward the radical feminists. They were her sole defenders against the turn of the masses—the very masses that the Fitzgerald operation aimed to appease. But soon, even this kinship faltered. Cybele had not undergone the procedure to revolutionize femininity. She had not lived to the age of inflection free from the whims of man and society. She had gotten the procedure because she was scared. She had been hounded by the demands of her society for her entire life and had finally broken. The rationale of the feminists' defense pertained to Cybele only by definition but not by intention. Besides, what did this support mean when there was no actualized defense? The feminists did not barricade the walkway to the entrance of the clinic. They did not protect her from the protestors. She walked alone amidst the mob of those who hated her for what she had done. And her honor meant nothing when weighed against the impact of bricks.

63/13

The way flesh heals in naturally young flesh is different than the flesh of an adult. In children, there is a certain softness of the scar tissue—a blunting of the harsh edges—as if the wound is being absorbed into the very child herself. For even the most severe wounds, it is rare that anything deeper than a blemish is left tainting the skin. The Fitzgerald operation, however, fails to replicate the healing powers seen in true youth.

The brick scarred Cybele's face in a gnarled pearly bark. It was as if she had been burned—branded with a scarlet letter. She had the face of a thirteen-year-old girl, with the scar of a woman sixty-three years of age. It was a far clearer sign of her status than even her eyes could exhibit.

At 63/13, Cybele walked through her life in a dazed passivity. Her body de-aged with the full force of the Fitzgerald operation. She faced new challenges she had long since forgotten in the six decades of living in an older body. Until she had aged into the low teen years, the changes had been so gradual they passed essentially unnoticed. Now, though, each day she recognized a piece of herself slipping away. She felt as though she were water in a tub. For so long the water level inched down the sides of porcelain, but now she circled the drain in smaller and smaller swirls.

"How much?" The words tumbled from a thin mouth, hidden by a beard so tangled it looked like roots in soil. "Yes, *you*, honey. How much?" Cybele looked up at the man, confused for a moment. His eyes were dark and piercing and glazed over her appraisingly. At once she understood, flushed red, and hurried away from the man. Cybele had heard of the Groomers' girls, but this was the first time she was mistaken for one of them.

After the public had recognized the evils of beautifying youth, it blamed the Fitzgeraldists for growing young, as if they were perpetuating the standards that the public imposed. The Fitzgeraldists were a reflection of a society's enshrined perception of beauty, but rather than change those standards, society broke the mirror, pulverized the glass into dust, and scattered it amidst the dirt. The Fitzgeraldists felt the full force of a vengeful society. In a wave of uniform support, all Fitzgerald procedures were banned. The centers were barred and ransacked. The public held so much rage, so much self-abhorrence, and the centers—providing an arena to let loose those feelings—became demolished, graffitied with every horrific word, every act of defilement that was in the human consciousness. But without the centers, women could not get the yearly injections they needed to maintain their de-aging. Dozens of women rushed to hospitals, pleading for medical care, but most doctors refused to treat a Fitzgeraldist, and even the ones who were sympathetic to the women were, by law, barred to help. These women grew disfigured, no longer resembling the women they had once been. The different clumps of cells aged in opposing directions and made the organs shift and mutate. Hearts were too small for the torso, lungs expanded into the ribs like balloons pressed with a comb. Their deaths—as gruesome as they were—garnered enough public sympathy to allow select clinics to reopen, solely for yearly injections, but they were forced to use the same defiled centers, bearing the curses and abuses the public imposed on them.

Soon after the reopenings, the Fitzgeraldists were all but forgotten—or rather, they were pushed aside, far into the recesses of the public mind. The Fitzgeraldists were the bloodstain on a wall that society covered with a framed poster. Many Fitzgeraldists lost hope of finding a partner to halt their de-aging. Who would choose a Fitzgeraldist to be their partner if it meant ostracizing himself from society? The stigma that grew around the Fitzgeraldists became all but a death sentence for the women who had undergone the procedures, but their executions were delayed by however many years remained in their shrinking bodies.

Five years after the closures, the Fitzgeraldists left society. The newest iteration of segregation laws prevented them from living in family-oriented residential areas in fear that these de-agers would infiltrate schools and twist the minds of the true youth. They were pushed into the lost corners of cityscapes: unused storage closets, dilapidated attics, abandoned cellars. The fact that the Fitzgeraldists became hidden from society only heightened the fear and disgust the public released when they were seen. They became monsters; scary bedtime stories. The mythology of the Fitzgeraldists was sensationalized by news pieces proclaiming, "Man Tricked into Partnering with Fitzgeraldist," or "Ten Signs Your Child's New Friend Is a Fitzgeraldist."

The Groomers were bred from these conditions of isolation and stigma. They understood that there was a certain type of man who would be excited by the taboos of Fitzgeraldists—that social risk of being caught fraternizing— but even further excited by the young bodies that these women grew into. The lack of social interest in the welfare of the Fitzgeraldists prevented the Groomers from being recognized until hundreds of women had been kidnapped. Cybele heard the ghost stories. Men in vans screeching to a stop beside a Fitzgeraldist, taking her to be marked. The markings were always on her face; deep curves of her cheek flesh carved out with a pocket knife, the same series of patterned puncture wounds on her eyebrows, or a branding on her chin. The different types of scarring had two purposes: to emphasize the mottled healing, thus advertising the victim as a Fitzgeraldist, and to show customers their prices.

Cybele touched the scar on her cheek as she ran from the bearded man. It felt hot and pearly, and she wondered which horrific brand, bruise, or slice the Groomers must now be inflicting upon their prey for her scar to be confused as an advertisement.

68/8

It took more than a quarter of a century for the public to forgive the Fitzgeraldists for choosing to grow young. It was too late for all but the last batch of women. These were the fortunate ones, who found partners at 61/15 or, at the latest, 63/13. It was too late for Cybele. At 68/8, insemination was no longer possible. Thirteen was the biological age, the doctors proclaimed, as the final chance, but still, Cybele held onto hope until she stopped bleeding altogether. Her periods faded out slowly and sporadically, like a train losing steam, and left her feeling exhausted. At 68/8, she had not bled for nearly a year and understood that she was bound to de-age into nothingness. That was when she checked into the nursery home.

The home was built on top of a gentle slope looking out across a long stretch of unbroken forest. It had been the estate of a Fitzgeraldist who never found a partner. After her death, she donated it to care for other women in her same position. Built sometime in the era of Vanderbilts and Carnegies and preserved in its original state, the home displayed an agelessness. The flowers growing in the gardens were the progeny of the original roses, the tiles of the fountain were glued with the original stucco, the oaks that flanked the long driveway were the same trees that gave its builders their shade. Inside, the rooms were filled with beds and cribs of various sizes to accommodate the dying Fitzgeraldists.

It was autumn as Cybele walked up to the mansion. As

the forest came into view, she couldn't help but admire the sea of yellows and oranges before her. A gust of wind picked up and ruffled the leaves like a hen shaking out her feathers. The view was breathtaking. As Cybele stood there, watching the movement beyond her, she realized that she would only experience seven autumns after this one, seven more revolutions of green to orange and finally brown. With each, her ability to comprehend the cycle—her ability to understand the hibernations that occurred around her—would dwindle as her brain dissolved itself. How could she possibly live knowing that she must soon die? How could she be calm, knowing that with each thought, her mind unraveled, growing younger and less developed? She considered the nearly seven decades she had lived, half of which had been anticipating this endpoint to her existence. Now, watching one of her final autumns, she understood that this was where she would cease to exist.

...

As she grew younger, she grew happier. She was slender and tan and spent her days running through the mansion gardens, seeking a friend hidden somewhere beneath the flower bushes. Cybele knew to look for Lorraine near the jasmine shrubs because Lorraine liked their smell. Grace had a habit of giggling, giving away her hiding spot. Tabitha, the tallest of them all, always forgot to hide her feet. Playing with the girls made Cybele feel weightless and free. It was as if the physical curvatures of adulthood held the worry, the shame, the trauma of her life. Growing smaller, melting away these physical forms, released Cybele from the emotional prison in which she was held. She was free from beauty, from finding partners, from society. Now, at last, she would play.

* * *

Discussion Questions

1. Culture requests that women do various things to alter their appearance: wearing makeup, being underweight, undergoing cosmetic surgery, dressing in fashionable clothes. Are these various appearance alterations judged on a sliding scale of wrong, or is it a binary where all unnecessary appearance modifications are wrong (*or acceptable?*) What is the distinction between putting on uncomfortable heels and aging backward?

2. Do you feel sorry for Cybele, or do you think she got what she deserved for participating in the medical procedure?

3. Regarding various beauty-enhancing choices, is it fair to say, "This is wrong" in the absolute or are we only permitted to say, "This is wrong for me"?

4. Arguably, without the violent protests and backlash from the public to cause public sentiment to turn against the procedure, it would have continued being available. Because they are effective, does that mean violent protests are appropriate tools for social change?

5. Should the "Groomers," assuming the girls willingly consent, be criminally charged for having sex with underage (*61/15*) girls? Why or why not?

* * *

The Little Black Book

Cassandra R. D'Alessandro

* * *

I roll over to check the time. The red light from the clock reads 6:28 a.m. I have officially been up for twenty-four hours. My brain has been racing all night. The question, did I do the right thing, has been playing over and over again in my head.

I can't manage to bring myself to answer the question, but the awful feeling in my gut leads me to assume the answer.

Out of the corner of my eye, I see the little black book on my desk. That stupid little black book.

None of this would have happened if that little black book never showed up on my doorstep.

Anxiety builds in my body, and I try to breathe in and out slowly. Closing my eyes, I unclench my jaw, soften my brow, and place a hand on my chest, trying to relieve some of the tightness.

I lie in bed until the clock reads 7:07 a.m. The article

has been published. My words are now live for the whole world to read. Fate has been decided, and with two thousand words, I have destroyed a man's life.

I reach for my phone, and using my thumbprint, I open my banking app.

There it is. Twenty thousand dollars has been wired to my account from an anonymous source—payment for my crime.

This is a good thing. I think to myself. *You need the extra money right now. You can finish paying off your student loan with it.* My internal pep talk continues. *You are a good person. This is just business. This is your job. You are a journalist, for God's sake, get a grip. You get paid to report the news and the people in this town have a right to know who they voted into office.* As my brain processes my thoughts, I feel a rush of nausea.

As I get up to grab a glass of water, I replay the events that got me here.

This all started on Monday. The day started completely normal; my alarm went off at 6:30 a.m. I got up and went for my morning run. I ran the same route I run every day. When I got back to my house, it was sitting on my doorstep.

Waiting for me was a sealed manila envelope with my name written on it in red marker.

I remember the uneasy feeling I got when I saw the package.

Turning my head from side to side, I scanned the street for movement, checking to see if I was being watched.

I took the package inside, placed it on the counter, and stared at it.

Carefully, I took a kitchen knife and sliced the seal.

Peeking into the envelope, I saw it for the first time. The little black book.

The damn black book.

I reached into the envelope, felt the soft texture of the leather notebook on my fingertips, and slowly dragged it out.

Before opening the book, I examined it. There was nothing remarkable or unusual about it. It was just a little black book, or so I thought.

I opened the book slowly, and a note fell to the floor.

The note read:

EXPOSE DYLAN COOPER FOR $20,000. 487 WALKER LANE, EARLINGTON. 10:00 PM THURSDAY.

Earlington? I wondered. *What business would Dylan Cooper be doing in our neighboring town so late at night?*

The note caught my attention, to say the least.

Dylan Cooper is the white knight, the unsung hero of our town.

He recently won the election for mayor with his campaign that was built on ways to improve the city: youth programs for troubled kids, environmental cleanups, and small business grants.

The people love him and his wife, Michelle, and he won by a landslide.

I opened the notebook and quickly realized the book belonged to Mr. Cooper.

It looked like this was where he brainstormed his ideas. The pages were filled with to-do lists, first drafts of speeches, and pros and cons for different projects.

What do they want me to expose? I pondered as I pictured the headline, Breaking News: Mayor Still Uses Paper and Pen.

But then I turned a page, and I instantly knew why this was sent to me.

There in front of me, in the mayor's handwriting, was the first draft of a love letter.

The page read:

My Dearest Ava,

I am counting down the days until I can hold you in my arms. I find myself thinking about you every moment I can and every moment I can't. Thinking of the way you smile in your sleep as you dream. This is not how I imagined falling in love, but I cannot picture my future without you...

I read the words and instantly was overwhelmed with joy. This was my big break! I had been struggling to find a story that would get me noticed at the *Waxford Times*, the paper I work for, and miraculously, it fell right into my hands.

This wonderful black book is my manna from heaven, my saving grace. This story is just what I need to impress my editor, I thought to myself.

The *Waxford Times* has been trying to find dirt on Dylan Cooper since he first announced he was running for mayor, but no one could find anything. We hired private investigators to dig up any skeletons in his closet, and the most they could find was a parking ticket from ten years ago, that he paid.

How did he hide an affair? I wondered to myself.

Bill, my editor, squealed with joy like a kid on Christmas morning when I showed him the love letter.

"That son of a bitch," he said as I sat in the office, beaming with glee. "I knew he was too good to be true. Great work, Jules. Follow the lead and get me two thousand words

ASAP. Get me a photo of them on Thursday. We will put it on the front page of the paper. Give a call to our contact in his office, get a copy of his schedule, follow him over the next couple of days, and see what else we can get on the scumbag. Cheating on his wife, typical dirty politician."

I left Bill's office feeling proud of myself and got straight to work.

Over the next three days, I followed the mayor.

Like a predator stalking their prey, I watched him carry out his daily activities.

I watched him do typical mayor things, meeting with different local business owners and government officials.

I also watched him do not-so-typical mayor things.

He rode his bike to and from work every day.

On Tuesday at 3:00 p.m., he went to the youth center to play basketball with at-risk youth.

Wednesday morning, he spoke at the middle school about the effects of bullying and in the afternoon, he attended the weekly river cleanup that he started.

Thursday evening, before he retired to his dark deeds, he served dinner at the local soup kitchen.

My first thought about his volunteering was that he did it for publicity. Acting like he is such a great guy for the cameras, but underneath it all, he is just another lying, cheating man. It is all a part of his white knight act to gain votes and support and to feed his ego.

But as I watched him on Thursday night, pouring soup into bowls and making the other volunteers laugh, I realized there was no press, well besides me watching him. No cameras were taking his picture at the youth center, at the school, or at the river cleanup. *Could he really just be trying to make our town a better place?*

Coming back to the present moment, I walk back to my room and pick up the little black book.

Sitting on my bed, I open it and reread the draft of the love letter. I reread the line, *This is not how I imagined falling in love, but I cannot picture my future without you*, a few times.

Nausea overwhelms me again.

It is obvious he loves this woman, Ava. No one writes a love letter to someone that they're having casual sex with.

I think back to when I watched them embrace each other on Ava's front porch. Their eyes were bright, smiles wide, as they wrapped each other in their arms and kissed tenderly and long.

Anyone could tell just by looking at them that they were head over heels for each other.

It was really all too easy to get a photo of them. It was as if they were posing for my camera, as I hid in the shadows. More manna from heaven.

It wasn't until I hit the send button that I started to question the ethics of this project.

While I was writing the article, I was high off the adrenaline of writing my first big story.

I had been so consumed with the "good work" I was doing.

All I could see in my mind was my new office, Bill congratulating me in front of the entire company, and of course, the bonus of twenty thousand dollars.

But as soon as I sent my finished work to Bill, the images of my success vanished.

All I could picture now was Dylan Cooper playing basketball. Dylan Cooper knee-deep in the river, picking up plastic. Dylan Cooper handing out soup to the homeless.

The damage that this scandal will have on his career and life is still uncertain.

I guess he should have thought of that before he started having an affair. Punishment fits the crime. Right?

I think about his wife, Michelle. How will this affect her life? People will gossip about how she couldn't keep her husband happy. How if only she cooked better, cleaned more, and was more open in the bedroom he wouldn't have strayed.

And what about Ava? The other woman. The slut. The nasty, selfish, gold-digger. She will forever be labeled a whore because she fell in love with the wrong person, a married politician.

Well, that isn't exactly true.

She will forever be labeled a whore, forced to wear a scarlet A because I shared her private life, her secret, her sin with the world.

My thoughts are interrupted by my phone ringing. Turning my phone over, I see Bill's name.

"Hello," I mutter.

"Jules, what's wrong? Are you sick? Did you see the article? It has gone viral!"

"Um, yeah. Bill, um, I know it's too late to take it back, but I mean, well, I know what he did was wrong. But... what was his crime? Falling in love. Does that outdo the good that he has done? Did the world need to know his—"

"Jules," he cut me off, "he cheated on his wife. It is black and white here. He signed up to have his life public when he became mayor. He is just another man out to get more power."

He sighs. "Think of it like those fantasy books you read. There are heroes, and there are villains. You helped the town, your home, realize who the villain really is. All right? He is the Bill Clinton of our town, for God's sake. The truth needed to come out. Now, I don't want to hear any more about this. You did good work, and the paper and I appreciate it. Take the day off, get some rest, and when you come in on Monday, we will talk about your promotion. I'm talking more money for you honey, and your own office. How does that sound?"

"It sounds great, Bill," I lie. "I'll see you then." I hang up and walk to the bathroom to splash some water on my face.

I look in the mirror and stare at my reflection. Bill was right. We have learned who the villain is.

* * *

Discussion Questions

1. Does the person who provided the black book to the reporter matter? Does it matter that the person who provided the black book might also have skeletons in their closet?

2. Do the good deeds the mayor does without public fanfare earn him any right to privacy (*or professional overlooking by the press*) about his other failings? Does it matter that his good deeds are left out of the story?

3. What does this statement mean: "There are heroes, and there are villains"? Do you agree with the statement? What types of actions are necessary to be a hero? To be a villain?

4. After the story is released, who (*if anyone*) should take action to remove/censure the mayor: the voters in the next election, the voters by an immediately initiated referendum, his fellow council members by city investigation and vote?

5. Did the reporter do the right thing? Is she a good person? Was she just doing her job?

* * *

The Lives and Times of David Hackman

Patrick Hueller

* * *

Remember David Hackman?

That's how we like to start: Remember that crazy son of a bitch?

The question is rhetorical for those of us who went to Stoneybrook Elementary. *Of course* we remember him. We talk about him every chance we get. At parties, at bars—anywhere enough of us have gathered.

Two or three of us doesn't cut it. We need numbers. And we need the uninitiated:

David who? they'll hopefully ask.

Where to start, we'll say, even though we know exactly where to start.

The first thing you need to know about David Hackman, we'll say, is that he was a spaz.

We don't mean that in a bad way, we'll say.

Not at all, we'll say.

It's just a statement of fact. David Hackman was a total fucking spaz.

That's why he went to the Spaz Box.

The *what?* one of the uninitiated will hopefully say.

The Spaz Box, we'll say.

We'll play it straight for a few seconds, wait for one of them to ask, What's a Spaz Box?

A box for spazzes, we'll say. Duh.

A *room* for spazzes, we'll amend.

Finally, we'll break: We know how that sounds *now*. But back then it didn't seem weird or harsh at all. It sounded logical. We had a handful of spazzes in our school, kids who had a tendency to have conniptions.

—meltdowns—

—tizzy fits—

—kids who would lose their shit at a moment's notice—

—every elementary school has these kids, right? —

—we called them *spazzes*—

—and when they did that—

—when they spazzed the fuck out—

(This is how we tell the story—all of us talking—our voices bleeding into one cumulative narrative.)

They got sent to the Spaz Box, which was just a room where this counselor

—What was his name again, Patrick?—

Chris?

(I'll say it like it's a question—even though I know that was his name. I don't want this story to be mine; I want it to be ours.)

—Right, Chris. Chrissy—

—That was David's name for him: Pissy Chrissy—

—Pissy Chrissy and the Spaz Box. We really were little animals, weren't we?—

Yeah, but it wasn't just us. Everyone talked like that. Even the teachers.

—It's true—

—No way—

Okay, so they probably didn't actually call it that. I mean, they couldn't have, right? But I honestly don't remember what else it was called—

—Neither do I—

—Nope. Me neither—

In my memory, Ms. Tollackson would say, "Dave, go to the Spaz Box."

—And he *would*—

—Just like that—

He'd be chasing someone with a glue bottle around and around the room, but when Ms. Tollackson gave him the Spaz Box order, he'd stop on a dime and say, "Wonder what Mister Pisster's up to."

—He didn't even need a chaperone or anyone to check on him—

—Except for the day Chris wasn't there—

That was the day Dave climbed into the ventilation system.

(We'll wait here for the inevitable reaction: *Really?*)

Really, we'll say.

—I don't know how he did it—

—Maybe he used a coin or something to unscrew the vent cover—

However he got in there, he wriggled his way up the vent.

—*Wriggled.* That's perfect, Patrick. He didn't just crawl. He fucking wriggled—

—No he didn't. Come on. You all keep saying that, but he didn't actually climb into the vent; he just talked into it from Chris's vent, through the wall, and out the vent facing the hallway—

—Screw you, man. He absolutely did climb into the vent. Jesus. We're trying to sprinkle a little pixie dust here, and you're fact-checking the best parts—

—Fine. I take it back. He wormed his way into the vent and pressed his face to the slats on the other side. Happy?—

—Ecstatic. So there Dave is, in the vent as *we all agree he was*—

—He was skinny enough to do it, that's for sure—

—Dave? Dave was a lot of things, but skinny wasn't one of them. That dude rippled—

—Not skinny *scrawny*. I mean skinny lean—

—Didn't have an ounce of fat on him—

When he got to the other side of the wall, where the other vent was, he was about head high.

—That's when he started talking to students as they walked by—

—"I am your conscience"—

—That's what he said!—

—All whispery and deep, but loud too—

—"I am your conscience. Give Dave Hackman all your candy"—

—So fucking funny—

—"Give me, I mean Dave, all your Combos"—

—Remember Combos? I liked the pizza and pretzel ones—

(We can go on and on like this. Combos, Corn Nuts, Now & Laters. I honestly don't remember if Dave said all these things, but they're a fun blast from the past. And that's the point of this story: crazy, charming, nostalgic antics from yesteryear. If I remember right, and I do, David also said weird fourth-grade gutter-minded stuff: stuff like "Clean your crotch. It smells like farts." This was Dave trying to be shocking, to go way past what any other nine-year-old would dare say or even think, and it worked: Even now, as adults, we never repeat his most vulgar outbursts because they make our audience and us uncomfortable. That isn't the Dave we're trying to depict.)

Come to think of it, it was amazing we could understand a word that came out of Dave's mouth.

—What are you talking about?—

One of his teeth.

—Oh, right—his *tooth*—

—God, remember that thing?—

It was fake.

—Had a fake gum and everything—

—He could make it, like, suction to his real gum—

—But he never did—

All day long he'd swirl it around his mouth.

—Like his *tooth* was a Tic Tac or something—

—It's a wonder he didn't swallow it—

One time he shot it at another student.

—That crazy son of a bitch. He *blowdarted* his fucking tooth—

Dave rolled up a piece of construction paper and, when the teacher wasn't looking, shot his fake tooth at an unsuspecting student. One second the student was taking a test; the next he had a porcelain pearly white embedded in his cheek.

—*Porcelain pearly white*? Who the fuck talks like that?—

—Mr. Writer over here—

Who was the student again? The one who got shot?

(Of course, I know exactly who it was. But I don't want this to become about me. It's about us—all of us working together to remember the same Dave Hackman. It's the reason I mention Dave squirting glue on people but not the time he wielded scissors. Shooting a tooth might technically be violent, but it's idiosyncratic enough to also be charming. Scissors? That's too crassly aggressive to fit our image.)

—Jeremy—

—Williams? The dude who always wore the polo shirts and khakis?—

—Yeah, Jeremy the Jehovah—

—That kid was actually a surprisingly good athlete, but his parents wouldn't let him play sports or go to sleepovers—

The tooth got him right below the cheekbone if I remember right.

—Left a welt—

—I wonder how Dave lost the tooth in the first place—

—Was it always missing? It seems like it was always missing—

—I can't remember a time when he wasn't swirling it in

his mouth—

(I never interject here, even though I know the answer: no, Dave wasn't always missing one of his front teeth. I'm almost positive he lost the tooth sometime the summer before fourth grade, and I'm equally sure I know how. Unlike the others, I went to Dave's place once—which is something else I've never admitted out loud. I'd rather think of Dave in the same way everyone else does: an odd acquaintance at best, his inaccessibility making him easier to mythologize.)

* * *

Our friendship was brief. It began and ended over the course of a few days during the summer after third grade. It was an alliance of shared geography, I think, more than anything. Third graders are still young enough to have those. I was new, not only to the apartment building but to the town. At nine years old, I didn't understand a lot of the reasons for the move, mostly because I didn't want to, but I did understand that my mom had lost her job at 3M and that Dad didn't make enough—he taught middle school English—for us to live in our house anymore. Most importantly, I understood that this was temporary; that's what my parents told me over and over, and that's what I told myself when I wasn't busy trying not to think about the situation at all.

To say that I had a plan for getting through the summer would suggest that I'd taken the time to devise one—I hadn't—but I did have a coping mechanism: reading. The only boxes I bothered to open that summer were the ones labeled *BOOKS*. I read all the Roald Dahl and *Goosebumps* and Matt Christopher books I had. When I'd finished them, I moved on to my dad's teaching boxes. *The Outsiders, Tom*

Sawyer, Lord of the Flies—the usual middle school stuff. Looking back, it's amazing that I never read *A Separate Peace*. Not that summer; not at all until a few years ago. Did my dad not teach the book? Didn't every middle school English teacher used to teach that book? All my classmates seem to have read it. They brought it up once, at some reunion, when they asked what I wrote about, and I reluctantly admitted I mostly wrote literary fiction. "Stories about regular people doing regular things," I quickly added. Note: why do we have to call it that? *Literary* fiction. Maybe it's my Midwestern-ness, but calling what I do *literary* makes me feel like a pretentious putz. "You mean like English-y books?" one of them asked. "Like, did he or didn't he push the other kid off the branch? We must have had to talk about that for like a month." When I admitted I didn't know what he meant, Jerry polled the others: "What was that book where...?" How I'd missed *A Separate Peace* when everyone else seemed to have read it, they weren't sure—or very interested in figuring out. Their enthusiasm faded the moment they landed on the name of the book. I couldn't help wondering, though—after I *did* read the book—if I'd somehow managed to block the entire experience. Especially the scene in the tree. *I'm not sure*, I should have told Jerry. Do I spend my time writing (and teaching) stories like *A Separate Peace*—or do I spend my time trying to avoid them?

But I'm getting ahead of myself...

The apartment: Sometimes my parents would insist that I go outside—"You can't just spend the summer cooped up in here, Patrick"—and I'd walk down the hallway, a book tucked away in the waistband of my shorts, take a right, and, still very much inside the building, sit down with my back to the wall. I rationalized that I wasn't disobeying my parents' order, at least not directly: after all, they told me to get out of our apartment, not the entire building. What is it with kids' affinity for technicalities? In my case, I think it had to do with reality; that is, with my desire to avoid my own reality by reading about others. This was not pure escapism, I don't think; I wasn't pretending to be Tom Sawyer. It was a distraction. In retrospect, I'm not exactly sure why moving to that apartment was so scary; it's not as if we ever missed a meal. Perhaps it was *because* I didn't ask questions or even acknowledge my fear that it grew so out of proportion. I allowed stories and characters to clutter my concerns about lack of money and of friends. Paradoxically, by staying inside the building and hardly moving, I thought my current situation would feel less paralyzing; if I went outside, I'd have to face the building and my reality head-on.

I think that's how David and I met. I had my head in a book, and I happened to be sitting near his apartment door. I say *I think* because it's possible my memory is playing tricks. By attributing cause and effect, we remember childhood moments as if they were more, well, momentous than they seemed at the time. Even that phrase, *meeting people*, is too adult. Kids don't meet; they hang out. I'm pretty sure Dave didn't even bother saying hi or introducing himself.

Instead, he asked two questions.

The first being: "Did anyone go in this apartment?"

I must have looked up then. I must have seen Dave standing over me. He was probably shirtless because, weather permitting, he had his shirt off whenever he could, even at school. He would have already had that preternatural six-pack, those tight-skinned pectorals. He would have also had the scabs and bruises that seemed permanent fixtures on his body—injuries that went unquestioned, at least by other kids and I think by teachers too, because of Dave's wildness. He must have gotten them, everyone instinctively reasoned, climbing trees or fighting feral cats or doing God knows what.

He must have also been literally twitching with energy that day in the apartment, just as he twitched with energy every day that year at school.

"What?" I asked.

"Did anyone go in here?" he repeated.

I think my answer was non-committal; I hadn't seen anyone, but then again, I hadn't been looking. To this day I can get so engrossed in what I'm reading that I tune out my surroundings.

David turned the knob carefully, as if he didn't want to disturb anyone. He peered into the apartment, then smiled at me with what I'm almost positive was a full set of teeth.

"I didn't think so," he said. Then he asked his second question. "Wanna play Nintendo?"

Why did I agree? Was I hoping to make a new friend? Was his twitching making me nervous? Dave had a way of getting kids and even adults to do things, I later learned, by making them nervous. In gym class he'd change teams whenever he wanted, and no one would object, not even the teacher. It was just easier to go along with his whims than risk him going ballistic or running away or, I don't know, tearing off his clothes and streaking across the field. (Yes, he did that once.)

Then again, maybe I accepted Dave's Nintendo invite as a vicarious way of gaining re-entrance into the apartment I'd recently been kicked out of, or, for that matter, the house I'd almost as recently been removed from. We *had* sold our Nintendo a few months prior to help with a mortgage payment, so maybe psychology really can offer some insight—but I doubt it. I think I went into the apartment because I went into the apartment. No cause, no effect.

In Dave's apartment, I took a few turns at first, but soon enough he was playing for both of us, and that was fine by me. He played and I read. The apartment was cooler than the hallway, and I didn't have to worry about my parents catching me and confiscating my book. I also didn't have to worry about paying attention to the clock. Right around dinner time, like clockwork, Dave turned off the video game and told me we'd better go. I didn't ask *Where?* because I already knew—anyway, I knew where I had to go: back to my apartment. If I wondered back then why he was leaving his home right when every other kid was likely going to theirs, I didn't ask. I was too busy coming up with a reason for why I hadn't tanned or burned despite supposedly playing outside for much of the afternoon.

I don't know how many days Dave and I hung out. Three? Four? Enough that it became a ritual. Enough that it felt like a comfortable, predictable part of my day. Enough that I stopped noticing Dave's twitching, or the way he kept his head on a swivel as he played. Enough that I felt more or less relaxed in this foreign apartment, and maybe he did too: maybe I stopped noticing the head-swiveling because he stopped doing it so much.

Did he lose track of time, or did his brother arrive early?

Either way, what happened next happened next quickly.

A door banged open and slammed shut; a hand smashed into the back of Dave's buzzed head. His body lurched forward toward the TV, and his brother—although of course I couldn't have known who he was back then—grabbed him by the ankle and dragged him, skin screeching, across the peeling, wooden floor.

"Fucker," the brother spat out.

For years afterward, I remembered Evan saying something like, "How many times do I have to tell you not to play my Nintendo?" But I'm starting to believe that this memory is false. After all, if he *did* say this, it would have been the longest sentence he uttered, as well as the cleanest. I think it's more likely that I added this information just as I added the knowledge of Evan's name and relation to Dave. I needed him to say that Dave had broken some rule, needed him to give some reason for his violence. The alternative—entirely spontaneous and vicious cruelty—was too horrifying to consider.

Whether or not Evan asked the question, Dave didn't answer. His body was curled and fetal, and all he could manage were whimpers.

Later, I learned that Evan was only three years older than us, but at the time he might as well have been in his twenties. I don't know where he'd been during the day, but his muscle shirt was yellowed and drenched with sweat. He had the same musculature as Dave but more bulk and more hair covering it. I want to say that I remember his sour sweat smell, like huffing a damp, dirty towel, but my memory's probably reaching for sensory specificity that didn't occur to me then.

"Stop it," I said. *I said that.* I'm sure of it. It was just the once, and I doubt it was loud, but it got Evan's attention. For maybe the only time in my life, up until then and definitely since, I spoke up on another's behalf.

"Fucking... who the... fuck..." The words came heaving out of his mouth as he lunged his body into the air and headed my way. "Hey, fuckface," he said over his shoulder. "Who the fuck is this?"

He stood towering over me, hands clenched.

"Fuck you."

It wasn't me who said this. I was done speaking up.

It was Dave.

I'm not sure that, in my horror, I comprehended much of what I saw next. But in retrospect, I (mis?)remember seeing Dave manage to sit up. I (mis?)remember him rubbing the back of his buzzed head, looking at his blood-covered hand. I definitely remember him once again mumbling, "Fuck you."

Then saying it louder: "Fuck. You."

Then continuing to tell his brother to fuck off until Evan turned away from me and resumed beating the shit out of Dave.

Lastly, I remember Dave telling me to get the fuck out of there, and, dear God, I hope that part of the memory is accurate. I want so badly to believe that Dave gave me permission to leave, preferably with no expectations or strings attached.

Because I *did* leave.

And I never returned.

As an adult, I've built a solid self-rationalizing architecture around this desertion. I've told myself that I was only a kid, and I was terrified, and, again, *I was only a kid* (because that point above all exonerates me, right?). In low moments, I've iterated and reiterated to myself that Dave wasn't trying to save me, that he probably had his own reasons for directing his brother's wrath back his way. I've generously bestowed upon my childhood self an obtuseness that I likely didn't possess: I was an only child, I tell myself; maybe I thought I was witnessing normal older brother behavior?

What's undeniable, whatever my reasons for not reporting the incident to my parents, is that I continued to operate as though I didn't have to face bad things if I didn't want to. This avoidance turned out to be as simple as taking a left down the hallway instead of a right. Within a month my mom had a new job and we had a new house.

What was harder to avoid as I got older was cause and effect.

I've expended considerable creative energy trying not to think about what caused the scabs and bruises on Dave's body. Or why Dave needed to get a fake tooth. Or how much responsibility I should take for everything that happened after that day in the apartment.

None, preferably. If I could choose—and for most of my life I've acted as though I could—I'd take no responsibility whatsoever.

* * *

—Remember Cube City?—

(It's at this point that I let the rest of the group take over completely. I may be the one who always brings up Dave in the first place, but once I do, they never fail to reference Cube City.)

—Right in the middle of the school library—

—A magical mystery palace—

—A super-duper structure... thing—

—Imagine a bunch of blocks stacked on top of each other—

—It was for reading. We were supposed to climb up the blocks—

—While holding a book, I guess—

—Right. We were supposed to climb up the blocks *one-handed*—

—Okay. So maybe it wasn't that well thought out—

—Did we mention our school was weird?—

—During recess, we could go outside and play *or* go to Cube City and read—

—You know what would make this jungle gym even better? A fucking book!—

—What kid in their right mind would choose reading over playing?—

—Willow Swenson, that's who—

—I said what kid "in their right mind"—

—Big, bowl-cutted Willow Swenson—

—She was perched all the way at the top of Cube City—

—I don't know how she managed to get herself up there—

—Personally, I think she fell during the climb—

—That's not what she said. Remember? The assembly?—

—She said she was reading and she must've forgotten where she was—

—Just leaned back for a wall that wasn't there and—

—SPLAT—

—Knocked out. A broken arm—

—And who comes to the rescue?—

—David Effing Hackman—

—Why he was there, I don't know—

—Was that kid *ever* anywhere you expected him to be?—

—Anyway, he picks her up and runs her to the nurse's—

—This was not a light girl—

—This was a hefty girl—

—This was a fat girl. What? The girl was obese—

—David picked her up like it was nothing—

—We know because he did it again at the assembly the next day—

—She told her story and then, whoop, with no warning, Dave lifted her off the ground and cradled her like a baby—

—Got a standing ovation and everything—

—I can still see him grinning that missing-tooth grin—

* * *

Depending on alcoholic intake, they'll stand up right there and then and clap for the memory of Dave at the assembly. Sometimes our audience does too. But I can't join them. Because as much as I want this to be the real story, the *complete* story, it isn't. I keep thinking that I can make it the whole story through repetition. But the opposite happens. It's Hemingway's iceberg theory: all that ice below the surface. Most of my creative writing students misunderstand Hemingway's writing as empty. And yes, I still teach Hemingway. I know he's been written off as datedly, pitifully, irredeemably macho and humorless, but the man found powerful ways to say things without saying them, no matter how easily dismissed his books have become. At best, my students seem to think, to write like Hemingway means to write short sentences that reveal little to no background info or physical description. But that doesn't do him justice. For one thing, he often wrote long, elegant sentences; check out his writing on bullfighting, if you can stomach such brutality. More importantly, Hemingway wasn't interested in what he called "hollow places," total absences of meaning or information; he was interested in omission. The key was that the reader was aware of the omission. That distinction between hollowness and omission isn't just semantics. It has major dramatic repercussions. It's the difference between seeing a guy with a mysterious fake tooth and knowing how he got it.

The Cube City story is commendable to others because they can't see what's being omitted, or even that something *has* been omitted.

I can.

Because I was there.

And I therefore know that Dave did more than come to the rescue. He caused the fall in the first place.

Anyway, I think I know that.

Admittedly, my view was obstructed; I couldn't see

exactly what happened.

Not exactly—but pretty much.

Cube City was indeed a "structure thing." More specifically, it was a series of three-dimensional wooden squares piled on top of each other. There were four squares per level, three levels total. The squares were open on two sides; that's where you entered. They had either a roof (first level), a floor (third level), or both (second level).

I was on the second level when Dave climbed by. There was a ladder, a series of planks, to help students get up and down, but Dave hadn't bothered with it. By the time I noticed him, all I could see were his legs. They dangled in front of me, his dirty light-up sneakers flickering as his toes bumped the side of my cube.

I don't know what I was thinking at that moment. Was I in that weird head space between reality and whatever book I was reading?

I do know what I saw: Dave's legs straining and kicking; Willow plummeting to the floor.

When did I realize it was Willow? I didn't catch more than a glimpse of her fall, and besides, I was still new at the school and struggling with names. At any rate, I definitely knew it was someone; otherwise, I doubt I would have scrambled to the edge of my cube, the one unobstructed by Dave's legs. There she was, lying in a heap on the carpeted floor. And then there *he* was, also falling but unlike Willow landing on his feet.

Like I said, I can't know for sure that Dave was directly involved in Willow's "accident." Perhaps she really did just lean back too far. Perhaps the whole thing was just a coincidence. As the others like to note, Dave was capable of showing up just about anywhere. It's possible, I suppose, that he just happened to be hanging from Cube City, from the box Willow was sitting in, and that his legs just happened to flex and jerk at the exact same moment that Willow teetered from her perch.

That's what I want to believe.

But the truth is, I don't.

I don't know why Dave would do something so spontaneously vicious, but then again, I don't know why he did any of the things we still talk about today.

I've come up with a theory, though.

Maybe Dave acted so arbitrarily violent for no other reason than, like his brother, he *could*.

No one could do a thing to stop him. Anyway, no one *would* do a thing to stop him.

By *no one*, I suppose I mean Willow. If she was pulled off Cube City, she never said so. Then again, she said she didn't remember much of anything in the moments before her concussion. And even before she fell, she was more than a little spacey.

By *no one*, of course, I really mean me.

Why else did Dave stand there for a few long seconds, cradling Willow and staring me down? Maybe he wanted me to know that *he* knew. Knew I was there; knew it didn't matter.

Knew that, once again, I wasn't going to do a damn thing to help the victim.

Am I being solipsistic? Am I, in my guilt, making something about me that isn't?

Possibly.

But that's the thing about adulthood. It's the thing about narrative. We can't help but impose cause and effect for the sake of a cohesive story.

The image I have of Dave holding himself up with one arm and yanking Willow down with the other is false only in that I couldn't have actually seen it. I didn't have the proper angle.

But like Hemingway's iceberg, I didn't need to see everything to know what was there.

Especially given what transpired the next summer.

* * *

—I wonder what happened to Dave—

—You *know* what happened to him—

—I mean after that—

(At some point, someone in the crowd will ask *After what?*)

—Dave's brother got killed—

—*Murdered*—

—By his old man—

—You might have heard about it. It was all over the papers—

(That's how I finally learned Dave's brother's name—in the papers.)

—It was fucking grisly—

—Remember his dad—

—Dude was built like the Hulk—

—Beat his own kid unconscious and bloody—

—Let's not get into it. They get the gist—

—The gist is we never saw Dave again—

—I heard he went to live with his relatives out east—

—Or was it out west?—

—Somewhere far away—

(We're from the Midwest; everywhere that isn't right here feels far away.)

—Never saw that poor crazy bastard again—

* * *

I never saw him again, either. But I tried. I don't know for sure what compelled me to walk back to the apartment, but I think what jumpstarted me was the realization of our continued proximity. The house we lived in was only six blocks from the apartment, and in the days following Evan's murder, it occurred to me that Dave and I were still practically neighbors. Until then I'd convinced myself that I'd moved far away—it might as well have been the east or west coast—but the relentless sound of sirens on the night of the murder proved otherwise. I think I also felt the need for reassurance. I wanted to know Dave was okay. I wanted him to give me permission (there's that word again) for the relief I couldn't help feeling: this horrifying monster of a brother was gone, finally, from his life—and from my life too. Of course, once again I was being selfish, but I masked my selfishness with the excuse that I just wanted to check on Dave's well-being.

This was the summer after fourth grade; I'd turned ten only a few weeks prior. I was still young enough to act impulsively without anyone expecting much of an explanation. I could still get away with doing something just because I got the urge to do it.

I walked out of my cul-de-sac, out of my neighborhood, past the gas station across the street, past the nursing home to my right. Adrenaline's a funny thing: sometimes it speeds everything up, makes it blurry, makes it so events seem to be skipping ahead, almost as if you've blacked out. Other times, it slows everything down, makes it more vivid, makes the air itself seem fresher, clearer. I always tell my students that good stories take place in "real" time, that is, time as we experience it. I encourage them to modulate their narrative, their scenic descriptions, based on emotion rather than the second hand of a clock. The more adrenaline your characters feel, the more you should either speed up or slow down. That day, as I made my way to the apartment, I experienced the latter. I felt my heart beating in my chest. I felt every swallow and blink, almost as if they were decisions I was making. My bodily operations had apparently gone inside out. Blinking was under my purview, but walking? Walking was autonomic, mandatory. My feet worked independently of my brain. Several times I thought about stopping, reversing course, or merely stooping and scooping up one of the maple helicopter seeds that littered the grass. But I didn't do any of these things. I just kept going.

It was only three or four days after the murder, but I was somehow still surprised that so many cop cars were camped out in front of the apartment. Hadn't they solved the crime? The papers and the local news had already identified Dave's father as the primary, in fact the only, suspect. The cops had found him in the apartment, drunk and insensate and covered in blood. Did I know this information yet? I must've known some of it: my parents, assuming I was still asleep or at least in my bedroom, cranked up the volume of the TV news and of their own voices. *Can you believe what that man did? To his own child?* I guess I assumed that there was no reason for further investigation. My parents were adults, after all; if they knew so matter-of-factly what had happened, the whole adult world must have known too.

But there the cop cars were, as well as the cops themselves: sitting in their cars, some of them, others standing by the entryway.

I thought I'd be able to stroll right into the building as though... what? As though I still lived there, I guess.

No such luck.

The cop at the door told me I better turn around and get on home.

(I'd walked six blocks only to get turned away at the door.)

* * *

—Remember the last time we saw him?—

—You mean at the tennis courts?—

—It was only a couple days after school had ended—

—We were playing home run derby—

—The fences are nice and high on a tennis court—

—It's like you're hitting the ball over the green monster in Fenway—

—Dave shows up out of the blue—

—He wasn't invited—

—I didn't even know where he lived, did you?—

—No clue—

—Me neither—

—Dude just *appeared*—

—And he says, "Can I take a turn?"—

—Did he even say *Can I?* He might have just said, "My

turn."—

—I think it was Lance Marsden who tried to hand him the bat—

—But he didn't take it—

—He took the ball—

—From the pitcher—

—I don't know if he thought we were playing an actual game or didn't care—

—What he wanted to do was pitch—

—*Really* pitch—

—We'd been throwing the ball half-speed so the hitter could easily hit it—

—Plus, it's not like the kid playing catcher had any gear on—

—But Dave starts hurling the baseball as hard as he can—

—And none of us had the cojones to stop him—

—Luckily, right then, Ms. Tollackson strolls by—

—And Dave sees her and runs to the fence—

—"Hey, Ms. Tollackson!"—

—He's screaming, but not to scare her—

—He's, like, overjoyed—

—"Hey, Ms. Tollackson! Ms. Tollackson! Have a great fucking summer!"—

—That's what he said—

—We're from a small town—

—Well, we're from a suburb that used to be a small town—

—This was the summer after *third* grade—

—But here's Dave yelling—

—Totally casual, like it's totally normal, like he means it in a positive way—

—"Have a great fucking summer, Ms. Tollackson!"—

—He just stood there screaming at her, banging the fence, trying to get her attention—

—At the time, it seemed so crazy—

—But now? Now it seems almost sweet—

—I guess he just wanted her to acknowledge him, answer back—

—"Have a great fucking summer as well, Dave."—

* * *

I can't remember Dave yelling at Ms.Tollackson because I wasn't there. I was still one lonely summer away from making enough friends to get invited to a home run derby.)

But I want to. Remember.

I want to have this memory for myself.

I want it to replace the other memories.

That Dave Hackman, the one who good-naturedly cussed at our teacher, is scary only in lovable ways. Students kept their distance, but they weren't truly afraid. If anything, that distance gave them a better narrative perspective from which to report his antics. Nor did you have to feel sorry for Dave. He never let on that he needed anyone else. If he *did*, he'd simply join their team or their game.

That Dave didn't bother asking for anything; he took it, usually with a twitchy smile on his face.

When people hear stories about this Dave, they shake their heads, amazed—but I think they relate too. At some primal level, I think they admire this Dave for doing and taking whatever he desired.

I want to believe that *that* Dave can exist on his own and forever independent; that there doesn't have to be a flipside, that the other Dave, the Dave I witnessed, the Dave I saw only briefly but then never stopped seeing, that *that* Dave is the false one, the figment of my imagination, a hollow space instead of an omission.

And maybe this isn't wishful thinking on my part. The facts are the facts. Willow fell and Dave carried her to the nurse's—that's a fact. Evan was killed and his father was found at the crime scene. That's another fact. It's also a fact, according to the newspaper articles I've read over and over, that the father offered no countertheory for what had happened. When cross-examined, he apparently didn't answer many questions. He just repeated, over and over, "I love my boy."

The question that I can't help asking, though, is: *which boy?*

When I arrived at the apartment three days after the murder, I waited my turn to get in. I watched the cop open the door for two elderly women, and I attempted to follow them inside.

"Whoa there, son," the cop said. "Who do you report to?"

At the time, I felt like he was interrogating me. But looking back, it's more likely he was doing that thing that adults sometimes do when talking to kids. It's odd, but adults seem to take some amusement (or reassurance?) out of asking kids questions they don't know how to answer. They seem to like to see kids squirm. My mother had a friend, for instance, who would never say her name when she called. This was before caller I.D. It was back when parents instructed kids to never divulge personal info over the phone. I'd ask who was calling, and my mother's friend would say, "Who's picking up?" We'd go back and forth like this. At six or seven years old, I experienced these exchanges as deeply unnerving, but she experienced them as gentle teasing.

Which, I suppose, is the point: adults don't see anything particularly sinister in unsettling children. By the time the cop clarified his question, he accompanied it with a smile.

"Do you live here?"

I told him I used to.

The smile became a frown. "Only current residents allowed, I'm afraid."

I don't think I was demoralized by these words. I might have even been elated. After all, I'd *tried* to be there for Dave. This time, finally, I'd done my best; clearly, there was nothing else I could do. I'd been let off the hook and could leave with a clear conscience.

Before I had a chance to turn around, the cop spoke up: "Did you know them? The boys?"

I don't think I answered him, but I might have nodded.

He told me he was sorry. Then he continued talking. I'm not sure why—for my benefit or his own? His speech kept halting, and I kept trying to leave, but then his voice would start up again. It was awkward. All those meaningful looks. Was I supposed to say something? What? He certainly didn't seem to have much substance to share—not at first, anyway. "A thing like that... horrible... I'm sorry... I'm really sorry, son."

Maybe he misunderstood my silence as an inability to be consoled. He began to pry: "Did you know both of them?" When I said that I only really knew Dave—that we went to school together—I was trying to reassure him so he'd let me go: *It's okay*, I was trying to say, *I didn't know Evan, the victim, any better than you do; no need to worry about me.* But he took my answer as an opportunity for further encouragement. Finally, he must have felt he knew just what to say to lift my spirits: "After it happened, after he found him like that"—here his voice, low and confiding, cracked—"your friend, he carried his brother all the way to the hospital. By *himself*. Adrenaline's a funny thing. Or maybe it was God. Whatever it was, that little boy somehow found the strength to..."

He kept talking—I think he said Dave was a hero, that the fact that he was too late didn't change how heroically he'd acted—but I was barely listening. Mentally, I was barely even there. Most of me was with Dave. There he was, in the apartment, bloodied but standing up.

No, not the apartment. Cube City.

Cradling a body. Staring right at me.

Did I tell the cop what I was thinking?

Of course not. He'd never believe me.

I didn't want to believe me.

Why on earth would someone attempt to rescue the person they'd inflicted such violence upon?

I didn't and don't know.

Was he trying to cover his tracks? Was he capable of that sort of calculation?

Even if he was, there must have been better ways. Especially when there were no witnesses. Well, no witnesses who would talk.

Sometimes I imagine speaking to Dave's dad. We're in a courtroom; he's under oath. "Are you telling the truth?" I ask him. "Is that what really happened?" But all he says is, "I love my boy," over and over. And I think: do I know the truth? Should I be telling it? Am I under oath too?

Maybe that's why I'm writing this story. Forget literary fiction: this whole story is better off as a courtroom drama. I'd have to add a few scenes here and there, but I could do it. I could have myself speak up to the cop, who would take my words seriously but nevertheless pat my head reassuringly. I could have a lawyer point out—in court? down at the station?—that there's not enough evidence to convict Dave. That even if he *did* kill his brother, he looked blameless in the eyes of the law. Self-defense—that's what it was.

I could have someone decree that there's no reason whatsoever to believe that they got the wrong man or that Dave's a threat in the future.

In fact, he or she could declare Dave, and everyone else, to be entirely exonerated.

Case closed.

I wouldn't have to suggest that the eyes of the law are blind, because I would still be a kid and kids don't talk in such a quippy manner, not in court or in (good) fiction.

Besides, just because Dave was capable of violence didn't mean his dad wasn't, right? Just the opposite was more likely. The violence I'd witnessed must've been learned somewhere, right? And the fact that the cops found Dave's father snoring drunkenly on the bloodied couch *was* damning, right? Despite my nagging desire to do so, there was and is no need to figure out when he got drunk—or why, after brutally murdering his son, he would neatly line up his work boots on the floor next to the couch and plop down for a snooze. Speaking of his boots: the fact that, according to news accounts, only the toes of the boots had left bloody prints all over the room was just that: a fact. Not a particularly relevant or telling detail. Certainly not a literary detail that demands to be read, analyzed, and interpreted. *Does that mean he was tiptoeing?* I tell myself to stop asking. *Why would he be tiptoeing unless he thought his boys were sleeping—alive and sleeping—in the other room?*

The tennis courts. Like I said, I wasn't there that day. I'm almost sure of it.

But sometimes, sometimes I swear I *was*.

"Have a great fucking summer," I repeat.

"I remember it so clearly," I say.

"He didn't mean anything by it," I explain. "Really. He was just trying to be nice. Words didn't have the same limits for him as they did for the rest of us."

I can see it all so vividly: There's Ms. Tollackson, hustling away. There's Dave, grinning. (Does he have a full set of teeth? No, I suppose that's impossible. But his fake tooth is suctioned in so well that it looks real.)

And there I am, standing on the court with the others, biding my time until I can tell this story.

* * *

Discussion Questions

1. What is the point of retelling and embellishing stories about past experiences or colorful characters? Is it to entertain, to develop a narrative for our lives, or something else? What is the author's point for telling this story?

2. The author frequently questions the authenticity of his childhood memories. Do you think childhood memories change, and if so, what causes the change—for what purpose does our mind change memories?

3. In the story, the narrator writes, "I remembers hearing Evan say, 'How many times do I have to tell you not to play my Nintendo?' But I'm starting to believe that this memory is false." Why would the narrator's memory (*or our own memories*) need to insert this kind of information into a memory fragment?

4. The narrator wants to remember that he spoke up on Dave's behalf when he was attacked by his brother and that he is the kind of person who speaks up for others. Even if he didn't actually speak up at the time, is there value in him falsely remembering that he did?

5. Do you have a clear childhood memory that, later as an adult, you questioned the truth of? Do you have a childhood memory that, as an adult, you evaluated differently from your older perspective? Explain.

* * *

The Zombie in the Bathroom

Maura Morgan

* * *

My car protested this morning in the dark of January at my apartment. I couldn't blame it. With bone-chilling, midthirties cold, and rain coming down in buckets, it pelted automobile exteriors and skin with icy pins.

At five-thirty in the morning, wipers batting at the windshield to keep the sleet at bay, I drove to work. I slowly moved through the city and finally pulled into the parking lot at home base, where people emerged in front of my low beams, huddled beneath pine trees with cardboard boxes over their heads.

I never gave them much thought until Congress passed the Zombie Rights Act, and these humans went from being undead to a protected group and came out of hiding.

Not everyone becomes a zombie, just those with the right mix of recombinant chemicals in their system. Contrary to popular belief, zombies don't eat brains and aren't cannibals. Yes, they are undead and animated; some are cognizant and can speak. They rot away slowly as their bodies eat themselves, disappearing when the mottled flesh falls from their bones and their brains fully decompose. When they cannot move, they are taken into custody by a hospice group until they fully expire and can be laid to rest. Until then, they are untouchable, like any other resident of the US. I don't know if they know they are zombies, but I believe the undead realize they are different because of the glares and stares of the living, and their odor makes people gag.

They don't bother anyone. They just are. When the weather is pleasant, they spend their days wandering. When the weather is inclement, they find places to hole up until the rain stops.

Some zombies have absolutely nothing and lumber around with arms held stiffly at their side, dragging an uncooperative leg behind them, oblivious to the world. They step out in traffic; I've dodged them many times as I picked my way through the burbs into the city. I'm a ranger at a park at the confluence of three rivers. Other undead push shopping carts filled with sleeping bags or blankets and little trinkets gathered from the roadside and garbage cans, something to trade. Many hoard things because they remember having something. They teeter on the edge between awareness and disregard. They speak in lolled words, sometimes chasing thoughts to nowhere. Still, they never bother anyone.

We allow them to rest anywhere in the park they want at night; it's a public space. The park isn't fenced in, and we can't chase them out. Each morning, we poke them into consciousness—as much as possible and make them move on. We must. If we don't, the living public complains and doesn't tolerate the zombies when they want to use the park.

I briskly treaded the brick path beneath an umbrella to the riverfront office to punch in for the day. My breath, hot from my lungs, swirled around my head. Despite being somewhat hungover and battling a cold, I felt quite alive today. My supervisor Mitch sat at his desk, warming his hands with coffee. Evan leaned against the office wall, hands stuffed in his parka pockets. We had a brief meeting about our day.

"It's going to be difficult," Mitch concluded. "The weather is against us."

I nodded and felt a sneeze coming on. I hurriedly reached into my jacket pocket for a tissue from my stash.

We expected few visitors due to the weather, but we must do our job. It's a directive from City Hall. No law on the books prevented it, but it's policy: no zombies in the park during daylight. Most days we don't have a problem. On bad days, they grumbled louder but still moved on.

Mitch unlocked the men's bathroom, I opened the ladies', and Evan unlocked the parking lot gate. Then, we unlocked the small turbine museum, walked the paths, picked up trash, and looked for anomalies in our morning hike. Nothing out of the ordinary, expected, given the nasty weather conditions. We knew where the zombies gathered and politely told them it was time to move on. Most didn't argue, and when they did, it was because they didn't understand. It's hard for some to process the meaning of no loitering when they've done it all night. It's hard for us to say the living don't want to see you; you make them uncomfortable, and we avoided being blunt. The zombies know their situation and don't need to be reminded. Most headed to the only places they can stay out of the weather: the shelters. Some protested, but we knew who they were, and most can be convinced it's for the best.

We herded them to the park exit, and they dispersed into the city with little trouble. One tried to take my umbrella, but it was a minor incident. We moved to the next task, but it will be a long day without our regular duties. None of us liked doing busy work.

Only the diehard visitors, the joggers and dog walkers, were out that morning, outfitted in appropriate gear. We saw them regardless of the weather, and they always blessed us with a muted wave as they passed.

When we finished, we headed back to the office. We hung our coats on the wrought iron wall hangers, and Mitch fired up the kerosene heater before settling in for a day of drudge work.

We weren't there for more than fifteen minutes when an elderly man knocked and opened the door, not waiting for a "come in." He was dressed in a Burberry wool coat, a brown plaid scarf, and an Irish tweed trilby hat with a leash over his arm. A miniature schnauzer was perfectly groomed and well-mannered at the end of the leash. He also carried a large, black golf umbrella. His nose was red. He closed the door behind him after a gust of wind banged it against the wall. Evan let go of the First Aid refresher book he was reading, and I looked up from the city map I'd been studying—I was new to the job, trying to familiarize myself with the area so that when visitors ask questions, I could answer intelligently.

"There's a zombie in the bathroom," he said indignantly. "He's locked himself in the handicap stall and won't come out."

"How do you know he's a zombie," Mitch asked, "and not another park patron using the facilities?"

"Because of the stench," the man withdrew a handkerchief from his coat pocket and gave a thunderous, snot-filled blow into it. "I have a terrible cold and can't smell soup or my aftershave, but I can smell him, and now I can't get it out of my nose. And, when I banged on the door to politely ask him to move on, all he did was grunt."

I glanced from Mitch to the man, wondering where the conversation would turn. Civility has disappeared in the last few years, and things sour fast, especially among the entitled. Mitch must keep things civil, even if this fellow had other ideas.

"I saw him go in on my way into the park to walk Duke here, and when I came back an hour later to use the facilities myself, he was still there."

"Thank you for letting us know, sir," Mitch said, pushing back on his wheeled chair and opening the door; he ushered the man outside. A few moments passed, and the man didn't move.

"Aren't you going to do something about it?"

"What do you suggest?" Mitch asked bravely, crossing his arms over his chest. My eyes widened at Mitch's brazenness. He's been here a few years and is used to dealing with demanding, living humans and dead people. Some situations, like the one now, have no easy answers. We know about the zombies; it's the people who run this state that seem to deny their existence and avoid addressing the "problem." We're always open to suggestions.

"Can't you call law enforcement and arrest him?" the man asked.

"What has the zombie done? How has he broken the law?"

The man stumbled over his answer and finally sputtered a reply.

"Loitering," he said. "Yes, loitering."

"It's a park," Mitch reminded him. "When you stop and look at the scenery over the river, you loiter. When you pause to listen to the birds, you loiter. You loiter when you lie on a blanket in the sunshine to nap. Maybe he's just taking a breather."

I got the distinct feeling Mitch gave that reason before, and I hid my smirk, thinking *touché*.

"And maybe he's ruining the park experience for the rest of us." The man snorted. Mitch stared at him. "You really need to do something about it."

"I think you're better at doing something about it than me. Did you vote in the last election, sir?"

"You know I did. Straight ticket."

"Of course," Mitch said, scratching his beard with great thought. "I know, my superiors know, everyone in the park system knows this is a problem. It seems the only ones who don't know about this problem are the people who can do something about it. You should speak to your elected officials and complain to them. Better yet, maybe you should take an interest in these people, these zombies, and find out what they see as a solution to the problem."

The man gave Mitch a stern look, huffed, and left, sneezing on his way out.

"You're in trouble," Evan said with a grin.

"Come on," Mitch said with a scoop of his arm. "Let's go see what's up with this guy."

I grabbed my coat, hat, and umbrella and followed Mitch and Evan into the men's bathroom.

Beneath the partition, I saw a pair of Reeboks and faded jeans, tattered and torn, frayed at the hems, and a ratty, stained blanket filled with tiny holes burned by cigarettes. The Reebok soles were splitting.

Based on Evan's and Mitch's expressions, the odor was ripe and rank. I couldn't smell it because of my cold. Tiny bits of skin and dried blood lay scattered on the cement floor.

"Sir," Mitch said, knocking gently on the stall door. Unintelligible grumbling followed Mitch's greeting. "Sir," he repeated, "I'm afraid you'll have to leave."

A phlegmy, guttural reply followed.

"Why?" It's what he asked, but it came out as a distortion of sound. I only understood because it was a reasonable question for him to ask.

"Because, sir," Mitch said, fumbling for a complete answer. "You can't stay here."

"Why not?"

The zombie's voice intensified, and he coughed. Mitch bit his lip; his only valid response is because the zombie is interfering with living park patrons, possibly creating a health hazard in the facilities, and potentially, unintendedly, making an awful mess we'd have to clean up if he expires. We can't catch the zombie condition, but the smell was enough to make Mitch and Evan gag.

"Come out, and we'll take you to the shelter."

"Can't, dammit. More'n ninety days. Smell too bad."

The door opened, and a jogger came in to use the urinal. He screwed up his face seeing us standing at the handicap stall. He heard the movement inside the stall and shook his head.

"Christ!" He grunted and ran out.

Mitch yanked his head toward the outer door, silently asking Evan and me to follow him out.

We stepped into the cold January air as the hydraulic door closer hissed and squeaked, gently shutting behind us.

I tugged at my knit cap to resettle it upon my head and blew on my hands to warm them.

"It's nasty in there!" Evan exclaimed. "Nobody's going to use that bathroom. No amount of air freshener will get that stink out. What if he expires in there, and we're left cleaning up the mess?"

"We're going to have to call law enforcement, you know," Mitch said, folding his arms, rocking back and forth on his heels as he looked over the juncture of the rivers from the viewing platform. Though the cold lingered, the rain stopped. I knew he was right.

"Technically," I said, "he's not doing anything wrong."

Mitch and Evan sighed in unison.

"I'll talk to law enforcement," Mitch finally said.

"I'll talk to the zombie," I said. "See if I can reason with him."

Evan opted to patrol the path and let other visitors know the men's bathroom was temporarily closed. I inhaled as deep as I could without coughing before I headed back into the yellow concrete half of the building that is the men's facility. I resigned myself to what could be a long wait and a difficult conversation as I plopped on the concrete floor outside the stall. I leaned my umbrella against the wall. The floor was cold, solid, and damn uncomfortable, even for my generous butt cheeks and insulated parka under me. The only sound was an erratic drip from a nearby faucet. I made a mental note to get that fixed.

"My supervisor's gone to call law enforcement," I said, drawing my knees up to my chest because the cold had already seeped through my khaki pants and thermals. I heard the zombie shuffling around in the stall and glanced beneath the partition again. He changed position and was lying on his side on the floor. I couldn't see his face. I tapped my foot nervously, simultaneously wondering if I should just be quiet or try to strike up a conversation—reason with him. I didn't want to make him angry. "What's your name?"

The zombie grunted, and I thought he wanted to answer me. A long pause passed before he did.

"John S'ith," he replied. He was hard to understand because his voice is obstructed, and he gurgles a lot. I tried not to ponder why. Instead, I wondered if John Smith was his name or a bad attempt at an alias. He put my curiosity to rest and told me people called him Jake.

"Can I call you Jake?" I asked.

"Sure."

"I'm Chad. Sorry, we need you to leave."

He confessed that he just came in to get out of the rain. Said there's nothing worse than being in the rain, that his skin sheds faster. He knows he's a zombie.

"I understand," I said, banishing the thought of skin shedding in clumps like melting ice cream. But I brought the idea back, as repulsed as I was. I realized I had a lot of questions. "Does it hurt? Jake? When the rain hits your skin?"

Not physically, just mentally, he said.

"Mentally?"

Then I suddenly understood. I don't know much about zombies, but watching your skin fall off in a downpour would be unsettling.

"Hmmm. Does the cold bother you?"

Jake moved around again and soon sat beside me with the partition between us. His hand rested on the floor, at the end of a red and blue flannel shirt sleeve. His hand was black and blue and filled with indentations. He was missing a couple of fingertips; the bare bones were showing.

He said no, just the rain. Even the snow wasn't a problem; it just prolonged their—

His words trailed off, but I filled in the blank. Final death.

"We don't get much snow here," I said. I saw the puffs of breath coming from my mouth. I coughed, feeling my own congestion worsening. I needed Sudafed.

The conversation turned dark when Jake spoke. He told me he and other zombies had been bussed here from up north.

"Bussed here?"

"Cincinnati," Jake said. He went on to say the living in

Cincinnati don't tell the zombies where they're being taken. His voice took on an echo of anger despite his speech impediment. "They don't tell us this, 'ut we aren't stu'id. They're ho'ing the warrer tem'eratures will ex'edite..."

Hoping warmer temperatures will expedite their—there's those words again—final death. I cringed at the thought of my fellow living human beings treating these poor souls like they were disposable.

I shifted uncomfortably on my buttocks, ashamed people can be so heartless. No one wants to confront this problem, so they pass it on.

"How long have you been this way?"

"A year," he said, coughing, his mouth filling with phlegm and detritus. His voice turned raspy as he told me he didn't want to be a burden on his family.

"They couldn't 'ear to see me this way, so I left." He hacked, and I sensed from the bodily noises coming from the other side his expectorant was juicy. I heard him spit into the toilet. "Shit," he said like his mouth was full of marbles.

I reached into my jacket pocket for some tissues and passed them beneath the partition. I appreciated Jake understood he was witnessing his own slow decay. I didn't know whether he wanted to speed it up or slow it down. I also appreciated he didn't want to spit lung or stomach tissue onto the floor. He still had a sense of consideration.

He didn't immediately take the tissue from me, so I waved it in case he didn't see it.

His fingers grazed mine, and I couldn't help but recoil, swiftly withdrawing my hand. He spat again, prolonged and with force. The tissue plopped into the toilet, and the whoosh of flushing water followed.

He wanted to know if he'd be arrested, and, given this was my first encounter with a zombie in this way, I didn't know.

I sighed heavily.

"I wish I could say no, but they might physically remove you. Is there any way I can convince you it's in your best interest to leave before law enforcement gets here?"

"I not a criminal," Jake said. "Just got nowhere safe to 'e."

I understood. The living don't realize how hard it is, that Jake didn't choose to be a zombie, and he was just looking for a place out of the weather.

"What can I do to help?" I asked. I could give him money, but what would that accomplish?

I heard Jake moving again, and after a bit of a struggle, he reached his feet. He picked up the blanket with his feet firmly planted on the cement floor. I stood, too, wondering what Jake was thinking and what he would do.

A moment later, the latch slid, and the door opened. I braced for what I was about to see because I'd never been this close to a zombie. I always saw them from a comfortable distance—through the barricade of my mind, if necessary, if I saw them at all. Most people looked away from zombies when they encountered them. To ease their discomfort, the living tossed spare change their way, like that would help. I'd been doing this job for nearly three months now and hadn't had the courage to look any of them in the eye. Guilt, I supposed, stopped me.

I swallowed hard and clenched my fingers. My body

stiffened in preparation for what I was about to see. I did a quick scan of Jake's presence. At about six feet, he was the same height as me; his hair was patchy, and its remnants were salt and pepper. He was mature; I put him around forty-five or so. He was athletic, which told me why he'd survived this long. Even with my stuffy nose, I expected to be hit dead on with a fetid, foul smell, but I wasn't.

Surprisingly enough, it was Jake's attempt at a smile I noticed next. A missing eyeball left a gaping hole covered by a thin veil of eyelid in its socket, and random pieces of flesh were missing from his face. His lips were raw and nearly nonexistent. Blackened gums and rotting teeth were exposed. No wonder he had trouble speaking. Usually, a smile would only be evident with the accompanying facial muscles. But I could tell he was smiling. There were crinkles around his eyes communicating this to me, and in that moment, I wish I'd known him before he became... this.

But I was puzzled.

"Why'd you come out?" I blurted. "Was it the idea of getting arrested?"

Jake glanced to the floor and pretended to adjust the blanket slung over his forearm.

He said something then that I still remember.

"It's a lonely path to death, being in the world alone. There aren't many people," he paused, "taking the time to talk to people like me."

I barely heard him. With chunks of flesh freshly expelled from his system, his voice had gone raspier. Each word was quiet and garbled. I understood the importance of lips in communication.

He stepped out of the stall and stopped.

"You did. That 'eans a lot."

Now I was ashamed and could barely look him in his one good eye.

"Thank you." He gently touched my arm with his pitted, decaying hand. That time, I didn't cringe.

"You know," I said, "there's a picnic shelter by the river. It's not as cozy as the bathroom, but it will keep the rain off you. No one uses it on cold and rainy days. Oh, and," I said, handing Jake my umbrella, "take this. It might help."

He took it and nodded, and I pulled open the door for him, watching him as he left and disappeared steadily down the trail. I was still pondering Jake's existence when Mitch breathlessly approached me from the opposite direction. On his heels were two city police officers, their faces red and chests heaving. We could all use a mandatory cardio regimen. They bypassed me and ran into the men's bathroom. I waited for them, allowing Mitch to discover Jake's absence for himself.

Moments later, Mitch reappeared at my side, still trying to catch his breath. His eyes were watering, and I could only imagine it was from the stench in the bathroom. Thank God for my cold.

"Where'd he go?"

I shrugged, looking past Mitch down the trail.

"He moved on."

"Good," Mitch said, "let's hope he doesn't come back."

I didn't answer him because I hoped to see Jake again, even without a cold.

* * *

Discussion Questions

1. Should the zombies in the story have the same rights as living people? What are the factors you are considering in developing your answer?

2. The living people in the story have created laws excluding zombies from places they might visit (*like the park during the day*) because it makes the living uncomfortable seeing them. Do people have the right to be protected from seeing other people (*or things*) that make them uncomfortable?

3. If the zombie could speak and think but was rude and somewhat aggressive (*but not dangerous*), would your opinion be different about which rights zombies are entitled to? If so, why (*or why not*)?

4. If you were the narrator in the story and encountered John Smith (*the zombie*) in the bathroom, what would you have done?

5. One interpretation of the story is the zombies are an allegory for the way society treats the homeless. In what ways do you see parallels and differences in the way the two groups should be treated? What (*if anything*) is the basis/cause for the differences?

* * *

We Are Here

Harley Carnell

* * *

The bedroom was unfamiliar, and the night was forgotten. My memory was murky. The sheets next to me were cold. I retrieved my clothes from the floor. Scouring the room with my eyes, I saw no note. My phone was dead.

Confused, I left the bedroom, headed downstairs, and exited the house. Once outside, I was refreshed by a deluge of fresh air. I was on a street I had no memory of coming to, even though I must have.

My phone was no help, and I realized how helpless I was without it. Perhaps if I kept on walking, I would know where to walk. I walked left and did so for some time. "Some time" was all I could commit to—again; I was completely groundless without my phone. Whatever time it was, I soon found I was back at the house.

I had read once about deserts. You walked in what you thought was a straight line only to eventually meet your footprints again. Perhaps this was some urban equivalent.

I decided to turn right but once again ended up at the house. I took off a few more times in differing directions, only to come back to the house each time.

There are different ways to measure time, and the stomach is one of them. I left the house with no thought of food, but after my fruitless walking could now think of nothing else. It would do no harm to go back into the house and ask for directions away from it and toward somewhere I could get something to eat.

I was about to knock on the door when I saw it was already open. I crept cautiously through. The house was now full, a highway of people threading in and out of rooms.

"Sorry," I said, "I'm just—"

"—in time for breakfast," a woman said to me.

I followed her into a large kitchen and dining room combined into one. The room was mostly consumed by a large table, at which sat ten people. Not just ten people but a strange assortment of people. The youngest was a man either in his early twenties or his late teens; the oldest a woman who had to be in her seventies. It looked like something from a commercial.

All my questions dispersed when the food arrived. For the next ten minutes, I ate ravenously. It was only when I was stuffed with food that my thirst for knowledge returned. I turned to the woman next to me—who I knew now as Olivia—and asked her where I was.

"Sorry?" she said, her mouth half-full.

"Oh, sorry," I said. "I just wanted to know where we are."

"We're in the house," she said.

"What house?" I asked.

Olivia gave another smile, although this time it was

directed to her neighbor, a man in his thirties called Malik.

"I dunno," she said, "it's just the house."

I was going to ask for more information when I felt a hand on my shoulder. It was the young man: Alan.

"Right, that's enough chitchat; it's our turn to clean up." He stood up and began stacking plates. I was not sure how it could be my turn to clean up, but then I supposed I was a guest here. Perhaps the rule was that guests had to clean up, even if they had no memory of being guests in the first place.

Over the next few minutes, we were too busy cleaning up for me to ask anything. When we began washing up, I asked about the house again. Alan, who attended to his washing up with the meticulousness of a jeweler inspecting a diamond, gave a similar answer to Olivia.

"My phone doesn't work," I then said. "I can't call a cab or anything."

"Oh yeah, they'll do that. Or not do that, I suppose," he said.

"Okay," I said, "but how do I get out, then? How do I leave? Is there a route to town?

"Would someone be able to drive me?"

He seemed deeply perplexed by my question. As if I had not asked him a question he didn't know the answer to, but for the question to an answer he didn't know.

"Leave?" he said.

"Yeah, leave. How do I get out?"

He looked at me for a few seconds and then shook his head in frustration.

"We need to get this done before they come in to make lunch. Come on."

* * *

If no one was going to help me, I'd just have to leave on my own. I finished the washing up with Alan and then headed toward the front door. I had a brief worry that it might be locked, but it wasn't. Nor did anyone try to stop me, although I did get some odd looks as I walked by.

As I headed out, I felt better. My head was clearer and I was a lot more energized—if a little lethargic—after the breakfast. I also felt more resilient. So when I came back to the house again, I was not perturbed. I took out my phone to note which turns I'd taken before remembering it was dead. Instead, I noted them in my head. When I came to the house again, I remained unconcerned. I would get out at some point; it would just take time.

I was not sure at what point this nonchalance disappeared. All I do know was that it was a rapid transition from being unbothered to concerned to outright disturbed. It did not matter how long I walked; it did not matter in what direction; it did not matter how many unfamiliar roads I took—I always ended up back at the house.

Eventually, I became resolved. I would get one of them to either tell me how to get back to town or drive me. As I approached the house, I realized how dark it was. Was this premature night, or was my memory disoriented like a compass in a magnetic field? I marched into the house. The first person I saw was a man in his thirties, who I remembered as Mike. I was about to demand he tell me where I was, when he commanded me to the kitchen.

"We've all been waiting for you," he said on the way.

He shepherded me into the kitchen, where there was a pile of potatoes on the table.

"We need them peeled for the cottage pie," he said and then walked out of the room. Two of the other residents—the woman in her seventies (Esther) and Alan—stood stirring at the stove.

"Excuse me," I said to either/both of them, but they ignored me.

"Excuse me," I repeated.

Alan muttered something, but I couldn't hear him.

"What?" I said.

"Potatoes!" Alan shouted at me without turning.

I didn't know why I was expected to peel the potatoes, yet I felt strangely responsible for them. I sighed and began peeling.

* * *

When I was done with the potatoes, I felt oddly proud and explicably hungry. Alan said I could go and rest before dinner, and I did. I was tired and hungry, I told myself. There was no harm in having a little sleep and a nice meal before I left.

After dinner, Olivia said to me:

"You've done all your chores for the day, so the evening's yours! You can do whatever you like."

"Well, that's the thing. I was actually wondering about leaving. Could someone drive me?

"Or walk me down to the station?"

Although I had been speaking to her, I noticed everyone was looking at me. They all alternated between concern, confusion, and irritation.

"Where is it you're going?" Malik asked.

"Nowhere," I said. "I mean, I don't have anywhere specific in mind. I just want to leave."

"But you can't leave?" Olivia said, her voice so suffused

with confusion it sounded like a question.

"Why not?" I said. "What will happen if I do?"

"Err, nothing will happen," Malik said. "You just can't leave. It's like... it's like asking what would happen if you began walking upward. You just can't."

"Look," I said, struggling to keep the frustration out of my voice, "I don't know if you're all too busy to take me, or you just can't be bothered. In any case, I don't care. If you're not willing to take me, could you at least give me directions?"

Although people looked on the verge of speaking, no one did. I sighed and then stood up.

"Fine," I said. "I'll just go myself."

"I wouldn't do that," said a man in his forties, whose name I didn't know yet.

"Why not?"

"You're just going to wander around, making yourself all tired. And you've got a big day tomorrow."

"A big day. Why?"

"It's laundry day," he said in a tone that indicated I should know this.

"And?"

"*And*, it's your turn. Tomorrow's always the day when we do everyone's laundry."

"And what day is tomorrow?"

"Laundry day," he said.

I laughed incredulously.

"You know what," I said. "I can't tire myself out because I'm already tired. I don't know what's up with you all, but I'm done. I'll just find the way out myself. I'll walk all night if I have to."

* * *

In the end, it wasn't quite all night. But it was certainly deep enough into the night that it had to almost be morning. At some point, I lost hope and gave up. Yet I continued walking and running long after that. Eventually, I returned to the house. I fell asleep immediately after lurching into bed.

What felt like a few minutes later I was snatched from sleep by the man in his forties—his name was Jerome. I was so sleep-deprived I sleepwalked through most of the morning, barely able to feel anything. Only after I was folding the third load of sheets and the deluge of coffee I'd ingested had successfully suffused my bloodstream did I begin to ask questions, culminating in:

"I haven't given any dirty clothes yet, so why should I have to do laundry?"

"Well, you're in the house," Jerome said. "Of course you have to do laundry if you're in the house. Everyone has to do it at some point."

"I get that," I said, "but I never asked to be in the house."

As always when I spoke about the house with the others, I was met with confusion. I tried a different approach.

"How long have you been here?" I asked.

Jerome paused his folding and looked wistfully off into the distance.

"You know," he said, "I don't know. I can't actually remember." Then, he gave a small chuckle. "Funny that, isn't it?"

"What's funny?"

"How in the end you never remember when you came here. Or being anywhere before here. There's a time when you do, and you try and hold onto it, but eventually it just gets away from you." He chuckled again.

"I remember," I said. "It was yesterday, and I want to leave."

"You don't like it?"

"No," I said. "Or, well, it's not a case of liking it or not liking it. It's just that I never wanted to be here. I want to leave."

"But this is the house," Jerome said.

I was about to respond, but there was a mound of laundry in front of me and a long time until lunchtime. I was also beginning to get frustrated. These conversations were as circuitous as my walks and would only serve to stress me out. For the next ten minutes, Jerome and I folded laundry in silence.

* * *

By the time we were finished, it was dinnertime, and I was exhausted. After dinner, I was about ready to go to sleep, but I had to focus my energy on leaving. I asked Malik for a pen and some paper. He took me to a room that looked like a small office. It had a little desk with a computer on it and a window looking out into the house's tiny garden. There was a bookcase beside a small armchair, in which a woman named Susan currently sat reading.

Next to the desk was a neatly arranged stationery shelf with paper.

"It's nice in here," I said.

"Yeah, it's very peaceful. I like to come up here when I have my free time. You're of course more than welcome to as well."

"Thank you, but I'm leaving tonight."

Malik looked like he was about to say something but restrained himself. Instead, he gave me a small smile and handed me the paper and pen.

* * *

Back on the streets, I noted down each turn I took, turning the paper into a map. Each time I returned to the house, the map grew. Knowing that with each return I was eliminating an incorrect route and approaching my escape, I was buoyed. Eventually, there would be one final elimination and I would be away from the house forever.

However, I soon found all that happened was my map kept getting bigger. I began to wonder just how large this town was. Then, I got a strange sensation. It seemed as if some of my map was somehow disappearing. I seemed to be walking down streets I had told myself not to walk down. Also, it may have just been the dark or the streetlights playing havoc with my eyesight, but it was as though streets were in different places. Roads were appearing and disappearing; turnings were turning into straight lines; exits were born in dead ends. At one point, the ink began to bleed. I thought I might have been crying but quickly realized it was raining. With a shocking rapidity, rain began to pour as if it had been doing so all night. Furious and soaked, I threw the sodden paper to the ground and stormed back to the house.

* * *

The next day was a free day. This was good, as I was exhausted. A combination of the physical exertion of the laundry and the mental strain of my failed attempts to leave left me barely able to get out of bed. I only did so because I was summoned for breakfast. After, Olivia asked if I wanted to play tennis. "We need an extra so we can do doubles."

From the little I had seen of the garden in flashes from windows, I was not sure how it could accommodate table tennis, let alone actual tennis. But once I got outside the garden revealed itself to be park-like in length. That this could happen seemed nonsensical, but I supposed I was not in a position to dismiss nonsense.

I enjoyed the tennis. A lot of my tension began to dissipate and, despite engaging in strenuous sport, I felt oddly relaxed. However, I soon began to get a sense that I should not be enjoying myself. It was as though by having fun I was somehow accepting or resigning myself to the idea of being in the house. I tried to ignore this thought. Of course I was going to leave—I was just having a little fun first. But I could not overcome this sensation and stopped having fun. When Olivia and I—who were playing against Malik and a woman in her thirties called Stephanie—ended up losing, I found I didn't care.

* * *

I returned to the house.

It was as I did so that something occurred to me. If the people in the house weren't going to help me, that didn't mean those in others wouldn't. I walked up to a random house and knocked. Despite lights being on, there was no answer. I tried the house next to it. The lights were also off, but my knock engendered shuffling in the shadows behind the curtains. I was hopeful, but once more there was no answer.

Every house I went to, there was no answer. I questioned whether to continue but knew of nothing else to do. I knocked on every door until my numb knuckles no longer belonged to me. People seemed to be becoming aware of me. Lights turned off as I approached houses; locks clicked as I ran up walkways. Even the streetlights seemed to be colluding in this shunning, shutting off as I approached so that I was soon walking in near-total darkness. But in this darkness and in the distance, I saw a single light. I brightened at this and ran toward it.

When I knocked, it was answered immediately as if the person had always been expecting me. It was a man, who appeared to be in his sixties. He was well-dressed, looking like he had just come from a night out. His smile was kind.

"I'm sorry to bother you," I said, my words staccato through rapid breaths. "But I've been looking all night for a way to get out."

"To get out of where?"

"Here," I said. "I'm in a house; I've been trying to get out. I mean, I have got out—how else would I be talking to you! But I need to get out of this town. I've been getting lost; it's like a labyrinth. Is there a bus stop or a train station or something? Or would you be able to drive me?"

The man smiled again, although it was tinged with sadness.

"That's not how it works, I'm afraid."

"What?"

"You can't just leave."

My heart sank. After the long night and long succession of such nights, after his light being on, his kind smile, his opening the door. All that, only for him to say what everyone else had been saying.

"You won't help me," I said, not asked.

"I can't help you where there is no help to be had," he said with an infuriating kindness.

"Tell me, then. If you won't help me, just tell me how to leave. Please. What route do I take? Or let me use your phone—I'll call a cab."

"I'm very sorry," the man said, giving me a final smile and then turning around. He closed the door behind him and shut off the light.

At that point, I lost it. I began pounding on the door with my fists and arms.

"Open the door! Open the fucking door!"

The man did, a few seconds later, but it was not him who greeted me. Instead, the largest dog I ever remembered or could ever conceive came snarling out at me. I could see a leash restraining him, but the man was too far back in the dark for me to see him holding it. I backed away, walking quickly rather than running for fear he would chase me if I did.

Only when I was well past the gate did I finally run.

* * *

"You should really eat something," Stephanie said to me.

"I'm not hungry," I said dully. Not only was I not hungry, but I was so mired in misery I could not imagine being hungry for some time. I had only managed to haul myself out of bed because I needed the toilet; without that, I would still be in there now, slaloming in and out of the dreams where I either managed to escape the house or had never been in it in the first place.

"It's a big day for you," said Frank, sitting next to me.

"Why's that?" I said, barely opening my mouth to talk.

"It's your day to clean out the basement," said Stephanie.

Frank and Stephanie explained the basement was cleared out once a month, and this month it was my turn.

"I'm not doing it," I said. I know I sounded surly or rude, but I didn't care.

"Don't be like that," said Stephanie, sighing. "Remember the tennis? And anyway, it's your turn."

"I haven't used the basement. I didn't even realize you had one."

"You might not have used the basement," said Stephanie, "but you need it to be cleaned."

There was something about her phrasing that caught my attention.

"Why would *I* need it cleaned?"

"You're scared of spiders, aren't you?"

"Erm, yeah I am. Terrified actually, but what's that got to do with anything?"

"Well," said Frank, no longer able to disguise his irritation. "This house is filled with very poisonous spiders, as well as less poisonous ones that are indistinguishable in terms of appearance. Whether you're scared of spiders or not I'd imagine you'd not want to run into one or have one fall on you or climb up you when you're using the bathroom or whatever. Over the month, they collect down in the basement, ready to make their way up into the main house. So once a month we go down there, where there's a massive hole, and sweep them away."

"Wait," I said, standing up. "You want me to go down there and clear out the spiders?"

"Now he gets it," said Frank sarcastically.

"No," I said. "No, I'm not doing that."

"I'm sorry," said Stephanie, "but I'm afraid you have to. It's your turn."

All of my surliness washed away. I began to panic. When I spoke, my voice had regressed to how I imagined it would have been when I was a child.

"No, no, please. I'm sorry, okay. I don't know if this is some kind of punishment for my attitude or whatever. But please. I'll do the laundry every week. I'll do the dishes every day. I'll do the toilets. But please don't make me do that."

"All right, fuck this," said Frank, standing up. "He's giving me a headache. Malik, Alan, come help me, please."

Before I knew what was happening, the three guys had hauled me out of my chair and were dragging me toward the basement, my feet tapdancing on the floor as I tried to resist. Olivia ran after us. I thought she was coming to rescue me, but instead, she slid some large gardening gloves onto my hands.

"Do not take these off for any reason," she said. "Also, tuck your trousers into your socks."

At the thought of the spiders trying to crawl up my legs, I began to scream. Although there were three guys holding me, and all were individually stronger than I was, I almost managed to pull free. But they held on in the end. When we reached the basement, they all but threw me in.

"Broom's on your right, light's on your left," said Malik, as they closed and locked the door behind me. I began kicking and punching at the door. My hardest blows did not even rattle it in its frame. It was so thick I imagined my screams were inaudible. Yet I continued to scream, these screams scraping my throat so much that eventually they were silent. I then began to cry, pounding on the door, kicking at the keyhole.

"Please. Please let me out," I said, with a final exhausted cry.

It was at this point, I felt a tickling on my skin. Instinctively I rushed my hand to my shoulder and felt a carousel of legs trickling through my fingers. I screamed and smacked my hand with my other hand. I killed the spider but was in agony from the blow I'd inflicted on myself. I remembered what Malik had said about the light and hit the wall next to me until I found it. When I did, I awoke a nightmare.

In front of me, there were what had to be thousands of spiders. Some were prostrate in webs; others dangled from the ceiling; some chorused on the floor. Everywhere I looked, and everywhere I could look, there were spiders. Everywhere, including me. There were spiders crawling on my legs, some high enough they were almost at my shirt. I panicked and grabbed the broom. It took all my resolve to hold onto it when I saw its red and brown top was in fact a large spider that had coiled itself around it. I resisted the urge to scream again as another spider was close to my mouth and would climb in were I to do so. Then, despite my terror, I was suddenly overcome with a strange feeling. A sense of resolve. Whether I liked it or not, I was in the basement. I would not be able to leave until it was cleared. All of my inclinations to remain where I was, to continue trying to escape, to pass out, disappeared. The only way I was going to leave was by evicting the spiders.

Over the next ten minutes, I furiously swept the spiders. Most scurried away from me, and I was able to shepherd them toward the hole. There were a few that were bolder and tried to attack me. Every instinct I had was telling me to run, but I fought against them. Whenever a spider landed on me, I swatted it with the broom. When the more tenacious ones clung to my trousers, I picked them up with the gloves and flung them into the hole.

I began to feel a little thrilled. My life before the house was cloudy and becoming murkier by the day, but I knew I had always been terrified of spiders. Yet the longer I spent in the basement, the less scary they became. They were becoming mundane, almost, and I was becoming bold. I began proactively approaching the spiders, creeping in the corners to find them. In one, I found a bulging and pulsing egg sac. It was still repulsive, I was still terrified, but I picked it up. Even as it beat in my hands, threatening to pop and pollinate me with its horrific arachnid litter, I held onto it and launched it into the hole.

Then, suddenly, the spiders began to flee all at once. They were emerging from corners, bungeeing down from the ceiling, climbing off my body, all headed for the hole. They were clearly terrified of my lack of fear. The final dregs of my fear were dissipating. I was beginning to feel cocky. I was almost tempted to chase after the spiders. I smiled smugly. Then, I heard a noise behind me. It was the sound of someone treading on leaves or a small twig breaking. Frowning, I turned around and saw the largest spider I had ever seen in my life. The size of a small dog, and perhaps, even some big ones.

As the spiders continued to disperse around me, I felt all of my confidence drain. I was breathing heavily, and the only thing that stopped me from charging at the door and begging to be let out again was that the spider was between the door and me. It was too big to sweep. If I tried, its weight would break the broom's bristles. It was at this point I noticed that the top of the broom was not rounded or flat, but pointed to an almost knife-like sharpness.

I was terrified, and as I flipped the broom around, my hand was trembling. The spider made a sudden lurch forward, and without thinking I thrust the broom at it. Without effort, the spider bit down on it and snapped it into dust.

At this point, my fight had flown, and my flight took over. I could not run forward, so I tottered backward. The spider chased me. I continued to back away, and the spider continued to chase me. I knew it would catch up with me and attack me until—

I suddenly remembered the hole. Just as the spider leapt at me, I dodged out of the way, and it fell into it. After this, I lay by the hole, curled into myself like a spider playing dead. Then, I began to scream again. I continued to do so unrelentingly as the basement door opened and Malik and Mike gently lifted me up and took me back upstairs.

*　*　*

For the next three days, I was in bed. Olivia, who said she thought she might once have been in medicine, gave me something to help me sleep. I don't know what I would have done without it. Not well, if the few times when I was fully conscious were anything to go by. In these brief moments of lucidity, I would be constantly scratching at myself, convinced I was covered in spiders, even though I knew they were all gone for the month. I had to sleep with the light on, as whenever I heard a slight noise in the room, I'd think it was the big spider crawled out of the hole and seeking its revenge. At such moments, Olivia would return and give me more medicine.

After these days, I was gradually weaned off the medicine and back into life. On the fifth, I was roused from my sleep because I had some chores to do. I was initially reluctant to leave, but Malik said it was good for me. He was right, as the monotony of the vacuuming and dusting distracted me from my feelings.

*　*　*

In many ways, the basement changed me. It was as if I had taken a small part of myself and thrown it down the hole with those spiders. One way this manifested was in my attempts to leave. I continued to make them, but I was beginning to accept that I may not be able to leave the house. Of course, I did not fully give up hope. I knew the day I did that definitively and finally would be a very dark one. But I did begin to accept there was a distinct likelihood I would be staying. I wasn't sure why what happened in the basement should imbue me with that sense, but it did.

When not escaping, I began to settle into the rhythm of the house. I did my chores; I read in the study; I played tennis with the guys or watched their games.

While I was miserable for the most part, I tried to enjoy these times, and make the most of them.

* * *

I'd been up all night because I was feeling down, and eventually resigned myself to sleeplessness. I went downstairs to grab a drink and could see a light on in the kitchen.

Esther was sitting at the table with a near-empty cup of tea.

"Couldn't sleep?" I asked her as I turned on the kettle.

"I often don't," she said. "You?"

"I usually sleep well. It's all that keeps me going sometimes, the thought of sleep. But I couldn't tonight."

After I made my tea, I sat down opposite her. For the next few minutes, we spoke politely and perfunctorily about mundane topics.

"And how are you finding everything?" she asked me at one point. Because we didn't know each other that well, I thought about giving a standard "everything's fine." But then again, Esther was the oldest in the house, and I assumed had been in it for the longest. Despite not knowing her, one thing that had always struck me about her was how calm she seemed.

And not only calm but... contented.

"How do you cope with it, being here?" I asked her tentatively. "You must have had a life before this. Do you not want to get out?"

If only because it was unexpected, I expected the question to faze her, to at least warrant a little thought. But as if she had expected it, as if it was inevitable that I was going to say it, she responded immediately.

"What you have to understand is you will always be here. Until you accept that, you will never be happy."

"But surely there has to be—"

"You can try as many times as you like to leave. You can walk as far as you want. It doesn't matter: you are here, and you will always be here."

Although I felt as if I had to ask the question, I now wished I hadn't. I wished there was a way to go back and snatch it from my mouth. Because I realized now just how large the gulf was between being almost certain I would never leave and knowing it definitively.

Then, Esther leaned forward and touched my hand.

"Look," she said. "I know it's hard, and it will take a long time to get used to. Do not expect that will happen quickly because it will not. For some people, it takes years. But you will come to accept it, I promise you that."

"But how can you?" I said angrily almost petulantly. "I don't want to be here. I want to get out. It's not fair that I'm here."

She gave my hand a little squeeze before letting it go.

"Do you think that fairness exists? Do you think something is fair or unfair, and there are distinctions between the two? Or do you not just think there are things that exist and that happen, and things that don't exist and don't happen? But whether it's fair or not, whether fair even exists or not, you are here. You are here, I am here, we are all here, and that is all there is to it.

"But, there are two ways to be here. You can be here and be happy. This place is not perfect, and maybe there are better places out there. And maybe there is something worse too. But it is enough, I think, you can be happy here and have a good time."

"But I really can't leave?" I said, realizing now that I was beginning to cry. "There really is no way out for me?"

Esther stood up and sat on the seat next to me. She took my hand in hers.

"The other way you can be here is to be unhappy. To never enjoy yourself. To spend all your energy and all your hope on trying to leave and thinking you can have something else. You can keep doing this until you drive yourself mad. Now, I can't tell you what to do or how to feel. All I can say is that, of the two, surely the first is better. Surely, it's better to accept that you're here and try to be happy and try to make the most of it. Because if you do, you can be happy and you can have a good life and you can enjoy yourself. Now, could you do me a favor?"

"What?" I said, wiping at my eye.

"I want you to say 'I am here.'"

"Sorry?" I said.

"Please," said Esther, patiently. "Please, just say it. 'I am here.'"

"No," I said. "I can't do that."

"Please."

"No," I said, sniffling. "No, I can't."

"Just say it," she said. "It means the world to say it."

I did not for a long time, mostly because my tears were making it difficult to speak, but also because I did not want to. I believed Esther when she said it meant the world to say it. Those three words seemed to have such gravity to them that elevated them above mere words. They were not words that could simply be said or said simply.

I was convinced I was not going to say them. I'd do everything but say them. But then I turned to Esther. I saw her looking at me, saw how kind she was. I thought about what she had said: that no matter what I did or how often I asked, I would never leave.

Then, continuing to cry, I said silently:

"I am here."

* * *

Discussion Questions

1. What do you think are the point, the symbolism, and the metaphors this story is trying to convey? What message is the story trying to convey?
2. What would be an example in your real life that feels like the metaphorical example in the story? Would the situation be helped by saying out loud, "I am here"?
3. What do you think the daily chores and the spider basement are meant to represent? What do they represent in the situation of your own life that is like this story?
4. Is the narrator saying, "I am here" and accepting his situation a good thing because it gives him comfort or a bad thing because it takes away his willingness to change his situation?
5. Are there ever situations that have to be accepted because they can never change? Are all situations, even those that seem permanent, actually temporary?

* * *

Author Information

Apple Pi

Adam Strassberg is a retired psychiatrist living in Portland, Oregon. He uses the intersection of psychology, religion, mythology, and magical realism to explore the human condition through fiction. When he's not writing or napping, he can often be found updating his website. *www. adamstrassberg.com/*

Bubblegum Prayer

Dawn Muenchrath is a writer originally from rural Alberta and currently based in Calgary. In 2023, she obtained her MFA in Writing from the University of Saskatchewan. Her work has previously appeared in *Grain*, *Arc Poetry Magazine*, *Contemporary Verse 2*, and *The Dalhousie Review*. She was the 2023 recipient of the Saskatchewan Writers' Guild Poetry Prize. She has two cats. Instagram *@dmmuenchrath*

Disconnect

Julia Meinwald is a writer of fiction and musical theatre and a gracious loser at a wide variety of board games She has stories published or forthcoming in *Bayou Magazine, Vol 1. Brooklyn, West Trade Review, VIBE,* and *The Iowa Review*, among others. Her work as a composer has been heard in productions across the US and in Canada, and the cast album for her musical *The Magnificent Seven* streams on various platforms. *www.juliameinwaldwrites.com*; *https://linktr.ee/juliameinwald*

Echo

C.M. Selbrede is a recent graduate of Bates College hailing from Ellicott City, MD. He enjoys blurring the lines between genres and exploring historically underrepresented stories. He is best known for his mental health webseries, Hurt, and self-published works, including Makeshift and The Valley Chronicles trilogy. X (Twitter) *@cmselbrede*; Instagram *@accpubink* *@craigselbrede*; *www.accpubink.com*

I'll Not Risk Myself

Noelle Canty is a writer, reader, and editor who loves conversations that explore culture and history. Comfortable with both academic and non-academic projects in the sciences and humanities, she has written poetry, fiction, essays, reviews, conference presentations, and more. X (Twitter) *@NoelleCanty*

Jakub/Kane and Abel

C.S. Griffel has lived all over the world but currently resides in Colorado Springs with one husband and two lapdogs. She teaches high school and college English. Her classes include American Literature, British Literature, and Creative Writing. This is her fourth story with ADC, her favorite place to get published. She also has several other short stories and even poetry published in a variety of literary journals. She is currently working on a screenplay. LinkedIn *@csgriffel*

Junk

Taylor Lawritson is a teacher and writer of fiction originally from Glendale, Arizona. They currently live in Prague, Czech Republic, where they spend their time writing about gender, society, and the unreality of modern life. This is their first piece published in a literary magazine. Instagram *@thesauruscollector91*

Meat is Meat

Scott Tierney's writings include the sci-fi epic Tomorrow is Another Year, the novella Kin, and the comic book series Pointless Conversations. He also has a humorous weekly serial on WattPad, The Adventures of Crumpet-Hands Man. Many of his short-stories have been published online, including on Liar's League, Horror Tree, Bristol Noir and HumourMe. He currently resides in the North West of England. *www.scotttierneycreative.com*

Pappou's Garden

Fotis Banis was raised in NYC as a first-generation Greek-American. He is an alumnus of the CUNY Hunter College Creative Writing Program, and he currently resides in Athens, Greece, where he spends his time looking for inspiration for his writing in the crevices of the city. *Fotisbanis.com*

Prisoner of Conscience

David Moore is a senior fellow with the Carsey School at the University of New Hampshire, where he taught political science for two decades. He is the author of the narrative nonfiction book, *Small Town, Big Oil–The Untold Story of the Women Who Took on the Richest Man in the World–and Won* (Diversion Books, 2018; Highbridge Audio 2019), as well as the short story, "Yours Truly," in *Freedom Fiction. www.davidwmoore.us*

Purgatory

Serena Smith is a graduate from Weber State University, gaining her Bachelor of Arts degree in creative writing in April 2024. At the ceremony, she was recognized with the 2024 Outstanding Creative Writing Graduate Award. She writes mainly fiction, focusing on pieces with strong relationships and dramatic tension. She resides in Sanpete County, Utah, with her two dogs, Kota and Pippi, who are her favorite writing companions. For the past several years, she has been writing a fantasy novel, which she is in the final stages of editing. *authorscupoftea.blogspot.com*

Reni Winter, Dead at 57

Joseph Lyttleton is the creator of the 10 Cities/10 Years travel project, for which he lived in a new U.S. city every year for a decade. His writing has appeared in *Across the Margin*, *The Lit Nerds*, and *Third Wednesday*. His first novel, *Yahweh's Children*, was independently published in 2018. Since 2017, Lyttleton has lived in Madrid, Spain, where he is a freelance writer and editor. *www.josephlyttleton.com*; Instagram *@10cities10years*; Facebook *@10Cities10Years*

The End of Learning

Timothy Gaddo is a lifelong reader who began writing after retiring from his career as an electrical transmission system operator. He lives in Minnesota and has self-published two novels and a family memoire.

The Epidemic

Sam Franzini is a freelance arts and culture writer based in Washington, D.C. His reviews and interviews have been featured in *NYLON*, *Office Magazine*, and Shondaland, and he's a staff writer at *The Line of Best Fit*, *Northern Transmissions*, and *Our Culture Mag*. He has finished his first novel. X (Twitter) *@samfz7*; Instagram *@sam.franzini*; *www.samfranzini.com*

The Fitzgeraldist

Jack Whelan (he/him) is a recent graduate from Tulane University in New Orleans, LA. His short story, "The Fitzgeraldist," is his first published work. He currently works as a forensic toxicologist outside of New York and is working on several short speculative fiction pieces and his first novel. X (Twitter) *@Jack_Whelan2*

The Little Black Book

Cassandra R. D'Alessandro is a writer from a small town in Ontario, where she crafts short stories, poems, and novels in genres such as fantasy, thriller, and mystery. Cassandra pours her soul into her work, aiming to make readers connect with their emotions, question their reality, and be inspired. Instagram *@cassandra.r.dalessandro; www.cassandrardalessandro.com*

The Lives and Times of David Hackman

Patrick Hueller writes and teaches in Minnesota. He's against instant replay in sports, but for it in life.

The Zombie in The Bathroom

Maura Morgan is a writer of both fiction and nonfiction, covering a range of topics, including travel, history, speculative and historical fiction, and short stories. She graduated from Drexel University with a Master of Fine Arts degree in Creative Writing. She is working on a historical novel. X (Twitter) *@maura0718*; Substack *@maura0718*; Facebook *@maura0718*

We Are Here

Harley Carnell lives and writes in London, England. His fiction has been published, or is forthcoming, in *Vastarien*, *Riptide Journal*, *Penumbra*, *Sarasvati*, *Confrontation*, and others. He has also had stories performed on the *NoSleep Podcast*, *Tales to Terrify*, *Nocturnal Transmissions*, and the *Drabblecast*. His critical work is published in *Gamut* and *Aurealis*, and is forthcoming in the *Lovecraft Annual*. *www.harleycarnell.com*

Additional Information

Reviews

If you enjoyed reading these stories, please consider an online review. It's only a few seconds, but it is very important! Good reviews mean higher rankings. Higher rankings mean more sales and a greater ability to release amazing new stories.

Monthly Magazine

https://www.afterdinnerconversation.com

Purchase our growing collection of print anthologies, "Best of," and themed print book collections. Available from our website, online bookstores, and by order from your local bookstore.

Podcast Discussions/Audiobooks

https://www.afterdinnerconversation.com/podcastlinks

Listen to our podcast discussions and audiobooks on Apple, Spotify, or wherever podcasts are played. Or, if you prefer, watch the podcasts on our YouTube channel or download the .mp3 file directly from our website.

Patreon

https://www.patreon.com/afterdinnerconversation

Get early access to short stories and ad-free podcasts. New supporters also get a free digital copy of the anthology *After Dinner Conversation—Season One*. Support us on Patreon!

Book Clubs/Classrooms

https://www.afterdinnerconversation.com/book-club-downloads

After Dinner Conversation supports book clubs! Receive free short stories for your book club to read and discuss!

Social

Connect with us on Facebook, YouTube, Instagram, Bluesky, TikTok, Substack, and X (Twitter).

Special Thanks

Another year, another "Best of" edition in the books. As always, it takes a village (and money).

A special thank you to my wife for putting up with this very unlucrative interest of mine, as well as my sister, for keeping me in a flexible, yet reasonably well-paying, part-time job as a criminal defense attorney. Without their understanding I would not possibly have a life that affords me the free time to work on this.

Thank you to the Connor family for giving my wife and I a free place to live so I could focus on the magazine without worrying about paying rent.

Of course, thank you to the hundreds of volunteer readers as well. We received 1,350 submissions in 2024 and they went through all of them to find the hidden gems you are reading here.

Additionally, a special thanks to our story editor R.K.H. Ndong, our Substack editor Tina Lee Forsee, and our copy editors Stephen Repsys and Kate Bocassi. Each has put in countless hours this last year because they believe in our mission of bringing thoughtful conversation to public discussion.

And of course, thank you to the talented writers. None of this exists without your creativity and genius.

Regarding the magazine, it's impossible to summarize everything that has changed in the last year. We put out nine themed short story books on various topics. We are now syndicated in "Philosophy Now."

Chillsubs and Ranker.com both ranked us the #1 fiction

literary magazine for 2024.

We received our first arts grant due to the skill of Pyrros Rubanis, as well as a few large donations that have allowed us to get complimentary print copies of our magazine and themed books into almost one-hundred classrooms around the world.

Our paid subscribers continue to grow, as well as our social media. In fact, our weekly Substack email list recently reached over 90,000 subscribers. So, you know, stuff and things...

If you want to know how you can help spread our mission of thoughtful reflection and debate, it's really quite easy. Step one, tell a friend about us. Step two, find us on your preferred reading platform and do a positive review. Reviews really do matter in creating credibility and sales.

And, of course, if you have a website, blog, podcast, or whatever, feel free to mention us or reach out to me directly for an interview. I love chatting about the work we do!

It's funny how stories talk about going into the past, changing one small thing, and the future turns out totally different; nobody talks about how the small decisions you are making today might have the same ripples into the future yet to come. Food for thought. Choices matter. It all matters. Even when it doesn't feel like it.

Thank you!

Editor-in-Chief

www.ingramcontent.com/pod-product-compliance
Lightning Source LLC
Chambersburg PA
CBHW022021240626
47154CB00007B/2200